I0660914

Eliza Mary Middleton Willoughby

The Story of Alastair Bhan Comyn

The Tragedy of Dunphail

Eliza Mary Middleton Willoughby

The Story of Alastair Bhan Comyn
The Tragedy of Dunphail

ISBN/EAN: 9783337049430

Printed in Europe, USA, Canada, Australia, Japan

Cover: Foto ©Andreas Hilbeck / pixelio.de

More available books at **www.hansebooks.com**

THE STORY

OF

ALASTAIR BHAN COMYN

OR

THE TRAGEDY OF DUNPHAIL

A TALE OF TRADITION AND ROMANCE

BY THE

LADY MIDDLETON

WILLIAM BLACKWOOD AND SONS
EDINBURGH AND LONDON
MDCCCLXXXIX

Dedicated

TO THE

LADY ELMA CUMMING BRUCE
(BARONESS THURLOW)

OFTTIMES MY COMPANION,

SOMETIMES MY GUIDE,

ALL TIMES MINE OWN FAMILIAR FRIEND.

PREFACE.

Dear Elma,

       Many years ago I promised you a versified form of the old family traditions, that, told by you in our walks and play-hours of childhood at dear old Dunphail, cast about the place a charm and glamour of romance that has to me never lost its force. It is so many years since I began the story, that you will almost disbelieve in its completion, and I feel half ashamed to offer it. Life with its changes and many storms, has come athwart our wish and will in the matter; and what with long, forced interruptings, a busy life, weariness of spirit, and the disgust at one's own incapacity, ever baulking those who would attain an ideal, I have often despaired of living to offer you a versified edition of Alastair Bhan Comyn's story. But now, after writing it through no less than three times, and feeling little more content with the last than the first framing, I give up all hope of satisfying myself, and confide it to your, perhaps greater, leniency. My notes, written for you, are mainly of family and local import; though they may interest also those who, outside our own circle, will read the tale.

The tale itself *is* interesting. It has archæological value as well as historical features; and had one only lived a century back—before the Gaelic language had died out in our county—much more might have been culled from now forgotten heroic ballads, and traditional tales in verse.

You will remember how, having through the kindness of his descendants traced in Sir Thomas Dick Lauder's papers the origin of his account of Randolph and Comyn struggles, in 'The Moray Floods' (namely, Miller the Minstrel's Gaelic traditions), your lord and I made an expedition one lovely June day, and visited many of the points mentioned in the ballad, realising others by sight; and with my scanty knowledge of Gaelic being able to render the modern translating of the old names, back into their originals. It was a grand triumph, and I devoutly wished the late Mr Cosmo Innes, and others who had endeavoured to question the authenticity of Sir Thomas' tales, had been in our company. I shall give the letters from the Rev. Mr Rose, minister of Drainie (near Elgin), to Sir Thomas—wherein he details Miller's story, at some length—in an Appendix, as they will show how tradition dies with a dying language, and also show (*mea max. culp.!?*) how I have introduced into the traditions a female element, and the character of Denys. But a tale is dull without women, and only a warlike element in the sterner sex.

You hold the scenes of much of the story; your children share the blood of the heroic Alastair; you unite in your own person the two rival families that, crowned or crownless, shook states and alarmed kings! So to you my book is most appropriately dedicated, and I ask that your children may never forget that they are also, in part, Cummings; and that through them, may honour once more accrue to that Race, from pride and greatness fallen.—Your loving cousin,

Eisa Gordon Cumming,
WIFE OF DIGBY, BARON MIDDLETON.

WOLLATON HALL, NOTTINGHAM,
May 1889.

To The LADY THURLOW.

CONTENTS.

THE PROLOGUE.

THE STORY OF ALASTAIR BHAN COMYN.

PROLOGUE

THE RIVER.

RIVER of Alders, Findhorn of my heart,
Distant thy dark stream flows ; but in my brain,
Through the lulled twilight, oft and o'er again,
Dwells thy dear strain !
And the bright morning knows, with mingled pain
And bliss, thy memoried song,
As aye along
By rock and bank, through mead and mazy holt,
Narrow and spread, and plunge and swell and dart,
Each after each, thou tun'st thy way ;
And I, apart,
Must ever hear thee, hear thee, hear thee—
A distant lover-lay ;
Through and above the festal melody
In halls of harmony ;
Blent with the voices bright
Of youth, in merry play, on winter's night ;
Through the cheered music of the hounds, and note
Of huntsman's horn through covert sounding,
When the curbed courser, bounding,
Ere, like a darting swift, or sling-sped bolt,
He speeds
By other waves, and woods, and meads,

Where still I hear thee, hear thee, hear thee ;
And would that I were near thee,
That I mote
But once again, there, by thy varied flow
Musing, those haunting raptures surely know,
And watch thy waters, downward rolled
In fused sardonyx, blent with liquid gold.

"VÆ VICTIS!"

OH! tragic race, that long thy bord hath trod,
Once kings in might, and—men say—lords of crime:
But have the o'erthrown e'er justice, when their fall
Was one from pride?
                         Our expiation's long!
Will the full years, round-rolling, not renew
The fortunes of our name?   Will He not soon
Arise, whose foot I heark for, 'mid the song
Of aye melodious waters, all in vain?
    He that, unblemished, shall our blame forgo;
    He through whose life our name shall honoured live;
    He that shall raise us, guide us, point us yet
    To days of worth; all chastened, humbled; sweet,
    Sweeter for pangs half-memoried, of our past,
    For pride more due, for power more wisely worn.

    I bid you not on bristling field of strife
    To flash, a meteor, 'mid the fainter stars,
    Nor in the statesman's chair make kingdoms tremble,
    Nor woo the marts o' the world with argosies
    Gold gath'ring.
                  Choose! don arms, a Gordon be!
    Woo statecraft e'en as Cairns or Iddesleigh!

Such lavished wealth as Peabody's can no man
Grudge him the culling.   Only remember this—
'Tis not the *deeds,* but chief the *life* that tells ;
'Tis less the *doing* than the *being* good.
Shine where you walk—no fitful gleam, nor flash ;
Be light that leads your way, and ours there-through :
   So men shall say, " He speaketh : it is truth ! "
And men shall note, " He doeth : it is well ! "
   Shine thus ! and be our beacon for all time !

I mark and test ye, men of my race and hour :
Weighed, and found wanting !   Who out your midst will rise
And nobly achieve the Life wherethrough names live ?
   These will not, and those cannot !   These are laid
In sloughs of sloth : those, stirred by bootless fires
Of selfish pleasuring, or excitements vain ;
Some bound in bonds, some weak of wit or will ;   .   .   .

  .   .   .   .

I test, I list ; and, strained and baulked, my sense
Knows He is not yet near ; and, tired, I turn
Once more to wholly heed, O Earn, thy voice,
That shall Him dulcet greet, in days unborn !

MORAY-LAND.

BRIGHT Moray of the North! thou queenly shire!
Still sov'reign thou; though not, in this our day
Of faded Chivalry, so fair thy crown
As when, six hundred years agone, the pride
Of England, round their long-limbed Edward, brought
Gold and the weight of arms, to instruct thy sons
In due submission!—
              When the cloistered Art
Tilled thy rich meads, and wooed thy bounteous clime;
And the fair Abbey throve, and Priories grand
Bade the deep glens rejoice, and multiply
Their generous product.
                Not in these swift times,
Heedless, irreverent, dost receive the meed
Of worship due to skies of sapphire hue,
And summer seas that whisper Italy!
No homage now, but just for careless using
T'wards pelf and lucre, at the world's refusing.

In this bright land of Moray lies a spot,
Above the fair most fair—a very star
I' the firmament of Beauty; a bright pearl
Laid in her opaline shell, whereon the wind

Breathes perfumed sighings, and the generous Sun
Bends graciously, as o'er a favoured child
A happy parent, beaming, smiles to bless.

    Lovely art thou, O hallowed airt of Earth!
There, where thy Homestead, set on sunny lawns—
On sunny sweeps of shrub, and laurelled lawns;
By bosky-circled, rainbow garden-ground
Environed; trimly shelters 'mid her trees,
Whose giant boles and branching canopies
Cherish this fondling of a later time
With ancient grandeur, whispering of abodes,—
There, ere thou wert, quaint-structured, homely bower!

    From this sweet nest, all over-rushed and spread
Of ruddy creeper, and of scented rose,
And feathered clematis; oh! what delight
To plunge in deepest forest, following down
The sombre Findhorn's wayward course profound;
Or, where the pine-woods t'wards the uplands rise,
Climb the moor-purpled crests, from thence to view
Eight shires, fair-spread, that mantling, laugh or frown
As skimming lights fleet kissing, or refrain,
And wood, and sea, and mountain vivid show
In the clear northern air! . . .

    Where lead the iron wheels, bewinged of steam,
Where sweeps the dainty barge on ocean furrows,
Lie lands of loveliness we know and praise:
Afric's bright North, where virgin-fair Algiers
Queens it, the pirate-freed; Kabylia's pride,
White Constantine, on thousand foot of rock
High-set, commands; and Egypt's memoried land,

Where lilac shadows glad the arid plain,
And Nile revives her Delta's glowing green
In yearly season, and old Cheops reigns
To mock our Modern : . . .
               These we know and praise !
And eke, bright Islets of the azure main ;
Sicilia, with her gem-like capital
Set in its golden shell ; Mallorca rare,
Whose sapphire crags dip feet in emerald depths
Of golden globe-hung orchards, sheltering
Sweet eld-time hamlets : these, and isles as fair :
Art-steeped Italia's shores ; the Rhine-cleft Teuton-land,
And many a clime of light, and love, and joy,
We know, we know, and praise ; but never yet
Dulls the dear North to our returning gaze !

  How shall I laud thee best, O wholly loved !
Say, that the dullest soul, most indolent,
Insensate, passionless, must own thee fair ;
Or self forthgone from that celestial sense
That kins mankind with angels, or the stars
Of morning, who arose to shout for joy,
Erst viewing the refulgence of the world ?

  Say, that thou art mine adoration's Shrine,
God's Highest Altar in this under-world,
Whereon I lay my love, my hope, my prayers ? . .
  For ye, my fellows, unto whom I owe
My heartis best, shall blame me naught in this,
Because, when, winnowed from its soil, our grain
Shall spring to Life in Heaven's amaranthine meads,
There will we company ; while this poor land,

Whose beauties bloom, like all of earth, to fade,
Shall blend its ashes with a ruined world.

What can I say ? or, saying, what avails
A helpless daughter, for thy weal and worth ?
Meseems, for century on century past,
Thy spell, like ever-drip from craggy height,
Hath worn a larger holding on each ledge,
Till it hath hollowed out, and brimmed above,
The basin where at last it dwells,—one heart.

Thy sons from thee in bleak indifference turn
To alien lands and loves of less delight :
I, powerless, lame of fancy, word, and wit,
Have hearked the winds and waters, till their sense
Bade me interpret here the tale they told.
So, writing of lesser lustres, Altyre mine,
I use thee, as a broiderer with beads
Bytimes sets a true pearl i' the robe, to lend
Value beyond the labour.   .   .   .
                              Fare thee well,
Thou rapturous memory of a living spell !

Song.

Sing not of hazel eyne, lad, in the dawning light,
When love awaketh, and waileth for benison,
But of the hue of those fair sun-sought water-ways,
But of my River, that leaps to the Sea!

Glows there a maiden cheek bright as the rosy cloud,
That ere sun-setting thy sea-tomb o'ercanopies?
Laugheth her sweet lip as smileth thy gladsome tide?
Oh! my loved River, that winds to the Sea!

Sing not of golden hair, sing of the tresses fair
Autumn-bright birkens drip down to the sombre pools;
Sing not of lasses with grace in their going; sing,
Sing of my River, that floats to the Sea!

Yourselves—wave makers of music—sing amain,
That I may catch your sweet, wild, woeful sense,
Love-aided, to interpret; and the Wind,
The ancient hoary North, comes to mine aid,
Out of th' abyssmal caverns of the past,
Bearing his memories down the sweep of Time,
Woven in wizard Rhyme.

NOTES TO MORAY-LAND.

" Bright Moray of the North !"—P. 7, l. 1.

THE History of the province of Moray, by the Rev. Lauchlan Shaw, minister of the Gospel at Elgin, printed in 1775, gives the fullest account of our native shire. He gives its extent as "From the mouth of the river Spey to the borders of Lochaber, in length ; from the Moray Firth to the Grampians, in breadth, including part of Banffshire to the east ; the whole shires of Moray and Nairn ; and the greatest part of the shire of Inverness. All which was anciently called the province of Moray, before there was a division into counties." He says, " Ptolemy doth not touch this point, nor doth any ancient writer that I know ; " but gives the reasons for his statement. He also gives as the rendering of the name, that the Highlanders called it Murav or Morav—from the Celtic words Mur or Mor, *the sea ;* and Taobh or Tav, *the side ;* and in construction, Morav, *i.e.*, the Sea-side. He pays worthy tribute to its charming climate, and the fertility of its plains and valleys, which has so justly earned it the title of "The Garden of Scotland " ; quoting the old saw, "That in the plains o' Moray they have forty days of fair weather in the year," more than in any other part of Scotland. The Gulf Stream is supposed to affect the Moray Firth.

" Their long-limbed Edward brought."—P. 7, l. 5.

Edward I., King of England, surnamed Longshanks, entered Morayshire with his army in 1296 — he was in the fifty-seventh year of his age and the twenty-fourth of his reign ; and again invaded the province in September 1303, in the thirty-first year of his reign.

" And the fair Abbey throve, and Priories grand."—P. 7, l. 10.

The Abbey of Kinloss, near Forres. Morayshire boasted, in the thirteenth century, of an abbey, three priories, and several monasteries.

" Quaint-structured, homely bower."—P. 8, l. 12.

The present house of Altyre is devoid of architectural pretension, having been added to and patched at various periods. It is none of it of great age. Tradition asserts there was an older residence or castle rather to the left of the present site. The Cummings seem to have lived at Dollas. Alexander Penrose Cumming (afterwards Sir A. P. Cumming-Gordon of Altyre) writes in 1801 : "The castle of Dollas—now called Torchastle—of which but a small piece of ruin now remains, was for many years the mansion of the family of Altyre, and in it my great-grandfather Alexander was born. On being divested of his family seat, or probably preparatory to it, or perhaps previous thereto, seeing his castle going to decay, he or his father set about building a house at Altyre, wherein the family resided till about the year 1789, when, my family being very numerous [he had sixteen children !], and Altyre insufficient to hold us, I bought the present house of Forres [from the Tullochs of Tannachy], where we have still resided."

Lucy Gordon of Gordonstoun (whose great-grandmother was that Lady Jean Gordon divorced by Bothwell to marry Mary Queen of Scots, and who afterwards married her cousin, Alexander Gordon, Earl of Sutherland) left by her marriage with Robert Cuming of Altyre an infant son, Alexander Cuming, who was the great-grandfather mentioned by Sir Alexander as being divested of his family seat in Dollas.

It appears that the infant son of Lucy Gordon and William Cuming was circumvented by his grandfather and guardian, Sir Ludovic Gordon of Gordonstoun, who bought from him (or, by some accounts, from his father) the barony of Dollas, about 1668, at a very low price.

Curiously enough, this barony returned to Altyre when, in the fourth generation from Alexander, the Cummings succeeded to the Gordonstoun estates, in right of the above "Lucie" Gordon.

So the present house of Altyre cannot, in its oldest part, be older than 1666 to 1668. But charters were signed at Altyre before that, notably a marriage-contract between James Cuming and Margaret, sister to Symon, Lord Fraser of Lovat, signed at Inverness *and Alter* November 1602. And Mrs C. Bruce mentions another contract between a son of Cumin of Ernished (Earnside), and a daughter of John the Grant, of marriage, at Altyre, *circa* 1581. "There had been," says Mrs Cumming-Bruce, "a warrant from the Crown in 1419 to build the castles and fortalices of Dollas and Earnside ; . . . it remained, therefore, for Sir Thomas [Cumyn of Altyre] to carry this into effect, and small castles were built at both places. The architect, it is believed, was Cochrane, the favourite of James III., by him created Earl of Mar. . . . Cochrane, it is said, built Calder, Kilravock, Earnside, and Spynie, and no doubt was master of the works at Tarnua [Darnaway] when James II. and III. took possession of it as a hunting-seat, after the attainder and death of Archibald Douglas, Earl of Moray, in 1455."

Cochrane's end was tragic, for he was hanged over the bridge of Lauder by a "hair tether," in August 1481. The barony of Dollas "marchis with" (*i.e.*, joins) Altyre, and the houses are about six or seven miles apart.

"Altyre mine."—P. 10, l. 15.

Pont, or Gordon of Straloch, who on Pont's decease was engaged to complete the 'Theatrum Scotiæ,' says : "Altyr, ad Cuminios spectans, quæ gens ante trecento annos omnium Scotiæ nobilium et supra omnes Scotorum proceres potentissima et numerissima," &c., which is thus rendered in Blaeu's Atlas : "Altyr, qui appartenoit à ceux de la maison de Cumines qui estoit, il y a plus de trois cens ans la plus riche et la plus puissante de l'Ecosse," &c.—Novel Atlas de Jean Blaeu, cinqme. part : Amsterdam, 1654.

THE

STORY OF ALASTAIR BHAN COMYN

THE DELL OF SLAGINNAN.

Treating of certain folk within a dell ;
And how their fateful meeting erst befell.

Rich is that deep late season, when the earth
Lies panting, burdened with her ripening grain ;
One blue alike the sky, the hill, the Firth
Clothes, and the heather purple, on the wane
But still delicious, drapes the misted moor,
And carpets firry forest ;—wherewith blent,
Swathes of rich yellowing bracken yield allure.
When on the Laigh the gilding corn is bright,
The plushèd barley floats, a mantling sea ;
And oats have golden ague, and the wheat
O'er vassal flowers sways sceptred monarchy :
When, in hot silences of afternoon,
Air is all weighty with a pine-wood scent,
And mazy buzzing of innumerous flies ;
Or a by-passing bee, in drowsy tune
Humming, the breathless quiet scarce belies,—
Such sounds enhance the stillness !

                    Ere this prime
O'er-rich of the year, when gentle June doth reign
In early matronhood, I, wandering lone,
Would seek fit haven for an idle hour ;

B

Then would I choose, to lull in soft delight
My jaded sense on Mother Nature's breast,—
A rocky dell I wot of, cool and deep,
Mossy and bowered o'er; oh, such a dell!
Haply a faëry country, hemmed about
With boulders, monstrous to the miniature
Of all within.

               No eye could scan its deep
From the above, because the pathway wound
(The footway of all wild and haunting things
That wonned there), wound in dense and devious way,
Now right, now left, then sudden dropped adown
To a rare spread of green and amber moss;
Nor there did cease, but split to many paths,
Twisting among the granite blocks, that wild,
In heaped confusion, strewed the place around.

   Fair, ferny plumes clustered in every nook,
And many-tinted lichens on the rocks
Drew dainty pictures, vague and various.

   No step but showed, for lute or limning, scenes
Fairer than other.   Here, 'neath a grey bare cliff,
Had fallen across the path a birken tree
Moss-cushioned,—dainty feathered all in sprays,
To form an elfin bridge : there, tiny pools,
Half hid by mimic rocks, lent tenderest hues
To greener mosses and more filmy fronds ;
While from a rock-rift sturdily issued forth
One austere Hollan, in whose martial arms
Nestled a white-bloomed Rowan.

   No unsubdued and rudely peering ray
Might cleave in summer the o'erarching boughs ;
But daylight glided in all softly green,—
All soft in mystic tenderness of gloam ;

And dream harmonics touched the attentive air,
Whisp'rous of musical waters wandering near.
   A further reach of quaintly sorted scenes
Wore-through the dell; when burst the invading Sun
In flash and flood through leafage on the rocks,
Striking to silver every ghostly birk
That threw adown the heights her tressèd shower.
   Still sang the music, and a gentle curve
Now in full radiant sunlight soon revealed
Its origin,—the rich and sombre flow
Of Divie's tide, that lingered 'neath the bank
(So lover 'neath his mistress' lattice lurks)—
As loath to leave Slaginnan's loveliness.

   She, all arrayed in weighty crimson robe,
And all enrobed in Beauty's witchery,
Moved through the dell.   .   .   .
And as her tiny tread imprints the moss,
Yon following train of crimson doth efface
The Ladye's track, as jealous of pursuit.
   Oh, beautiful !
A pale transparent loveliness—belit
To life by moonlight of her lucent eyes,
Beaming around in softest 'wilderment.
Her hair—like Findhorn's waters hued, when rays
Call golden laughter from the deep brown pools—
By golden snood was stayed; and from her hand
Hung 'broidered glove, and switch, and velvet cap
Crimson, bedight with heron's plume of grey.

   The stilly glen grew stiller, hushed to hear
The music of her motion.   Loitered she
In growing hesitation, gathering dread:

Now stayed to hark the river, for its song
Gave sense of company; now paced again;
Till, faltering at those mystical silences,
Half dazed, half daunted by the pallid day,
Strayed she aside, and on a lichened stone
Rested.

        Anon her voice made melody;
And, o'er her breath in quav'ring utterances:
    "Where have I strayed? Bayoumé, fatal steed,
To serve me so! Methinks thou art in league
With some Fay-guardian of this eerie spot!
What weird romance might Denys' fancy weave?
(Would he were here e'en now, or with him, I!)
Almost I see the dainty moulded car,—
Some fair cocoon, silk-lined and moth-forsaken,—
By lythe moor-lizards drawn, harnessed in wreaths
Of cran-flower bells that tinkle in the breath
Of soughing airs; and he, my spritish love,
With tiny beckoning hand invites me sit,
Cushioned on mossy verdure, by his side!
I'faith, I needs must dwindle ere I sit!"

    And through her faëry fancy losing fear,
She laughed aloud!
              A solitary bird,
Answering, harmonious chirped; and came, surprised,
One gentle sunbeam, glinting through the leaves,
To learn what cheered.
              But now an alien sound,
A tread, a stir of stones, alarmed the maid
And rising hastily, with tightened grasp
Of switch, and gathered garment for a flight,
She faced the intruder.

Through the soft green shade,
Adown the rough descent, he featly passed,
And moved with stately pace towards the maid,
Whose wonder o'erpassed fear. . . .

Did she behold the wooer of her conceit,
That faëry monarch, come to claim his bride
In guise most mortal? Or did heroic ghost,
The semblance of the invader Viking, slain
In combat with the Moray men of yore,
What time the beaks of galleyed War did plough
Yon smiling Firth,—did such return to mourn
Departed joys of pillage and of fray?

Not such this stranger, for his garb bespoke
No Fay-loom weaving, no Sea-king's array:
For the marled tartan round his girdle hanging,
Thence to his shoulder caught in draping folds
To's leathern vest affixed; the brogs, untanned,
Thonged to his shapely feet; the cap of hide
Poised on his brow,—might e'en have clad the form
Of any stalwart herd: nor mote the grace
Of his approach have marked him more than these,
For that free bounding step belongs to all
Who tread with limbs untrammelled the heathery moor:
But as from out the shade to sun he passed,
The golden glory of his head forth-shone,
And caught the beams (as golden waves reflect
In some fair amber tide the morning smile),
Crowning him king among the sons of men!
As rich their wonders gleamed from beard and brow,
Such locks of pride a fitting halo formed
To the proud face and noble, that from her,
Ydonea, wiled the remnant of her dread.

His blunt address showed more of camp than court;
For, scarcely vailing bonnet:
                              " Thine the steed
That, tethered, chafes, up yonder in the wood,
Ladye?" he said.   " Whence come you, and whither bound?
'Tis, sure, unsafe to roam these airts alone!
For wild beasts prowl, and wilder men do prey;
And in the darkling eve, creatures of dread
May haunt these solitudes.   You do not well
To tarry here all 'fenceless and alone!"
     Her lurking dread had vanished at his voice,
And soft she answered:
                              " Sir, I had no will
In seeking this enchanted dell: my steed,
The Barbary roan you spake of—lately mine,
Scarce yet to obedience tutored—fled away,
Frayed by the horn, and my poor strength o'ermastering,
Bore me out ken of the hunt.   At length he tired,
And I, in vain, sought out the homeward route;
For 'tis no pastime in these woods to prove
A track unkenned.   I strayed till voice below
Of murmuring stream gave hopes of clue, when tying
Self-willed Bayoumé to a tree, I came
Hither, and trust my homeward way to you!"
     Then Alastair: " Fair Ladye, tell me whence
You be? and claim such service at my hands
As may provide your safety!"
                              " I am ward,"
Ydonea said, "and kinswoman to John,
The Earl of Moray; and he makes abode
Even now at Forres, whence this morn I rode."
Smiled Alastair then, but courteously made speech:

" We had not heard that grim John Randolph housed
So fair a guest ! "
      " I left but late," spake she,
" 'Neath my true cousin Denys' wardenship,
Sweet sunny France—my motherland ! "
          " And I,"
Rejoined her questioner, " but now return
From personal assurance of the weal,
Round Inverlochy, of our Lochaber kin
(There now, alas ! no longer paramount).
Days have I sojourned afar, so may have missed
The stir of your arrival ! "
        " Sir, your name ? "
" Alastair Comyn, callèd Bāu (the Fair !).
My father's castle stands within yon wood."
 " A Comyn ! " cried the damsel ; " 'tis a name
That breathes of broil ! "
      . He laughed aloud, and bent.
" We will not bandy words o'er my descent.
I am a treacherous twig of traitorous tree,
Doubtless thou'st heard—if thou hast heard at all ? "
(And seemed he wished to hear that she had heard,
For she was beautiful, and he was young !)
But she replied not, save :
       " The day wears past,
I would be going ! " So he led her forth,
And helped her mount, and syne convoyed her on,
Speechless the twain, till, a wood-clearing reached,
He paused : " I hear the horse-hoofs, and I mark
Yonder the liveried varlets of your host !
They seek you, Ladye ; you are safe. Farewell."
 And ere Ydonea thanked him he was gone ;

While through the vista'd tree-stems rode to her
The pleasèd grooms, and prayed " Our Ladye's grace :
They had sought long, and joyed to find her well ! "

    And so they homed ; and through the forest glades
Ydonea seemed to spy a golden sheen,
And thought of nothing but a golden head,
And wondered much—and all of Alastair.

NOTES TO THE DELL OF SLAGINNAN.

"The dell of Slaginnan."—P. 17.

"SLEOCH-NAN-CEANN," or the "hollow of heads," assuredly won its Gaelic name from the tragedy enacted in the little ravine, and told towards the end of this story. I have seen it also spelled "Slack-kaunin," but have used the modern (and ugly) rendering.

"Of Divie's tide, that lingered 'neath the bank."—P. 19, l. 11.

A stream, tributary of the Findhorn, which runs by Dunphail and Relugas, joining the larger river below the latter place.

The destruction wrought by this little stream at Dunphail and Relugas in the great flood of 1829, is graphically told by Sir Thomas Dick Lauder in his 'Moray Floods.'

"Not such this stranger, for his garb bespoke."—P. 21, l. 13.

It is a favourite assertion among many whose study of the subject is at best partial, that the Highland garb and its composing tartans is of modern invention. This assertion is easily refuted.

Without quoting the 'Vestiarum Scoticum,' a work supposed to have been written by "Schyr Richard Urquhard, Knycht," about the end of the 15th century (wherein are described clan tartans as then worn), edited by the brothers Sobieski Stuart, authors of another

work on Highland costume ; or mentioning the well-known tradition
that St Margaret, wife of Malcolm Ceannmohr, and Queen of Scotland, taught her people to weave the marled stuffs with which she
clothed them,—I refer those interested in the subject to the 'Gazetteer of Scotland,' published in Glasgow in 1844, wherein appears an
excellent description of the Highland dress, under head "Highlands." It is too long to quote whole, but the editor utterly denies
that the philibeg (or kilt) is of modern invention, and that the truis
or trews was the dress of old.

It is probable that these were very ancient, but they were chiefly
confined to the upper classes, who used them for horseback.

Beague, a Frenchman, who wrote a history of the campaigns in
Scotland in 1546 (published in Paris in 1556), states that "they [the
Scottish army] were followed by the Highlanders : these last go almost naked ; they have painted waistcoats, and a sort of woollen
covering variously coloured." Lindsay of Pitscottie says also : "The
other pairts northerne ar full of mountaines, and very rud and homlie
kynd of people doeth inhabite, which is called the Reid Shankes,
or wyld Scottis. They be cloathed with ane mantle, with schirt,
fashioned after the Irish manner, going bair legged to the knie."
Much of this and what follows is gathered from Logan's 'Scottish
Gael.'

The 'Gazetteer' then describes the Breacan-faile, or "checkered
covering," as a plain piece of tartan, four to six yards in length, and
two yards broad, bound round the loins with a leather belt, the
lower side falling to the knee-joint ; and while there were *foldings*
behind, the cloth was double before.

The upper part of this cloth was fixed on the left shoulder with
a large pin. As the "breacan" had no pockets, a purse of goat or
badger's skin, or plain leather, and called "sporran," was worn in
front. Shoes and stockings are of comparatively recent date in the
Highlands. Stockings were originally of the same pattern with the
plaid—not knitted, but cut in web and laid up behind ; garters
were of rich colours and broad, wrought in a small loom now almost

laid aside. Martin (Dean of the Isles) describes the dress of the women in the Western Isles, which may be taken as worn also in the Highlands : " The women wore sleeves of scarlet cloth closed at the end, as men's vests, with gold lace round them, having plate buttons set with fine stones. The head-dress a fine kerchief of linen straight about the head. The plaid was tied before on the breast with a buckle of silver or brass."

The plaid, which, with the exception of a few stripes of red, black, or blue, was white, reached from neck almost to feet : it was plaited, tied round the waist by a belt of leather studded with silver.

Elsewhere we read : " The annals of the Iona Club have completely disproved the theory that the kilt and particoloured tartan plaid are of modern origin, and show that from the time of Magnus Barefoot [or föd, King of Norway], an. 1093, the Highlanders were always described as the 'bare-legged or red-shanked, wild, or rough-footed Scottis, clothed with ane mantle, with ane shirt saffroned ' [Beague's painted waistcoat ?] . . . their 'delight being in marled clothes, specially that have long stripes of sundry colours, and chiefly purple and blew.' The women's plaid differing only from the men's in its smaller size, being ' white, with a few small stripes of black, blue, and red.'"

Martin, Dean of the Isles, says in his History, in what may be looked on as a summary of his own and all previous observations on the question, that " every isle differed from each other in their fame of making plaids, as to the stripes in breadth and colour. This humour is also as different through the mainland of the Highlands, in so far as that they who have seen those places are able at the first view of a man's plaid to guess the place of his residence." The chiefs, besides the eagle's plume in the bonnet, often wore costly and richly dyed stuffs in their coats and vests, with slashed sleeves of scarlet cloth and gold lace, long plaited hair, and numerous studs and clasps of silver on their belts, and occasionally even a polished steel helmet. Green is now believed to characterise the tartans of clans having an Irish descent, as the Mackenzies ; red, of the pure

British Celt, as the Rosses and Clan Gregor; and yellow, the Danish clans, as the Macleods.

Miss C. F. Gordon Cumming, in her book on the Hebrides, says : " We had a glorious sail to Rodel in Harris, where we at once made for the old church, St Clement's Cathedral, which has a few quaint bits of old carving. The tower is the oldest building in Scotland, except, &c., . . . and those who doubt the antiquity of the kilt as now worn, may here see a most unmistakable sculpture of the garb of old Gaul. I suppose," she continues, "the use of tartan in remote ages was well proven, even before the appearance of that quaint old metrical version of the Scriptures, still preserved at Glasgow, which told how—

> ' Jacob made for his son Josey
> A Tartan coat to keep him cosy.' "

Logan, in his ' Scottish Gael,' quotes an account or charge of the Bishop of Glasgow, treasurer to James III. 1471, in which appears, "An elne and ane halve of blue *Tartane* to lyne his gowne of cloth of gold, £1, 10s.," and two other such tartan items.

And a contemporary picture of Mary, Queen of Scots, with tartan in her attire, was exhibited at the Peterboro' Exhibition, and was, I imagine, one I myself saw in Glasgow in 1888, where the Queen wears a whole mantle of Stuart tartan.

Dr James Taylor of Elgin writes to myself : " The dress . . . which went under the name of Breacan-feile—a tartan cloth from four to six yards in length, and so arranged round the body as to form both a kilt and a plaid—seems to have been the common garb of a Highlander in the fourteenth century." On a piece of ancient Greek sculpture, now in Rome, a *bagpiper* is represented dressed like a Highlander.

Logan says, "The Breacan in its simple form is now [about 1826- 31] seldom used. . . . The Highlander would require some assistance at his toilet if he wished to dress with requisite precision. . . . When abroad, he spread it on a sloping bank, and having the belt under it; laying himself on his side and buckling his girdle, the object was accomplished."

The late George Ross of Cromarty dressed in this fashion. My father (the late Sir Alexander P. Gordon Cumming) wore, when in full dress, a very perfect Highland costume. The coat was velvet, garnet-coloured, and gold-laced; the garters were gold, rich lace was worn at the neck and falling over the wrists, and among the gold and velvet belts hung the enamel powder-horn and stuck the inlaid pistols once the property of King James VI. (I. of England).

In my time—writing in 1888—the Highland dress is worn only by the upper classes, or by children in villages. Many, alas! of those who have a right to wear it, have given it up; and tourists and Southrons, with no spark of Scottish claim, have usurped the rejected honour. To look really well in the kilt, one must be to the manner born; and it is sometimes "carried" in a fashion that is neither dignified nor seemly! The Act passed in 1747, "that neither man nor boy, except . . . should on any pretence wear or put on the clothes commonly called Highland clothes—namely, the plaid, philibeg, or little kilt," &c., might be revived with advantage, for application to such cases as these!

I find an interesting correspondence with our kinsman, E. Dunbar Dunbar, of Seapark, and Glen o' Rothes (author of 'Social Life in Former Days'), on the subject of garbing Macbeth, when Gustave Doré proposed to illustrate Shakespeare.

It is too long to give (whole) here.

Mr Robert Young of Elgin says: "It is difficult to say how Macbeth should be dressed; probably in a species of chain-armour, stitched on a leathern tunic. The *kilt* is of modern date" (he means in its present *tailored* form), "but the checked tartan plaid was used at a very early date."

Mr Cosmo Innes says: "M. Doré enjoys the advantage of the question being absolutely open for him to dress Macbeth as he pleases; only, he did wear *some* dress, painting having been given up!!! I think his dress was a long tunic from shoulders to calf of leg, and some ornament like the Roman laticlave round the bottom of the robe ; . . . probably woollen, of dyes, furnished by our own hills, and varied almost *ad lib.*

" On high days . . . I guess a silk dress was substituted, and perhaps some gold ornaments round the skirt. For head-gear put a simple gold circlet with a few leaves as dress of peace. . . . The arms for defending the body might be rings or mail, fitting to the shape, though we have one fine instance of a sort of laminated silver dress of high antiquity. . . . Tartan (as we now read the word) is not admissible, nor any checked material. I cannot find authority at very early periods for the trews, or trowsers, which disappointed me. The instances which led us to adopt that as an early dress are those of men whose tunic, used on horseback, clung to the leg," &c.

Mr William Skene refers M. Doré to the work of the brothers Stuart, ' Costume of the Clans,' saying its letterpress contains every notice that exists regarding the dress from the earliest period ; and there are very accurate drawings of every representation of it, either on monumental stones or on pictures. It was published in 1845. The observations of Mr Robert Young appear to him, on this subject, very just.

Mr Charles Winchester writes from Rue du Dauphin, Paris, that Doré was much interested in these inquiries. " At the second interview he drew two figures for the mutual interview of Macbeth and Banquo, which showed that he quite appreciated the points set before him, so that we need not fear his producing either kilted Highlanders or Crusaders in plate armour. . . . It was marvellous to see the vigour of his invention, as with a stick of rough charcoal he sketched his notion," &c.

" Round Inverlochy, of our Lochaber kin."—P. 23, l. 9.

In the ' Origines Parles. Scotiæ' it appears that Inverlochy was the chief castle of the Cumyns of Lochaber. Lochaber and Badenoch came into the possession of the Comyns early in the thirteenth century.   The first chief of Lochaber mentioned is John Comyn, who is spoken of as party to an insurrection against the government of Edward I. in 1297.   It is stated that he had two galleys, larger than any to be seen in the Isles, anchored near his castle : "quod juxta castrum Johannes Cumin in Lochaber duæ magnæ galeæ fuerunt," &c.   This points to Inverlochy.—(Stevenson's Hist. Doc., vol. ii. p. 190.)   Gordon of Straloch mentions Lochaber among the Cumyn possessions : "Tenuerunt ea gens Buquhaniæ maximam partem ; Strathbogiam universam, Balvaniam, Badenochiam, *Lochabriam*, Atholiam, multaque alia in his oris.   Multaque quoque in australibus nostri regni provinciis, quæ mihi non nunc occurrunt."

The late Dr Taylor says Lochaber was wrested from the Comyns by Robert Bruce, and given to Angus Oich, junior of Isla, and to Ruari MacAlan ; "but it is pretty certain that the forfeiture thus made by Robert I. was cancelled when David Comyn, Earl of Athole, was fighting in the interests of Edward Baliol, and that Sir Robert Comyn, son of that Sir Robert assassinated at Dumfries in 1306, was reinstalled in his ancestral estate of Lochaber."   This Sir Robert was killed at Kildrummie with the Earl of Athole in 1335, and the estate probably reverted to the Brucean proprietors, from whom Lachlan Comyn was trying to recover it at the time of this story.   Inverlochy now belongs to Lord Abinger.   There is no assured record of the building of Inverlochy : a man at Fort Augustus, who "had but little English," told me of a tradition "that they will be tellin' round the fire in winter : how that the Comyns built Inverlochy long time since ; how they stood in a range [*i.e.*, row] from the hill to the place, and each man of them handed stones from the hill to his neighbour till the castle was builded !"   The ruins of the western tower are still called "The Comyn's Tower."   (The Gaelic name of Fort Augustus is Kil-na-Chumein, or Killiecumine as generally called, and is supposed to have been the burying-place of the Comyns of Lochaber.)   Mrs Grant, in her charming 'Letters from the Mountains' (1773), mentions an old tradition (evidently quoted from her by W. Rhind in his 'Scottish Tourist').   I give the passage whole. "You never saw such a castle [Inverlochy] in your life. I mused the whole night after I saw it, on the strange manner in which the inhabitants must have lived. It is large and square, and has the remains of four round towers. It is, built of round stones that never were touched by the hammer. You may guess its venerable antiquity from the circumstance of Achaius, 'our gude Scots king,' having signed a league with Charlemagne here in the eighth century. Only think how kings could choose such a residence! . . . It is somewhat singular that sixteen thanes or chiefs of the name of Cumming witnessed the league.

"The progress and declension of power is worth tracing, &c. . . . In these days the Cummings were unrivalled in the north, and potent everywhere. The wisdom and valour of some distinguished individuals no doubt procured this influence at first. When they acquired it they abused their power ; by their joint influence bore down every other name, till in the end they became the objects of universal fear and jealousy," &c. So criticises the bright correspondent, and no doubt justly.

I have been unable as yet to trace the source of her eighth-century tradition. Save the original keep, or "Comyn's Tower," what remains of Inverlochy is supposed to have been built by Edward I. of England. Lord Hailes, in his remarks on the History of Scotland, expresses in a long dissertation his doubts as to the historical evidence of the famous alliance between Achaius and the Emperor Charlemagne (note in Aikman's Buchanan, vol. i. p. 261) ; and further, quoting Lord Elibank's letter to Lord Hailes : "You tell us the only contemporary writer of reputation quoted in proof of it [the alliance] is Eginhart. . . . Your lordship admits that *missi*, or *nuncii*, as quoted by Fordun from Alcuin's letter to Offa, with the title of ambassadors, and you conjecture that the subject of the embassy was religious, &c. Eginhart was the chancellor and biographer of Charlemagne, Alcuin was his governor." Hill Burton mocks at the notion of such an alliance between a chief probably living in a krall of mud and wattles, and the Emperor of the world !

"Alastair Comyn, callèd Bān (the Fair !)."—P. 23, l. 14.

I have adhered throughout this story to the spelling perhaps most generally used in old documents and histories. Few names have been subjected to greater variety. In an old charter presently owned by the family, it is spelled five different ways in two lines. We have Comyn, Cumyn, Cumin, Comin, Commines, Cumeine, Cuming, Cumming (as now written). In Manx it is Comish, in Gaelic Chuimein, and in Gibson's Camden's Brit. I find, page 279, under "Gloucestershire": "Puckle Church: now it [P.] is only a small village, the seat of Sir Alexander COMING, by marriage with one of the co-heirs of the Dennises, whose family have been eighteen times High Sheriffs of this county." I should like to know if these Comings still exist. Spottiswood, Archbishop of St Andrews, spells it thus in his History : "John Coming, Earl of Bughan, and John, Lord Comin" (of Badenoch). As to the name in Manx, I find a letter from one J. G. Cumming, from Castletown, Isle of Man, in 1853, inquiring why Henry, Lord Beaumont, quartered in 1308 the three legs of Man, "in right of his wife, daughter and co-heir of Alexander Comin, Earl of Buchan," and saying that the landing and occupation of the island by John Cumming (*sic*) was in 1270, and that John de Ergadia, son of the Lord of Lorn, who had married a daughter of the Red Cuming, had large possessions in the island. He also says that a General Cumming of the Altyre family was, a few years ago, buried in the parish church *here* (*i.e.*, Castletown).

Shaw, in his 'History of Moray,' spells it "Cummine." He says it "is a surname of great antiquity in Scotland. Some deduce it from Hungary, others from Normandy, but I incline to think the name is a Scottish patronymic ; the learned Primate Usher shows that Comineus Albus, anno 657, was the sixth Abbot of I-Columb-Kill, from whom I would deduce the name. And the frequent mention of the Cummines in the eleventh and twelfth centuries is a presumption of a higher original than the days of William the Conqueror." (Why ?) Mr Shaw pettishly adds, "I have not seen the writs of this family [of Altyre], and therefore will not offer to deduce the genealogy of it." This was some quarrel with our great-grandfather, who refused to allow the worthy minister to rummage his family charter-room, and Mr Shaw, I believe, thought himself avenged by endeavouring to prove the younger branch of Relugas Comyns was older than the Altyre one. Many family histories are written thus, through personal feelings of individuals, to annoy or to please.

LUPOLA.

The orbèd moon unveils herself to see
The unveiling of a veilèd mystery.

WHEN Day was melting into tenderest Eve,
Ydonea rested in her chamber bright,
Where walls and daïs'd couch alike were hung
With needled tap'stry of France.
                                        The damsel sate
On a high seat, whose dark cut-velvet framed
Her listless form; a fauld-stool courted prayer
In a far corner, and the pine-polished floor
Was bare, save in its midst, where richly lay
An Orient rug, like autumn leafage hued,
In woods where gean and beechen fade and fall.
  A silver lamp four argent chains suspend
From the high roof unceiled; but scarcely gleamed
Its feeble ray above the shining eve
That penetrates the chamber!
                                        Mused the maid,
And on the carven table by her side
Lay a rich book of Hours; each sumptuous page
The last outshone, in colour, art, and gold!
  A robe of creamy samite fringed with gold

Hung on her tired and soft-relaxèd limbs ;
One small foot rested on a carven stool
Slippered in golden broidery, and one
Stirred dreamily, unshod, the hoary coat
Of an old wolf-hound slumbering on the floor.
    The eve declined ; Ydonea mused—and slept.

Then entered to Ydonea, with no word,
And with a soundless footfall on the floor,
A Woman, tall and white.
                 She stayed anear,
With folded arms, erect, and still no word—
Like a fair lawn-grown Pine, whose youth hath borne
The falling flakes throughout a winter's night,
And bride-like greets the morning. . . .
    From head to floor the stainless drapery fell,
And the warm glow of courtier clouds that showed
Their monarch sun to's mountain-screenèd couch,
Dared not to touch.   And still Ydonea slept ;
And in his slumber yelped the uneasy hound.
    Now the white Woman turned unto the light
A face right wondrous, in its marble chill—
Perfection.   Scarce the light-born hue of Life
Tinged its clear mould, save where the carven lips
Glowed red as berries.   Softly within the room
Crept the rosed light yet further, touching now
A tress, like Fay-spun copper blown with gold.
    So the white Woman stood ; and still the light
Crept wondering on, to seek what was that lacked
This statue-fair !   Not a responsive ray
Came from her beauty to its gentle quest ;
The Eye o' the World was closing—where—her gaze
Should glad expectancy with tenderest blue ?

Oh! were there eyne, or cruel vacancy,
She knew alone who wore those gauzy folds
In masking bandage drawn across her sight;
The outer world her sense might dimly reach,
But none without could read her inner soul.

Thus through her light veil gazing, till the glow
Of sunset faded from the drowsy land,
She stood, then hasty to the slumberers turned,
Waking old Corbred from his dreaming joys.
He from the floor upstarting, nosed the air,
And brake into a howling—plaintive, wild;
Scarce by his startled mistress' voice controlled,
But chidden, hied him far, and laid, and watched
With emerald eyeballs gleaming through the gloom.

"Ah, Lupola, 'tis thou! I dreamed, methinks,
And Corbred woke me with his sudden rage!
The hound will never love thee, Lupola;
Go, speak him fair; his wont is gentleness."

She called, but with a sullen sound of wrath
The hound shrank closer to the wall; and she
Named Lupola, with half-impatient gest,
Said: "Never heed, the hound concerns me not!
You were long absent, Ladye?"

"Ay: my steed
Sped his own errands in despite of me;
And when at last I checked his wayward course,
Found my lorn self vague in a wilderness,
Where-through, in ignorance wandering, I at last
Lit upon one who set my feet for home."

"Will you sup here, good Madam, or in Hall?"
"Here, Lupola, and then will I to rest.
I'll not require thy service; bid them 'quaint
The Earl of this my purpose. Give ye good night!

Thou leav'st betimes?   Provide thee with a phial
To hold such potion as thy leech prescribes."
     The serving-woman took Ydonea's hand
And fondly kissed it—passing from the room ;
And the great wolf-hound came from out his dark,
Suspicious scenting round, his tail erect,
His spine upbristled, cautious his velvet tread,
As would mark down a foe ; then prone he sank,
With sigh, but half content, his mistress near.

"Poor Lupola !" (and Corbred at the name
Pricked ears)—"poor maid !" Ydonea self-communed ;
"Thou hast my soul's deep pity.   .   .   .
The light of Heaven that is Heaven's best gift,
To thy pained eyes were better ne'er to be ;
Sweet Nature's gleam and glory only shows
To thee blurred dazzlement,—as when one sees
A forest flame through pungent mists of smoke,
And seems fair robing of yon couchant sun
Displeasuring hazes.   Thou'rt a right mad wench,
That stubborn so can hold against my will,
And let no leech amend thee ; but instead
Choose the fell Covesea witch-wife's caverned lore.
'Twould daunt, in sooth, a daring heart to face
The spells uncanny and the nameless deeds
In darkness wrought, thou'lt seek to-morrow's morn !"
     Soft in her cushioned seat the maiden leaned,
And back her memory bore, when on a day
She journeyed, in her Mother-land of France,
Dark forests through ; and lit on a ruthful scene—
A woodland croft ravaged by robber bands,
Where, 'mid the wreck of what was once a home,
They found a wilding maid of youthful years.

The child was very fair, but close her eyne
Were bandaged with some half-transparent veil;
And sore she plained, and fought who would remove it!
    Her tale of orphaned loneliness (that band
Of fell marauders had her grandsire slain),
So moved Ydonea,—orphaned late herself,
And in her dowered beauty fresh consigned
As ward to Moray's proud Earl, her father's kin,—
That she, with ne'er a question, took the girl,
And trained her youth in summers two or three
For personal service.
                    Through the rash Ladye's train
Passed discontented murmurings for a space;
For, at the nearest hostel, whisperings dark
Gave sombre colouring to her charity!
    For, seemed yon homestead bore an evil fame;
The gossips vowed its wreck a curse fulfilled;
And some, of shaken heads, made mutterings
Of Wolf-cubs being risky pets for play!

And further, since the maid to Scotia came
(Alone came she of all the Frankish suite,
When claimed the Earl his ward's fair company),
Her Ladye marked she held herself aloof
From all the Castle household, joying most
In isolated hours; but this ascribed
To joint infirmity of sight, and tongue
That scarcely mastered yet the Northern speech.
    And so Ydonea pitied; pitying, loved.

Passed Lupola within her lonely room—
A little room, all solitary, that gave
On a dark narrow stair, with brief descent

Down to the postern door. She closed and barred
Her own, then clomb the broad high window-ledge
And gazed across the forest and the Firth,
On soft, vague distance!
                          Mother, Mother Night!
Oh woo thy World-child, thou, to soft repose!
The Harmony of Silence should prevail,
And all rebellious sound discordant jar,
And every wakeful watcher feel condemned
As out of tune with Nature.
    What stirs at Night is evil, evil; save
The passing airs—the waft of angel wings
Laden with gentle dreams to bless the rest
Of Heaven's belovèd. Come, O Mother Night!
Soft arms, sweet eyes; my weary spirit fails;
Day-memories are so garish, gloaming's sloth
Breeds feeble discontent in my tired soul:
I call thee, Mother Night! a weary child
Who claims thy kiss for sleep!
                          The gloaming died;
And Light revealed from million starry thrones
His Ever-presence. Still sate Lupola,
Leaning against the stone as if asleep:
Fallen was the snowy veil from off her head,
And russet curls massed richly round her neck,
Aneath yon filmy binding of the eyne.
    Sudden she moved; and brake a low sad sound
Of wailing from her lips—so sore, so sad,
It might have been the winter wind, too soon
Harassing leafless woods; or moaning 'neath
Some ruined keep's dank walls. Then whispered she
Low, such lament as this, swelling in sound and woe:

" Oh, hellish period of divided time !
Thou Night, if blest to Earth, thrice damned to me :
Thou weird and weary time of witchery,
Hast thou returned to blight me with thy gloom ?

   Oh, double life ! oh, soulless hours of dark,
And hours of light all darkened by despair !
How long, ye Powers Above—if Powers there be—
Must I endure ? how late, ye lowest Fiends
(For that ye are, I doubt not !), must I serve
To represent your utmost ? Woe is me !

   Ah, Moon ! I loathe thy flat and sickly leer
When round thou wheel'st in Heaven, pitiless ;
No break, no kindly angle whereon to hang
One thread of hope ; thy full and perfect sphere
Contemns mine imperfection. . . .

" I do not quail, thou mocking Orb, to front
A death of dull oblivion ; but within,
Senses more strong than reasonings bid me live,
Fight on, endure ! Oft, oft I fain would yield
To that night Nature, and be wholly such
As thou compellest, and consort with my kind ;
But all my Human riseth in revolt
'Gainst the dread action that confirms my fate.

   " 'Twas said my mother prayed once, at her last—
One prayer, drawn forth by travail's agony,
Haply scarce wrought of sense ; but, said the Priest
Who chanced (unsummoned) on her dying hour,
And marked it—'twould bear fruit in aftertime ;
No cry from earth to Heaven e'er was lost :
—'Twould work me weal !—

                Once in yon wood of France,—

Whither my grandsire brought me from our North,
Our pine-grown land of rock and raging flood,—
When all the fearful crimes that 'whelmed our race
Brought human retribution on his head ;—
Once, in that wood, when all the land was blythe
At time of Noël [but it reached not us],
I, 'gainst a tree-bole leaning, saw a sight !

" 'Twas there I saw, or dreamed, that Vision rare,
That woke the spirit-craving first in me,
That showed me what I was—vile, infamous ;
By Sacred Purity   .   .   .
I saw a Gracious Figure, king-like crowned
In Light that shamed the sun ; but as I gazed
With painèd vision, dazzled ; did I mark
The radiance burst from points of many thorns,
As leaves break bud in spring-time.
                              Then-a-days—
More ignorant and brutish than the brutes,
So low in mental moulding that those nights
Scarce sunk my being baser than its day—
I wist not that I saw the Holy One !
He spake : ' O child ! a prayer is lodged in Heaven,
One prayer for thee.   Behold this golden thread
Reaching from Thence to earth ; lay hold and keep
Safe through thy weary span, this grip on Life—
'Tis called Endurance ; and its filaments,
Tight grasped, so wax and strengthen year by year,
That by this fragile cord aspiring souls
May climb at last to Heaven !   .   .   .
    Child of a race accursed,
Though Mercy seem no more, and Retribution
Stern Justice metes, yet learn My Sorrowing !

Is any like to that?   Behold I bid
Rejoice, who truly Endure!'   .   .

" The Vision faded, and I stood alone.
No more alone!   The 'rounding world that was;
The heavy, senseless, speechless world that was;
The world of dearth and nothingness that was,—
New life, new seeming wore: sound bore a sense,
And sight was more than viewing.   Nature lived:
In me high-leaped the pure humanity!
I shunned the brutish part: I craved a Soul;
A Soul, a part in Love—Eternal Hope;
A Soul to give me Life, who lived in Death!

" Me! mis'rable, with more than mortal's woe!
Whence to catch courage? who can give me laws?
Is life, or death, for me?   Wake, dreaming hills!
Start, ye dull woods, thou singing stream, thou sea!
Carest thou not, Nature, that thine offspring dies?"

She started up, as now a heavy cloud
Passed o'er the Soul of Night; and with a touch
Unloosed the binding from her eyes, and knelt
Up-gazing to the sky.   .   .   .

Shrink further into heaven, O thou moon!
And stars, hie down the deeps of blackest Night;
And lest your haste should fail, call wandering clouds,
Call purposeless and wandering clouds, to veil
The horrid spectacle!   Those steely eyes!
Those ringèd orbs all soulless in their glare!
Those hungering, craving eyes, that look at you—
What mean they?   Say, ye all-embracing eyne

Of staring Heaven! in your nightly watch
Have ye beheld the lion from his lair
Gaze outward thus?   The base hyæna so
Leer from his ruined shelter on the waste?
Or, from the Steppes the skulking wolf regard
Yon lunar Queen, and bay a vain protest
Against her shining?
   Ye have beheld and met a lover's gaze
All sharp with anguish from his last appeal;
Received the self-destroyer's frenzied glance
Of drowning pain from out the cold, black deep;
Ye have beheld the murderer's red regard,
When flying from his victim he uplooks
To see if Heaven be : but never yet
Was manifest to you a sight so dire,—
   A woman—with brute eyes!
                    Ah! Lupola,
Well mayst thou screen them from the sight of men,
But spare the stars!
                She drew their baleful light
Ere long into the chamber, and began
Herself to unrobe; and stood a moment there,
Her white charms lighting all the chamber's gloom—
As a pure lily, kissed of beamy moon,
Lights up the dusky garden.   There she stood,
A perfect woman in her primal garb
Of stainless beauty—save those awful eyes!
   She, with a shudder rending all her form,
Of loathing part, and part from chilly winds
That played upon her star-lit loveliness
Through airy inlets, seized her mantle swart,
And, draped and hooded, moved adown the stair,

And slipping past the sentry, fled away;
And clouds closed up, to baulk the wondering heavens.

There was a rock by the River,
  In the rock a deep cleft,
Wherein was a woman's mantle,
  Late in the darkness left.
Where, oh, where in the darkness—
  Where had she flown ?
And the River no answer
  Gave—but a moan !

NOTE TO LUPOLA.

" Of an old wolf-hound slumbering on the floor."—P. 36, l. 5.

THE stag and wolf hounds of Scotland were in great repute in the reign of David II., just about the period of this story, as he landed from France in May 1341. So great was their renown that they were even exported to foreign countries. " In Scotland are dogs of marveylous condition, above the nature of other dogs : the first is a hound of great swiftnesse, hardiesse, and strength, fierce and cruell upon all wilde beasts, and eger against thieves that offer their masters any violence ; the second is a rach or hound, verie exquisite in following the foote (which is called drawing) ; . . . yea, he will pursue any maner of fowle, and find out whatsoever fish (!) haunting the land, or lurking amongst the rocks, specially the otter, by that excellent scent of smelling wherewith he is indued ; the third sort is no greater than aforesaid raches, in colour for the most part red, with black spots ; . . . these are so skilfull, that they will pursue a thiefe. . . . These dogs are called sleuth-hounds."

There was a law amongst the Borderers of England and Scotland, that whoever denied entrance to such a hound, in pursuit made after felons and stolen goods, should be holden as accessory unto the theft.—(From the ' Miscellanea Scotica,' a collection of old tracts.) Our breed of black collie dogs (the oldest of all collies) hunt fish : brought up by shepherds as puppies, and chiefly compelled to seek for their own food, they acquire the habit ; and I have seen one of them spend hours watching the gold-fish in an ornamental basin on an English lawn.

Song.

Spring! Rosy Dawn, flamingo-like arise
From Night's drear fen, and tint the Heaven with Hope!
The base, dull bat is gone, and leaps the lark,
All mad with praising, up the glowing skies.

Laugh, mocking Morn; infect us with thy bliss,
Poor dullards, who'll forget the blythest day
Leads to mirk night; teach us thy buoyancy—
Sweet thy deriding, dealt us through a kiss.

Yet Night is frequent fair, and often kind;
Reign of sweet placid moon, of pulsing stars,
Soft-breathing ocean, gentle silences—
Soothing the nerveless brain, the tortured mind.

Fool us, dear Day; and fooled, we'll ne'er complain
If frolic revel leads to fainting force:
We'll quaff thy draught, Nurse Night, of poppied peace
Till deeper Dawns shall rouse, and make us fain.

COVESEA CAVERN.

Telleth how one, bowed down by weight of woe,
To seek unearthly aid doth seaward go.

Now laughed the young Aurora o'er the land,
And wild notes sprang from thousand gurgling throats
To do her homage. Zephyr lay abed,
So tired with daffing 'mid the leaves at night;
And nothing stirred—but music. Then the gates
Of Forres opened, and a scanty train
Of men-at-arms, and one esquire, came forth,
Convoying Lupola. The woman rode
In wonted muteness; and the 'squire decreed
His task a penance. Passed they through the peace
Of happy Nature; through the wakening woods,
And quiet fields, whose fatling herds of kine
Grazed, switching from their flanks the early fly;
Past orchard plots, where fair Kinloss did show
Her stately welcome to all journeying bands;
But none these craved: and onwards still they rode,
Nor turned by Elgin, where that city lurked
In maiden modesty behind the hill,
Uplooking with sweet reverence to the mound
Whereon, proud-set, her guardian castle stood,
Warning assailers with defiant tower,
Portcullised western gate, and fair chapelle

Of Holy Mary, sanctifying all—
Guarding the guardian! And, oh! city blest,
Where that Cathedral, "Mirror of the land,"
"The kingdom's glory," and sweet Moray's pride,
Stood, in maturity of perfect fame!

   Oh, fairest Fane! in ruin how fair; but then
Worthy to hold, if worthiness might be,
His Praise, Whose Inspiration sure bestowed
Such power for beauty on the unmeaning stone,
That here in forms of fairness effloresced,
Various as poet dreamings, heaven exprest;
Whose spire and pillar, like to holiest thought
Aspiring Heaven, and spanning Arch as broad
As Divine Purpose, glorified the soil!
   Oh, sacred Ruin! now in thy splendour lone,
And lonelier yet shalt be, as out of time
With the discordant novelty around,
When piece by piece, and pleading stone by stone,
Is all demolished, that the passing years
Have left about thee, nigh thy storied date.
   Like to some mighty monarch, hoar with age,
Who sees of all that hailed his crownèd prime
No soul yet living; but through some ordered spell
Is doomed in sumptuous sadness still to sit,
And know himself the left, the last, the lorn!
Stand then, oh, Grandeur! shrine of many prayers,
Whose incense clings yet round thee; may the hands
That raze thy humble sisterhood to earth,
That have despoiled, and ruthless still despoil,
From the once ancient city all of eld,
Rot, ere they wanton touch thee, reverenceless,
Though ne'er to such as they appeals thy loneliness.

D

So shunning Elgin, turned, me rather seems,
The band towards Duffus, passing closely by
That massy fortress, that the liquid plain
Commanded to proud Spynie, whence a breath
Of faintest blue went curling to the clouds,
Reminding every hungry voyageur
That Moray's lordly bishop brake his fast.

Nor might grim Oggeston, in its circling woods,
Tempt Lupola to turn aside ; nor recked
She that her escort fain would promise claim
Of dewy salads, fair roasts of fowl, and stews
Of fish from yon broad lake, and cates galore
Would be their meed where'er they chose to stay.
  But on they must, and o'er an upland rise
That showed them Ocean, in the gleaming joy
Of that late morning.
                    Then the cortége stayed,
And sought a tiny hamlet, built of sods
And stones and drift-wood ; mainly habited
By fisher-folk, whose simple poverty
Was known their best protection.   Lupola
Alighting, becked to her a gaping lass,
Half-scared at the beshrouded dame ; but sheen
Of silver guerdon drew her—part reluctant ;
And up the hill these passed.   Soon did the girl
Point out some guidance, and her steps retrace ;
While Lupola sped swiftly on alone.
  Laugh to the dappled sky, thou guileful Sea !
Thou guileless-seeming, sweet, deceitful main,
And tempt the silver gulls to sail thy breast
All fearlessly !
              Ruffle the tiny waves

Thy face, as smiles do ripple o'er the peace
Of slumbering infant's aspect; lave the base
Of the dream-hills across yon lovely Firth,
And sweep into the Sound of Cromarty,
Where glorious might the land's proud Navies ride !
Oh ! lip the foot of Moray with thy tide ;
Bring shells in fragile tribute, roseate weeds
And emerald tresses to adorn her shoon ;
Bear her bold sons in safety on thy breast,
And never show a frown ! For she is Queen !
Is she not Queen of all this worshipped North ?
. . . . . . Or wilt thou rage
And fight the howling, ravening wind, and rise
Dashing thy forces 'gainst her guarding rocks ;
Sending spray challenge hurtling through the airs,
As if thou couldst no longer bear the nigh
Of such dear loveliness, and not possess !
   Nay ! Be in peace, thou dreamy, tender sea,
For tenderness will woo her, patient sea ;
And never stirred thee such a storm as rends
Her breast, who threads the rocks that fang thy beach.

   Full painfully she picked her tangled way
'Mid the rough stones and boulders of the shore ;
Now slipped on weeds, or sank in trait'rous holes
Where myriad sea-snails drew their venturing horns
Home, and the living blooms of Ocean, hued
In tints of cream and ruby, their petals waved
Astonished, and forthwith sank sulkily
Into mere jelly 'neath the fretted tide.
   Above her glowered dark, rugged, beetling cliffs,
All cave-pierced and time-tortured ; while aloof
Tall fragments held their isolated state

In pillared pride; and aye that solemn sea
Plashed gently on the sand, or drew along
Rattling, the harassed pebbles.   Dissonant cries
Of skimming Moulets rang, and chattering daws
Haunted the niched and creviced rocks aloft;
And all along the solitary strand
These—and no human creature—held a sway.
   At length a rock abutment rounded she,
That bold and prominent stood; and soon espied
A yawning cave forth-belching clouds of smoke;
And as she neared the spot, a shrilly voice,
Harsh as those sea-birds chorusing its tone,
Came out the fume and made her stand to hear.
   " What comes," it cried, " disturbing my repose?
I see a veilèd woman; but mine ear
Did catch a stealthy tread of skulking beast,
Such as have prowled from out the landward woods
In white Decembers on our shore domains,
To find the sea most generous!   Who art thou?"
   "Methinks a woman in a piteous plight,
Who would consult thee!"
                              Forth from out the cave
Came a wild skirl, like laughter; and emerged
As wild a shape, all bent and bowed with eld;
A shrivelled hag, whose scattered hoary hairs
Incongruous mixed with chains of golden sheen,
Framing a visage like a withered fruit,
So brown, so wrinkled; but 'neath grizzled brows
Gleamed two black piercing jewels of a light
That, in such setting, startled him that saw
With most unthought-of brightness.   She was clothed
In coarse blue garments gathered to a belt

Whose clasp was golden ; and across her shape
An ancient fleece hung ; ragged, worn, and soiled.

   "And wouldst consult me, woman ? Ho ! ho ! ho !
(Rang the weird laughter wild amid the rocks).
   "Is't a love-philtre for young Donald's eyne ;
Is Colin faithless, Duncan fled ? and left
Thee such a soul-ache as must needs be borne
By maids that are forsaken ?"
                    Lupola,
Responding not, advanced, and tossing off
Her hood and bandage, looked with naked gaze
Into the other's face !

As one who sees 'mid mountain fastness lie
A silver cloudlet steeped in the matin beams,
And nears, admiring ; only to behold
Its loveliness unroll, and bare to view
The hideous night of some appalling gulf,
A very pit of darkness and of death ;
   So peered the hag, and raised a shielding hand
To guard her vision.   "This," she muttered, "this !
I've heard of This !   Come in, and I will speak !"

   She entered, ushering Lupola, the Cave.
A roomy cavern, narrowing into gloom
At its extremity—whose sandy floor
Was tramped all over with a many feet ;
For not alone the ancient Spae-wife wonned,
But had three stalwart sons, part fishermen,
All wreckers, who were rarely home by day,
But, like young chicks (or liker curses), came
To roost at eve, and quarrel o'er their prey.

Scant garniture the rock-house held, but here
And there, and round, such traces might be marked
Of Ocean's bounty, as proclaimed their trade
Bore profit on that dangerous Moray coast.
    Rich carpets, plashed and faded on the sand,
Lay tossed in corners; piles of cordage near;
Tall spars with heavy sail-cloth curtained off
At will the Cavern's deepest; nigh whose shade
Stood an oak-kist, huge, carved, and clamped with iron,
Charely ajar; bedazzling any look
That fell upon its treasures half revealed.
Such beakers peeped, embossed with cunning work,
Such graven dishes showed their laboured edge,
Such links of gold o'erhung the battered sides
Of their rough bed, as might have made the wealth
Of him that owned them.   Thou, O Miser Sea!
Not often dost disgorge from treasure-stores
Bounties so lavish: wherefore then to these
Surrender, all unworthy?   But the hag
Drew quick a sail athwart the glittering horde,
And motioned Lupola to sit, while she
Leaned 'gainst the rock before her, and began:

    "Chief of Unfortunates, I, here beholding
What reason almost denies, ask of thee, dread,
Art thou that mortal and material thing
Of shame-full centuries the embodied Curse?
That wretched victim to the ruthless ire
Of the avenging Power some men call God?"
    The woman answered: "Ye have said.   I, here,
I, who am, sure, Damnation all incarned—
Such a sur-natural and nameless wight
That I could deem me formed but to remind

Man that with Heaven is nought impossible ;—
Do bear that curse upon me,—I, the last
Of a wild Northern race, here represent
Epochs of changeless crime, when the Berserker rage,
Mead-wrought to ravage, left within their reach
Safety and peace unknown.   Fierce robbery
And rapine their profession, and their sports
Such as would make these walls sweat with the telling,
The shrieking infants flung from spear to spear,
By torch of burning homesteads.

       Quit such tales !
Hast, of thy Sorceress' lore, no woven spell
Would humanise ; no drug could give me share
In mortal joy and woe ?   Nay, not for Joy
Do I beseech ; let Sorrow be myself,
So I be human !   No tempestuous surge
Hath half my tumult ; though the ocean tides
And I alike are Luna's sport, whose orb
In sphered perfection works my utmost woe !

 And mark me, Witch ! when erst my damnèd doom
Revealed itself (that when this cruel light
Clads on her fullest splendour, I must wear
Another life, roaming unhumanised,
That Thing abhorred) ; a woman, wise as thou,
Warned, that if once in those dread periods
The Brute had mastery, if human prey
Suaged once in me the ravening appetites
Through 'nighted wanderer's fall, or feast, where shrines
In parcelled Mould, Humanity's decay,
I'd sign my doom in characters of blood,
And crown mine Evil victor o'er my Good."
" I read thee, thou wouldst abnegate for aye

The human part; so live the brute, so die!
Why not this choice? if that thy twofold nature
In contest o'erpass anguish!"   . . .

   "I had a vision once," the woman said,
"That woke such hope, forbidding life in death,
That I would rather now be dust, than live
Mere animal and wholly infamous!
   He Whom I saw bade me, like Him, endure!
Yet, oh! the days are long, the time is slow!
And oh! I weary: canst thou give no aid?"

She rose and neared the Spae-wife; and those eyes
Ungentle, yet had pleading in their glare,
As if the Woman pleaded through the Brute.
   Instinctively the crone spread forth her hands
In warding: Lupola retired a pace,
And bound her eyes, and heard the other say:
   "'Tis well, 'tis better, help I've none to give!
Take comfort; thou'st a Help above my ken,
Else hadst thou long been rotting in the ground,
As beast, or self-destroyer.   Go in peace!
I cannot help thee; miserable, go!"

   Low on the sand she sate, and cloaked her head,
And rocked her to and fro; while Lupola,
Forth passing from the Cavern, caught her moan
Of "Horror! horror! horror!"   And the Wind
Heard her at eve speak warning to her sons
Of vengeance terrible, though long delayed,
Ta'en upon sinners; and—these deemed her mad.

The woman hied her home, not hoping less—

Because she had not hoped ; beyond the thought
As nought of earth could help her anything,
Might so this witch, unearthly !

                      And she filled
Her phial from the bitter, bitter sea,
To show Ydonea, did she question aught
Anent her faring at the wild sea-cave.

NOTES TO COVESEA CAVERN.

" Where that Cathedral, ' Mirror of the land.' "—P. 49, l. 3.

" THE kingdom's glory," &c. "Speciale patriæ decus, regni gloria et delectatis extraneorum."

Bishop Barr, in his petition to the King after the burning of the Cathedral in 1390, describes it in these words (Reg. Ep. Morav., p. 204): "The beauty of its ruin sufficiently points to the grandeur of its prime." After its final destruction, many dykes, &c., in the neighbourhood were built of its remains. "Elgin Cathedral was founded under the auspices of Bishop Andrew Moray, a scion of the great and powerful family of De Moravia, who possessed the greater part of the district, and whose wealth and influence must have been very considerable, even in that rude period. . . . The original structure was founded in the year 1224, and probably completed during the eighteen years in which Bishop Andrew occupied the See. After standing one hundred and sixty-six years, it was burnt in 1390 by the Wolfe of Badenoch. Soon after, Bishop Barr began to rebuild it, and from the year 1414 the work was sedulously pursued till its completion. In 1506 the great steeple in the centre fell, and was rebuilt soon afterwards. Whether in the conflagration of 1390 the entire structure was demolished, has not been distinctly recorded."—Sketches of Moray, 1839, by W. Rhind.

> " *The band towards Duffus, passing closely by*
> *That massy fortress, that the liquid plain*
> *Commanded to proud Spynie, whence a breath.*"—P. 50, ll. 2-4.

Dr Taylor, writing of the province of Moray in the thirteenth century, says : " The county of Moray (le paiis de Moreuve) . . . presented in the thirteenth century a very different aspect from what it does at the present day.   Much of what is now fertile land, producing plentiful crops of grain and rich pastures, was then uncultivated, being to a great extent covered with wood. . . . Lakes and morasses occupied a considerable extent of the surface of the province.   The loch of Spynie was then an inlet of the sea," &c.   It was then possible to boat over the now richly cultivated plain, from Duffus Castle, an ancient hold of the De Moravia family, to the Episcopal palace of Spynie.   These places are now ruins.   My father, and the present Sir Archibald Dunbar, drained much of Loch Spynie in my own day.   The Rev. Lauchlan Shaw writes in 1775 (p. 78) : " The loch [Spynie]—except a few pits—in summer is not above five feet deep, and might be easily drained, could the gentlemen proprietors agree about the rich soil that would be recovered."

Very little water now remains, only on the property of Captain Brander Dunbar of Pitgavenny.

> " *Nor might grim Oggeston, in its circling woods.*"—P. 50, l. 8.

Now Gordonstoun, once the seat of a family called De Oggestoun.   Sir Robert Gordon, son of the Earl of Sutherland by the Lady Jean Gordon of the Huntly family [first, Countess of Bothwell, and divorced by her husband in order that he might marry Queen Mary of Scots], acquired from his cousin, Earl of Huntly, the lands of Plewlands and others ; and remodelling and adding to the ancient house or castle, whose traces still exist in the house now standing, settled there and created the family of Gordon of Gordonstoun. The daughter of this house marrying Cumming of Altyre, carried the estates ultimately into that family.

There are traditions of passages under ground leading to the sea-shore about a mile distant ; and the large cave, entered by a square doorway,—where the witch might have lived,—and now called "Sir Robert's Stable," may have communicated with these.

A Sir Robert is believed to have concealed his horses there during the Jacobite risings ; and it is not unlikely that the lordly Baronets may have found these natural storehouses convenient for smuggling purposes ! My grandfather, Sir William, destroyed secret stairs and hidden passages, finding servants, &c., dreaded the house. He also did infinite harm to the outside, pulling down cloisters in front, &c. His father had previously cut down much of the old timber to help to pay for the lawsuit with the Duchess of Portland, who claimed the property in right of the Scots of Scotstarvet.

" Home, and the living blooms of Ocean, hued."—P. 51, l. 26.

The sea-anemones abound on the coast of Moray. How we used to enjoy playing with them at low tide !—fat crimson fellows, or big buff ones with a blue edge. We cut up limpets to feed them, and used to watch the gradual absorption of the luscious fragment, and its spongy refuse thrown out after a while.

And how sure we were of their gratitude, and that they recognised and welcomed us, next low tide, if we had not severed them from their rock-bed, and taken them home—to die, alas ! in footpans or basins, where we had made them happy (?) homes !

" But, like young chicks (or liker curses), came."—P. 53, l. 29.

Persian Proverb—" Curses, like chickens, come home to roost !"

FORRES CASTLE.

Telleth of lovers, lily-pleasaunce, lays ;
And of an Earl ill-famed in byegone days.

"How far is't called to Forres ? " Mighty Will,
Thy voice hath taught the name to many a wight
Unconscious o't ; or yet what fame did fill
That fair far Northern Burgh, when the proud might
Of England rested underneath her walls,
And monarchs dwelt and died within her halls.

In this same Forres, named of Shakespeare's quill ;
High-placed, the royal castle graced a mound,
Within whose precincts Moray's Earl did dwell
This story'd date ; and with him presentlie
Ydonea, ward and guest. . . .
    Beneath the castle walls and by the burn
That flows from Altyre uplands past the town,
A little plot of ground was sweetly set
In dressed disorder, for a pleasaunce bright,
Or Ladye's garden. Small art had been used
In its creation (or the subtler art
That hides itself in Nature). There were seen
The silver linèd willows of the wave,
Blent with dull alders trimming down the tide ;

And there, too ('twas as if the gardener willed
Some homage to the Gallic strain of her,
Their visitor), tall Fleurs-de-Lys y-blent
Their iris-coloured beauties.   Up the slope
A perfect field of fair June-lilies waved,
And on the inner wall the ivy clomb;
And sweet Scots roses, with their amber eyne,
Bushed lowly round a sunken rock that formed
A humble seat at the fair garden's verge.

   Across the burn the woods lay deep and still,
Save where a gap would let the landscape through;
And from the height just 'neath the castle wall
Were gleams of sea, and shadowy ranges, caught.
But from the rocky rose-embowered seat
The world was hid, and scarce a sound was heard
Save singing waves, and little else was seen
Save wood, sky, lilies!
             Here, upon a day,
Came a youth wandering, fingering of a lute—
A youth of summers sparely o'er the score,
Advancing slowly, with a halting gait.
His garb was rich, to emulate the airs
By night empurpled, all with gold befleckt.
His visage spake of climes beyond the main,
Where the dim Olive and the Cypress flourish,
And azure Rhone floats through a sunlit land;
Where blows the Mistral,—cruel-keen to mock
Thy power, O Sun-God!—in the fresh-born year!

   Dark were his eyne, instinct with tender glow
Love-litten; and his sable locks, besprent
Adown his shoulders, bore no curl or wave,
But hung in soft luxuriance.   In his hands,
Long, slender, blanched, the lute was fitly held

And gave response to every tender touch
That spake no pupilage.   He sate him there,
'Mid the pale bowery roses, while anear
Drew, through the waning day, the North's pearled gloam.

A breeze that fitful tuned the willow stems
Hushed, for the numbers wrought of lute and voice;
And Denys, from a moment rapt of thought,
Arose and swept his strings, and dulcet sang:

    "Down from thy height of Woman, O thou Fair!
    Bend gracious to the level of my love;
    See how I tremble at thy high aspéct,
    And adoration combats with desire!
    Come down and be more mortal, lest I die!"

The lute wailed forth an echo, "lest I die!"
And drooped the minstrel's head upon his breast,
Feeble in worship's amorous ecstasy;
Then, as impelled by inspiration, struck
Denys a bolder chord, and chanted thus:

    "Spread forth thy light and beckon me, O Star!
    Lend low a woven ladder of soft beams,
    That I may climb thereby into thy grace,
    And cast my dross of nature far behind!

    "Or, being such a silver-fleecèd cloud,
    Such rosy mist of morn's ethereal birth,
    Envelop me, and steep my sense in light,
    Shrouding the earth and its material things,
    Till, from the centre of thine influence,
    All cleansed and purified, I may attain
    To thy perfection."   .   .   .

Hush! who cometh here?
E'en as he paused, his theme, Ydonea,
Swept through the lilies; and their stirred heads
Dusted with gold the crimson of her garb,
And from their hearts an odour faintly rich
Flushed the still air—sweet waft of her approach.
The tallest lily grew so tall, so tall,
And leaned so lovingly towards the maid,
That in a tender impulse scarcely willed,
She bent her head, and passing, kissed the flower.

"Denys, art there?"
                            Oh, sound! oh, scent! oh, sight!
On his wrought senses weighed so mightily,
That twice she called ere he found meet response,
And moved without the dense bloom-spangled bower
To greet his cousin.
                            Bantering cried the girl:
"Ah, Troubadour! ah, minstrel! thou art caught
All solitary in the garden hiding,
When thy poor playmate panteth for a share
Of all thy garnered melody!   Oh, sing!
Good Denys, sing! and I will sit me here
Amid these sleepy roses."   And she brushed
The swaying boughs aside, and sate her down;
And he, before her standing, preluded:

        "The sound of thy voice, O Love!
    Murmuring in woodland or whispering in hall,
            Informs my soul with a dream-like pleasure,
            And wiles my senses from Earth away,
            Like the languorous wail of a dancing measure,
            Or lingering charm of a chained love-lay.

"The sense of thy coming, Sweet !—
Be the touch of thy treading scarce heard at all !—
    Fair fills my being with soft emotion,
    Before mine eyes cull delight from thine ;
    As the wind, unseen, stirs the breast of ocean,
    Or Spring hails Nature with kiss divine.

"The waft of thy raiment, Maid,
As it holdeth the flower-sweet airs in thrall,
    Steals on my mood with a tender blessing,
    Like incense stealing through sacred fane,
    Or a breath of the myrtle groves caressing
    Kind Memory with bliss that is kin to pain !"

"Oh ! cry a truce to songs of myrtle bowers !
I love the old-time memories of our France
Right well ; but, Denys, art thou not content
In my fair father-Scotland ?   Breeds for thee,
This poet gloam o' the North, such dreams of love,
That thou'lt believe those by-past myrtles held
Thy heart, in love with loving.   For they tell
That poets fret their freakish fantasy
With 'hark-a-back,' what might or should have been ;
The sweet 'what was' mocking the ill 'is now,'
And in self-torture passed the vexèd hours !
  Forget thine emblem myrtles, and inhale
This deep pine-fragrance breathing from the woods,
And sing of noble deeds and lofty thoughts,
That are the North's ; for high's the North, and height
Is Heaven !"
        "But I can sing alone what moves
My spirit to tune ;" spake Denys, with a sigh ;

E

"Sweet cousin mine, take thou the lute, and bend
Thy fair conceptions to melodious end."

She took the lute, and sparkling on him, sang:

"Lilt ye, Mavis! and lilt ye, Merle!
Notes as round as an orient pearl,
Liquid and light as a maiden's laughter,
Soft as the echo that followeth after,
Long as the sunbeam's heaven-sent ray,
As hairst-blent poppies so bright and gay:
Lilt! no care from the future borrow,
Soon enough cometh night and sorrow.

"Lilt ye, Mavis! and lilt ye, Merle!
Morning and nature their charms unfurl,
Like a banner broidered in colours gleaming
As fair and rich as the sunrise seeming;
And hearts that welcome your joyous lay,
Throb with the bliss of the new-born day:
Lilt! the present hath light and flowers;
Lilt! the future hath gloom and showers.

"Lilt ye, Mavis! and lilt ye, Merle!
Time is a faithless and fickle churl,
Lends you a moment with soft caressing,
Shows you a hope, but withholds the blessing,
Leaves you a dream of evanished joy,
Mocks you, of Fate the rejected toy;
Lilt! while sunshine and morn are yours,
For only the moment her bliss secures!"

"Wilt naught of past or future, dearest maid?
So be it; let us joy in present peace.
But we were happy in our childhood's France
Those summer seasons, when our neighbouring homes
Taught the two mother-sisters how to plan
Sweet intercourse that rarely missed a day.
Life was so fresh, and Hope was hardly kenned;
For Bliss ignoreth Hope, who folding wings,
Lieth soft sleeping in the sun of joy,
To wake when jealous clouds, passing, obscure
Its brightness.   Ah! I love my myrtle past.
But didst thou mark my ditty's plaint alone?
Pleased thee no whit, the strain?"

                                    Smiling replied
The girl: "A tyro, I, in arts of love;
Thou know'st those subtle sentiments must be
Felt ere conceived; except by you, ye poets,
Who can dip deep into the human heart,
Noting scarce born conceptions.   You create
Some woman angelic, and exalt to Heaven
Your own Soul's Creature.   See now, that Florentine
Whose page thou'lt con for hours; his Beatrice,
Was she a very flesh? or some divine
Conceiving of his brain?   Doth Laura, she
Lauded from Avignon, live peerlessly?
Or is some trivial wench, invest with worth
By the great Mind that makes her?

                                    On loftiest Souls
Lies thirst to love a higher than their ken:
So fashion they their fulness.   It is well;
For Earth's pure loves are ladder-steps to Heaven!"

  In change of tone: "Me marvels whether bliss

Or pain tips Love's light wand ; nor wish have I
To test ! "
                    The minstrel thought, " Ah ! be it mine
To wake thy sleeping heart," and wooed his lute.

Through deepening twilight now the twain espied
A shape advancing towards them, with a step
That more pertained to clang and clash of war,
Than music through a lady's pleasaunce sighing—
A step that brooked or stay, or stop, no more
Than that fierce deluge from the melted hills,
Snow-charged, and murky in a ploughing flood,
That pours, mid-winter, Findhorn-channels down.

Nearer it came ; and now the failing beams
Of drowsy eve betrayed their visitant ;
Though hardly might that softening sheen impart
To yon stern face that met the cousins' gaze,
One touch of tenderness or softening grace.—
It was so cold, so dour, so still a face !
When from its brow and eyne your baffled gaze
Sought round the mouth some gentler mouldings, there
A grizzled beard was warder, and forbade
The search for sympathy !   .   .   .

Randolph, Earl Moray, was a man must stand
And move alone, as on a mountain-crest,
Whence he o'er-glanced the ant-heaps of the world
To far horizon of ambition's goal.
    Proud, on his chilly height, all solitary
He trode ; and did the winds of Heaven dare
To let his going, man or mage must lull them.
The stone that checked his foot, by-tossed, might start

The avalanche, and whelm a lower world—
What of that world recked he ?
                              Withal he showed
Not trivial base ; his nature, great of ill,
Had naught of meanness.   As the marsh-fire leads
Fain wandering feet o'er fen to losing end,
So did Ambition's false and mire-born shining
Point on a course from which no fair allure
Diverse, might draw him.   Grand in singleness
Of selfish purpose, almost he compelled
Rivals to admiration !

    Friends owned he none, and foes to him were foes
Less to himself than to his purposes !
Would doom the wight that baulked him with less ruth
Than hang a thieving cur, and then bestow
Fair largesse on his widow or his kin !
No passions stirred his guise; cold courtesy marked
The gay guest's welcome, as the victim's doom ;
And the gyved trembler, in yon dark aspéct
Viewed less his Judge than his embodied Fate.

    Towards Denys and Ydonea now he strode ;
His grand and buirdly bulk could scantly pass
Atween the lilies, down their narrow way ;
And so they bending, brake ; and that kissed bloom
All-hallowed by Ydonea's gentle lips,
That fain had Denys culled and kept his own,
Lay bruised and crushed 'neath Randolph's iron heel.
    He called : " Good people, I have sought ye far
Through hall and chamber; late are ye without ! "
He said, " My lady ward, thy presence sweet
I crave to-morrow, whom I would consult

On matters that pertain the soon return
Of my good Countess from her pilgrimage !
    And you, Sieur Denys, prick at morning-tide
And speak Kinloss' fat prior, who sends complaint
That hounds of mine harass the monkish flocks !
If true his plaint, defray the damage done.
    And now, I pray you, in; for 'lated hours
My Ladye Moray chides.   Give you good-night."

NOTES TO FORRES CASTLE.

" How far is't called to Forres ? "—P. 61, l. 1.

SHAKESPEARE'S "Macbeth," written in 1606.

There seems to be good reason for supposing that the "greatest William" visited Forres and its neighbourhood, where he describes the blasted heath, in or about the year 1601-02.

He is *almost certain,* says Mr Fleay in a letter to myself, "that he [Shakespeare] was at Aberdeen in the autumn of 1601. The town-talk there at that date would certainly be on two subjects: one the Gowrie conspiracy, the other the execution of witches, which had been more abundant there than anywhere a year or two before his visit. If these two things would not recall to him the old Macbeth play—which existed before 1596—we may give up all psychological investigation at once. Charles Knight has given other reasons for believing in this visit, but they are unnecessary. Shakespeare being thus at Aberdeen, and having his mind drawn to the Macbeth subject, I cannot think it unlikely that he then determined to write it. The whole play is full of flattery to James I.; and the compliment to his country of giving accurate descriptions of the scenery, would, I think, induce Shakespeare to go on to Inverness, Forres, &c. I shall at some time publish my argument in full, but you are quite at liberty to quote my opinion. . . . With many thanks for drawing my attention to a point I had almost overlooked, I remain yours faithfully, F. G. FLEAY.

"The Hon. Mrs WILLOUGHBY.
January 1878.'

I think, encouraged by so great an authority, we may feel justified in believing that the sacred feet of that Solomon of modern times trod the soil of Moray, and that the "blasted heath," now pleasant arable fields, was recognised by Shakespeare's own eyes.

"In this same Forres, named of Shakespeare's quill."—P. 61, l. 7.

The town of Forres lies about twelve miles west of Elgin, towards Nairn. In his interesting work, 'Edward I. in North of Scotland' (privately printed for the Literary and Scientific Association of Elgin), from which, as from his private letters to myself, I borrow freely, Dr Taylor tells us—"The town of Forres is first mentioned as a king's burgh, *temp.* David I. (*circa* 1124). Its castle is referred to as early as the year 966, when King Duffus was murdered therein by the governor, Donald."

It was also used as a royal residence by William the Lion, and by Alexander II., who respectively dated charters there 1189-98 and 1238. John Randolph, Earl of Moray, dated charters there the year of his death, 1346.

It is recorded that Edward III. of England burned Forres and the surrounding country in 1336.

The 'Inverness Courier,' when General Sir Lewis Grant, K.C.B., had just become owner of the castle and its grounds, says in May 1845, while workmen came on some portions of wall and foundations during certain excavations : "It appears from the foundations that the royal residence here was of much larger extent than is indicated by the remains of the ruin above ground. The ancient foundation wall, which is of run lime and small stones, yet as firm as a rock, extends on the north in a direct line from east to west 26 yards. It is 6 feet thick, and has included an area of 200 by 100 feet. On the outside was a parapet wall of betwixt 4 and 5 feet high, and at 20 feet distant, still farther to the outside, another parapet of 3 or 4 feet; a third wall skirted the moat which surrounded the castle, access to which was probably obtained by a drawbridge at the east.

" The western approach has been defended by strong angular turrets at the corners. As shown by the foundations, the old orchard—in close proximity to the castle at the south, was four acres in extent, and till within the last half-century was well furnished with fruit-trees, some of them so extremely old as to warrant the supposition that they had furnished dessert to the royal table. The grounds were intersected with ash, elm, and scyamore trees of a hoar antiquity, which were sold by the proprietor, and along with the others cut down by a wood merchant from Aberdeen fifty years ago, and the royal garden converted into an arable field ! At the south-west corner the workmen employed in levelling the present public road some years ago dug up immense quantities of bones intermingled with the antlers of various kinds of deer, which had doubtless afforded sport to our native sovereigns in the royal forests of Stronkaltyr and Tarnaway."

" Randolph, Earl Moray, was a man must stand."—P. 68, l. 23.

Lindsay of Pitscottie says : "Robert Bruce gave the Earldom of Moray to his awin sister sone, Sir Thomas Randell of Strathdoun, Knight, Chieffe of the Clan Allane, &c." Dr Taylor says that in designating him of Strathdoun, Pitscottie has made a mistake, repeated by Tytler and other modern writers. His heritage from his father, also Thomas Randolph, in the thirteenth century, was Strathnith, or Stranith, in Dumfries. The first of the Randolph family is said to have been a Celtic chief named Dunegal, who lived in the reign of David I. From him probably Randolph got the title, "Chief of Clan Allan." Barbour, in his "Bruce," has these passages (p. 218 of the Spalding Club edition) :—

> " Thomas Randol, for that he
> Was till the King [Bruce] in ner degr
> Of blud, for his sister him bar."

And again (p. 228)—

" Eftir Thomas Randol he sent.

.   .   .   .   .

And for till he his stat him gaf
Murref, and thereof erl him mad,
And othir sinder landis brad
He [Bruce] gaf him intill heritage.''

The John Randolph of this story was grand-nephew to Bruce, and succeeded to the Earldom of Moray on the death of his elder brother Thomas in 1332, and after the battle of Halidon was forced to fly to France, whence he returned to Scotland in 1334. He pursued the Earl of Athole, David (de Hastings) de Strathbolgie (whose mother was daughter and heiress of the murdered Red Comyn, and who in her right was head of the Comyn party on the side of Edward Baliol) to Lochaber that year, and was sent prisoner to England in August 1335. In England Earl John remained till the year 1341, when he returned to Scotland, and *between* that year and 1346, the events told in this tradition must have occurred, and not *in* the latter year, as said by Mrs Cumming-Bruce, in her work on the two families whose name she bore.

It was in 1346 that, being among the invaders of England, John Randolph was killed at the battle of Neville's Cross near Durham, in the month of August. Dying *s. p.*, his sister, the Lady Agnes Randolph—known as Black Agnes—wife of the Earl of Dunbar and March, assumed the title of Countess of Moray, and the earldom was confirmed to her second son. From the Dunbars was bought back Dunphail, by Sir Alexander Penrose Cumming-Gordon of Altyre, and by him left to his younger son, Charles Lennox Cumming, who assumed the name of Bruce in addition, on marrying the heiress of Kinnard. Their only daughter marrying James Bruce, Earl of Elgin and Kincardine, the union of the ancient foes and rivals was assured; and, oddly enough, Euffame, daughter of Thomas de Dunbar (second Earl of Moray of that name), and granddaughter of Black Agnes Randolph, weds Sir Alexander Cumyn of Altyre; her brother Thomas, third Earl, signing the marriage-contract as "Thomas, Earl of Murreff."

" Of my good Countess from her pilgrimage !"—P. 70, l. 2.

Euphemia Ross, Countess of Moray, was widow of John Randolph, and married " Robert the Steward," afterwards King Robert II., in the year 1355, and died in 1387. (She must have been the second wife of Randolph, as it appears certain he was also married to his cousin, Isabella Stewart of Bonkhill.) See Tytler's 'History of Scotland,' vol. iii. p. 5. She was sister to William, Earl of Ross, who alludes in writing to " My sister Eufamia, Countess of Moray (now Queen)." She had two sons by Robert II. The King grants land for masses for her soul in 1388 (quondam carissima consortis nostræ Euphamiæ Regina Scotiæ).—Robertson's Index and Charters, p. 132.

" And speak Kinloss' fat prior, who sends complaint."—P. 70, l. 4.

Kinloss Abbey was an establishment of Cistercians or White Monks, so called from their white cassocks. It comprised an abbot, a prior, a sub-prior, and twenty-three monks. The abbot was mitred, and had a seat in Parliament. It was founded by David I. in 1150, and was richly endowed by him and his successors, William the Lion and Alexander II. It had extensive estates and large accommodation. Its church, which was dedicated to the Blessed Virgin, had a nave, transepts, choir, and a lofty central tower as in cathedrals. . . . Its foundations can still be traced, and those also of the chapter-house, which stood near, and is said to have been pulled down for building materials in the last century.

Pennant describes its then larger remains in 1790. It had orchards and gardens, and in the early part of the sixteenth century was fitted with paintings, carved furniture, arras, and couches of silk, and was undoubtedly an establishment vying with that of the highest noble in the land, when Edward of England paid his unwelcome visit there. (Extracted from Dr Taylor's work.) It is said the Abbey had fifty-six feather beds ! and that the table was supplied with pewter brought from England at a great expense! The church was ornamented with paintings, statues, organs; and altars to St Jerome, St Anne, . . . and other saints.—Survey of Moray, 1798. "The laird of Lethan, who owned the Abbey at the time of the Commonwealth, sold the stones of the building to erect the citadel of Inverness." The remains of Kinloss Abbey—a portion of the prior's chamber, a cloister wall, two fine Saxon arches—now (1888) belong to Mrs Dunbar Dunbar of Seapark, near Forres.

DUNPHAIL.

Of a fair fortalice within the North ;
They who abode there, and their muckle worth.

STAND in thy ruinous peace, oh ! once of might,
While the light airs do lip thee languorous,
And kiss thee to content, through dreamy days,
And pensive nights, and tender starry nights ;
While Autumn gales, that boisterous war as year
Each year succeeds, shower on thine old grey walls
The gold and crimson of October death.
    Hast thou no memory of those yellow flames ?
Art thou oblivious of that crimson tide ?
That wrapt thee round, that flooded all thy hearth
That fateful Autumn of thy vanished past ?
    Hast thou a memory of the blasting war,
Louder than din of fierce autumnal wrath,
That whirled thee round and left thee—what thou art ?
Nay ! for the hand of oft-deluding Time
Hath so enwrought to cheat the gazer's sense
With vision of such sweet serene decline
As chideth History, and half belies
The tale that Randolph warred and Comyn fell.
    Thy Tower, all ivy-swathed, commands the steep,

And plumes of fern and soft grass-tresses wave
Where armour hung and cressets redly gleamed;
The stoat and weasel shelter in thy cairns,
And birds brood safely in thy storm-beat walls.

Deep in the night, when stoat and weasel rove,
And wild birds, slumberous, nestle head 'neath wing,
Ask of the bat and hooting midnight king,
That hold their revels 'low the darkling arch
Of mystic Heaven, if they wander yet,
Those Headless Ones? with woful, weary plaint,
Liplessly utterèd; with arms up-tossed,
And feet all aimless, faltering 'mid thy stones;
Seeking the speech and vision they had tyned
In woful doom and losing warfare, yond';
Seeking the brain and reason to direct
Some spirit scheme of deep, of dire revenge!

Revenge! on whom? oh, ye bereaved, betrayed,
                    Rest!   Rest!
Nor twin poor human hate to Heaven's ire;
For long sin-syne hath Retribution gone
Forth from her mighty Source in sum and tale;
And, in the whole wild North, no single lum
Volumes forth reek to mark the haughty hearth
Of one of Randolph's name; no acre fair
Of emerald grazing, not a sombre glade,
Nor 'chaunting reach of river, wandering on;
Nor reed-fringed lochan, where the heron dips;
No soft-eyed herds in verdant luxury
Knee-deep; nor moor-fed, black-avisèd flocks;
No joy of Nature, and no love of Man,
Are by a cursèd stock or held or claimed

Fathered of yon fierce Earl, who spread the tale
Of death and desolation round Dunphail.

But in those days (since when five centuries
Have glanced thee by), thou tost and tumbled tower,
Wert set full lordly on thy rocky throne;
A fortress small, but deemed of might to front
What power besiegers could of force employ
In those past seasons. Deep the moat, and wide
Around it lying: not the cragged ascent
Could tempt a foeman's foot to scale its stone;
And time, with famine, seemed the only force
Might drive it to surrender.
                    This was held
By Alexander, Knight of Comyn race,
The guard and warden in his own behoof
Of passes from the Highlands to the Laigh;
And bound in bond of kinship to the Chief
Of that great faction who beheld their fall
In Bruce's triumph.
                    Here with six fair sons
He lived the true, high life of Every-day
As the light prompted, of those ruder times,
And was himself instructor in the arts
Chivalrous; the guile of sport, the wile of war,
Of Alastair, his bright-haired first, adown
To the young stripling whose pate cumberless
Wore fifteen springtides as a wreath of May.

He of the sun-gilt locks, bright Alastair,
In birth the first, so first in love; untamed
Somewhat of spirit, ready to resent
On such as stirred his ire, their rashling raid;

Though led by times of Pleasure, where the voice
Of slighted Duty hushed within his breast ;
Yet, Youth on unfledged pinions e'en might bear
His weight of ill, nor cower, crushed with blame ;
And Time, alas ! and Trouble (woodman wise),
Would smooth such knops and twigs as roughed the bark
Of Alastair's rich life, while every germ
Of manly virtue flourished at his core.

   An open hand and heart, a filial spright
With man's rar'st virtue, self-forgetfulness,
And the true pride of lineage and race
That breeds high actions !
                    Such the lad whose name
The maids of Moray whisper with a tear.

Long years had swept Clan Comyn's fortunes by
Since Bruce' victorious rivalry achieved
Their bitterest undoing.
               Fallen low
From proud possessions in a many shires,
Their chiefest wealth to Bruce's partisans
Awarded ; and the followers of their pride
Like bees forsaking all the fading bloom
Whose sweets they sucked in summer ; the poor race
Rued, in its country's weal, its own decay.

Its country's weal ! for on the straight plank leading
To sov'reignty, when wrestlers twain refuse
Each one an inch to yield, progress is not,
And action numbs within the watching crowd :
   Or, when the panting victor, spent, attains

The further brink ; stolen round by other roads,
There, alien foes arrayed, his weakness wait !

So, Caledonia, showed thy likely fate,
When England ravenous gaped, to snatch the prey
From jaws oped in reviling.
                        But in ruth
For thine afflicting, Destiny decreed,
Ere long, one faction's triumph ; and the Bruce
Successful, drew the world that loves success
With him to counter England.
                       Thus the weal
Of Scotia seemed in Bruce ; and Bruce's aim
Was to confirm his kingship ; 'suring which
Had wrought the Comyn fall.
                     And so these rued.

But though in time a dull submiss to fate
Some yielded ; certain chieftains of the race
Rose on the holders of their once domains,
Upstirring divers regions to revolt
'Gainst the usurpers ; other some abode
In sulky silence, with an outlook veiled
For kinder chances.
               Thus the chieftains.   Where
The chief of all the clan himself abode
When Alastair, forthstraying from Dunphail,
Chanced on his Fair, my count imparteth not :
The wind hath never named him, nor the wave
Had marked his step beside it.
                 Now Dunphail,
A place of strong command, and circled round

F

With appertaining land and privilege,
Did represent a power within the shire
Too potent for a neighbour's pleasuring.

This was the Earl of Moray, unto Bruce
A nephew's son, whose father had acquired
The Earldom and its worthy appanage
Of fiefs, demesnes, and manors from his eme.

This son, from English durance late returned,
Beheld with jealous'd eyne the Comyn power
In Moray, and desired to make his own
The length, and spread, and fatness of the land;
But so with dull indifference masked his mien
These t'wards, that no suspicion marred their peace.

Thus, in their castled strength from neighbouring foe
Seeming secure, the Chieftain and his sons
Abode in happy union; now engaged
In martial methods, when within the forge
Sparks, cheerful glinting, spangle the blackened lum,
Where, wrought of blows, the weapon learns to strike:
Now on the walls devising strength to strength;
Or raiding west, from strath of feudal foe
The ruddy steer they harry—lowing loud
Such, for kenned scene and 'customed pasturage.

And first in forge or foray, surest tread
On muir or mount, true sight and steady hand,
Shone out, shone fair, the Roof-tree of Dunphail!

Up with the dawn the glossy trout to net,
Or salmon spear, he, for his sire's first meal;
In wood seek bough for Will's or Walter's bow;
And stalk the marsh-bred goose, whose pinions gave
Richard the quill to indite yon crabbed lore
He loved so dearly: culled he by fenny stream

Reeds for young Ian's piping, and slew the heron
Whose royal plume on Raynold's crest would speak
The urchin's pride of lineage.

                         Thus his life
Blythe sped with Alastair, till chanced he met
Ydonea in Slaginnan.

NOTES TO DUNPHAIL.

"*Dunphail.*"—P. 77.

SIR RICHARD CUMYN had a grant from David II., under the Great
Seal, of the lands of Dovellij, now Dunphail, with the office of
ranger of the forest of Tarnawa, . . . an office once held by Robert
Bruce himself, and by Sir Alexander Comyn in 1291. "David Dei
gracia . . . Rex . . . Scotorum . . . confirmasse, dilecto et fideli
nostro Ricardo Comyne, omnes terras de *devally* vna cum officio
forestarii foreste nostre de *ternway* cum pretinenciis in comitatu
Morauia infra vicecomitatum de . . . Inuernys." . . . "The charter
from David II. appears to have been given at the time the King was
ransomed in 1357 - 58 ; "—Dr Taylor gives the date as 1368 - 69
(after his capture at Neville's Cross).— Mrs Cumming-Bruce, History of the Bruces and Cumyns.

This Sir Richard Cumyn was eldest son of Sir Thomas, murdered
by the Shaws (*circa* 1365), by Helen, daughter of Hugh, seventh
Baron of Aberbuthnot, and therefore nephew of Lachlan, killed in
a skirmish at Inverlochy. Sir Richard's wife was daughter of the
chief of Grant, and their eldest son, Ferquhard, was the first de-
signated "of *Altyre.*"

"*By Alexander, Knight of Comyn race.*"—P. 79, l. 14.

"Alexander de Comyn," says Dr Taylor in 'Edward I. in North
of Scotland,' "the brother of John, the Black Comyn [Lord of

Badenoch, Regent and Competitor], mentioned in Rymer's 'Fœdera' as one of those prisoners who were sent to the Tower of London after the battle of Dunbar; appears from the Ragman's Rolls and Prynne's work to have accompanied Edward in his march northwards, and to have sworn allegiance on being released from his captivity when he reached Elgin."

Says Mrs Cumming-Bruce: "By a writ, dated Abergavenny, in Wales; Edward I., October 26, 1291, directed Alexander Cumyn, keeper of the forest of Tarnua in Moray, to deliver to Alan, Bishop of Caithness, Chancellor, . . . forty oaks." By a "writt" dated at Berwick, 10th July 1292, Edward directs stags to be sent to Alexander Cumyn ("probably," says Mrs Cumming - Bruce, "the old knight of Dunphail and his sons of 1341-46, killed by John Randolph"). No! I hold the old knight of Dunphail to have been the *son* of Alexander de Comyn who swore fealty to Edward at Elgin in 1296, as does really Mrs Cumming-Bruce, both in the pedigree and elsewhere in her book. "The laird of Dunphail," she says, "a man of considerable talents and great resolution, was advanced in years and had a numerous family of grown-up sons. . . . From the place they held of keepers of the forestry of Tarnua, with the fortress of Dunphail, we incline to believe them to have been *descendants* of Alexander, who held that position in 1291, two of whose sons, Walter and Thomas, fell at Kilblain amongst the *désenhèrétés.*"

"From proud possessions in a many shires."—P. 80, l. 19.

Besides all their possessions in Scotland, many English shires gave lands to the Comyns. William Comyn, grandson to Robert de Comyn, Earl of Northumberland, held one-third of the lands of Fonthill in Wiltshire about 1120.—(Mrs C. Bruce.) We know (*vide* note, "William, Scotland's Chancellor," p. 157) that the Comyns held the lands of Northallerton in Yorkshire. Camden says (Gibson's English edition, pp. 1073-74, under "Northumberland") : " In Tindale are Whitchester, Delaley, and Tarset, which formerly be-

longed to the Commins." (*Vide* also note from Camden, on Gloucestershire, p. 33, "Comyn.") And by a charter (recorded in the
'Abbreviato Rotulorum Originalium,' vol. i. p. 209) of the time of
Edward II., the King gives and grants certain manors in Notting-
hamshire and Northamptonshire to John Comyn (son of Red John
second, murdered at Dumfries), in consideration of the good deeds of
his father of happy memory, for his own sustenance and that of his
son "Aymer" (who died *vit. pat.*), and of his wife Margaret,
"quæ fuit uxor prefati Johannes."—(Mrs Cumming-Bruce.) And
through marriages, &c., other lands in the south belonged at different
times to branches of the family. Alexander, Earl of Buchan, Great
Justiciar and High Constable of Scotland, was summoned by Edward
I. to perform military service in England, in return for lands held
therein.

"*Successful, drew the world that loves success.*"—P. 81, l. 9.

Wyntoun and Hollinshed both attempt to vilify the Comyns.
Anderson in his 'Scottish Nation' remarks, ridiculing a queer
attempt of the former (as an "exquisite blunder") in trying to give
an English rendering of the name : "The antecedents of the noble
family were too familiar to be utterly forgotten in that age—about
1420—especially by the Prior of Lochleven. . . . But they [the
Comyns] had been the vanquished party, and it was the fashion of
that age to vilify the unfortunate. This incident shows how little
reliance is to be placed on . . . historians, especially where national
or party prejudices are concerned." Anderson may be wrong in his
genealogies (as he is in that of the Comyns in part), but his judg-
ments are wise.

"*Had wrought the Comyn fall.*"—P. 81, l. 14.

"Et quia, ut prædicitur isti Comynenses, præcipue fuerunt qui
contra Regem insurrexerunt, ideo nunc deletum est quasi nomen
eorum in terra, cum et tunc tanquam majores regni multiplicati

fuerunt supra numerum. Unde tunc computati sunt triginta duo milites hujus cognominis, qui uno et eodem tempore in regno militari accincti sunt cingulo. Ideo debent milites et magnates, attendere ad Apostolicum dictum majis accurate, videlicet, Regem honorificate."—J. Forduni, Scotichronicon, lib. x. cap. xi., vol. ii. p. 92.

"Never, perhaps, did a princely family sink so rapidly and decisively as that of the Cumyns. History has actually few such cases on record, for, be it noted by English readers, we here speak of no petty race of squires, heading but petty handfuls of vassals. The Cumyns were men who could at will raise armies able to meet in the field all the power even of the Plantagenets. The Red Comyn, who fell under the hand of Bruce, undoubtedly held sway over many Gaelic septs, afterwards better known and distinguished separately (?). 'He was,' in the words of a respectable author, 'the Lord of Badenoch, Lochaber, and other extensive districts, and (in all) the head of the most potent clan that ever existed in Scotland.' Upwards of 'sixty belted knights with all their vassals' were bound to follow his banner, and the chiefs of the family made treaties with princes as princes. One such compact with Llewellyn of Wales is preserved in Rymer's 'Fœdera.' It is for these reasons that we have thus fully told the story of the Cumyns. Some may ask how they came to leave so few of their name, if so powerful at one time. Like the Bruces, they stood too high to permit of their family designation becoming common among their followers. Besides, they flourished and fell ere patronymics were at all fixed generally in Scotland. And yet in the reign of Alexander III., according to Hector Boece, four great barons and thirty landed knights bore the name of Cumyn." — (Smibert's 'Clans of Scotland.') And I have often heard my great-uncle, Charles Lennox Cumming-Bruce, tell how Sir Walter Scott had assured him that he considered no family in history had been more hardly used than the Cummings; and yet he himself quotes in 'Waverley' the Gaelic proverb which appears hereafter in a note.

" The chief of all the clan himself abode."—P. 81, l. 24.

There can be no doubt, from all preserved tradition, that the Comyns considered themselves a clan, under a chief and chieftains. Though the Norman origin of the Comyns is indisputable, and our claim to Celtic descent obtained only through marriage with such families as MacGregor of that Ilk, Macintosh, Captain of Clan Chattan, the Lord of the Isles, Cameron of Lochiel, &c., and in later times, oddly enough, through the old Cornish Celtic race of Penrose; yet, whether their vast power and influence drew to them smaller septs and races who took their name, or whether there were tribes of a similar patronymic (what were those sixteen thanes mentioned by Mrs Grant, "of the mountains," long ere the Conqueror's kinsman became Earl of Northumberland?), when Richard Cumyn acquired lands in Scotland first, about the middle of the twelfth century; it remains a fact that they were a clan, wearing a badge and tartan, and regarded by their people as were regarded chiefs and chieftains of Celtic descent.

In the 'Vestiarum Scoticum,' supposed to have been written about the end of the fifteenth or early in the sixteenth century, by one "Schyr Richard Urquharde, Knycht," the Comyn tartan is thus described :—

" Cvmyne heth two wyd stryppis of greine vpon ane scarlatt fyeld, and withovt thir sayd stryppis twa lesser of ye samen, and throuch twa greitter stryppis ane spraing gwhite, and vpon ye myddest of ye redd sett ane sprang blak."

The badge, a very uninteresting one, is the saugh or common sallow, growing on moorlands. Buchanan calls them a clan. "Knowing what a powerful enemy he had to contend with, his first object was to collect all the forces he could from every quarter; but as the whole *Clan* Cumin, the power of which family has never been equalled in Scotland, either before or since, were inimical," &c. —(Aikman's translation.)

"Had marked his step beside it."—P. 81, l. 28.

The Earldom of Buchan (Comyn) having been merged in daughters, and Red John Comyn the second, Lord of Badenoch, having no male heirs (his sons and grandson leaving none), the descendants of his uncle Robert, murdered the same time as himself (*vide* note, p. 154), became the head line and progenitors of the Comyn or Cummings of Altyre, &c. The second son of the slain Sir Robert, also Robert, who entered and rose to distinction in the Polish service (according to Mrs Cumming-Bruce), was subsequently the head or chief of the Comyns. It might have been his son Angus (whose second son, Lachlan, was killed in a skirmish at Inverlochy), or most probably Angus's *eldest* son, Sir Thomas (who obtained from the Bishop of Moray, *circa* 1350, a lease of the lands of Rothiemurchus, formerly owned by his family), who ruled at this date. And yet he surely would have been more prominent in defending his relatives at Dunphail.

Sir Thomas was killed by the Shaws in 1365.

"In wood seek bough for Will's or Walter's bow."—P. 82, l. 29.

We know nothing of the names of these hapless youths, whose career was destined to be so brief, and whose end was so tragic. I have therefore given them names likely to be of family association. *Will* might be called after his great-grand-uncle, William Cumyn, Earl of Buchan, great Justiciar ; *Walter*, after Walter Comyn, Earl of Menteith, second son to above Earl of Buchan ; *Richard*, after his ancestor, the spouse of the Royal Hextilda ; and *Ian* (Gaelic for John), after the first Red Comyn, his great-grandfather. *Raynold* I have never found as a family name save in the following extract : "An Indenture dated Palmesunday, in the year 1259, in the reigne of Alex^r. the third, the place the Castle of Edinboro'. It is a contract of marriage (Douglas and Abernethie); the witnesses are Alexander Cumine, Earle of Buchan ; *Raynold* Cumin," &c.—(History Houses of Douglas and Angus. Maister D. Hume.) I do not know who this Raynold was, or whether it may be a misprint for some similar name ; there was a Raymond de Burg, and the De Burgs and Comyns had descent in common.

Sympathy.

I was a crystal clapper,
Hung in a brazen bell :
What quaint caprice had linked us,
I'faith, I cannot tell !

But I loved my shiney doming,
With its hard and burnished glare ;
   Who liefer hearks, than silver trump,
The brazen clarion's blare,
Errs ; but I had no needing
.Yet, of deep tones and rare.

It fell on a fateful morning,
Some Man of men had died,
And bells from tower and turret
Were tolling, deep and wide.

Then erst, the brazen clanging
I wooed, felt scarce attune ;
And I sought a tenderer music
From the polished lift aboon.

I struck with a deepened craving
For an answering tone, and sweet ;

But only a noisier clangour
My wistful sense did greet.

Harder, to harsh responding,
I struck the metal frame;
My crystal bulk all shattered flew :
   Of brass they hung a clapper new—
The bell rang aye the same !

"EXPRESSION IMPRESSETH."

So brave a presence, such a lovely face,
A spot so weird of meeting, could it chance
No dainty limning on their several souls,
Touched by the art of their romantic youth,
Should rest? .   .   .
Nay! when Ydonea to her wench refused
The tale in full, of how and whence she fared
That noon of Alastair; herself perceived
(And thereat angered) in herself a show
Of masking, all unwonted; and began
To brood thereon, and argue with her mind,
Then dub herself, for arguing, a fool;
And so, by subtle passages, did creep
From brain to bosom, sense to inner soul,
The picture in Slaginnan!
                                      Alastair
More frankly told his 'venture to his kin,
And lauding her, brought banter from the loons,
Heedless of threatened vengeance.   Raynold gibed
Of damosels distressed and errant knights,
Then dipped in saucy nimbleness to evade
His wrathful elder's arm, and danced away
With boyhood's shrilly mocking.

                                    Yet these gibes
Brought him Ydonea present, whence he drew
Desire to see again and be confirmed
In his first rich impression.   Soon was made
Excuse toward Forres, and by gentle chance
(Such chances form Love's arrow-featherings !)
Happed on Ydonea and her cousin squire,
On sporting errands bent.
                           Thence intercourse
Friendly arose and waxed the youths between ;
For Comyn Bān inclined in gentle wise,—
That tender woman-kindness of the strong,—
To Denys, feeble, who could only share
Sports with the maiden, not the hardier toil
Of martial duties, or the perilous chase.

   And Denys found a never-failing charm
In the wild songs and legends of the North
Chanted of Comyn, and would task his lute,
Rendering all sweet the savagery of song,
To numbers rhymed in France's dainty lisp.

   The Earl forgot them, save athwart his path
They chanced ; or when Ydonea's company
It pleased him claim as favoured first of all.

   Jealous'd his soul to Comyn race, but yet
Stirred by no active spite ; so Alastair
Found welcome courteous, there, nor looked for more.

Fluttering there came a gentle wayward joy,
And lodgment thieved within these alien breasts,
Thriving, like cuckoo fledgeling, to eject
All else, a naughty wight ; and spread and flourished,
Till days that knew no Alastair, as skies
Rain-dimmed to Ydonea showed : to him

Were dialless, for marked his calendar
Only those hours belit by her, his Sun !
   'Ware of his love was she ; but each betrayed
To Denys, shrouded in poetic dreams,
And living in a sphere himself created,
Whose light and worship was Ydonea's self,
Naught of their soul's profound ; nor came the youth
From air-realms to such finding ; in his past
Safely he dwelled, nor visioned days forlore.

   The Comyn hoped, and feared, and hoped anew,
For kind his Ladye was, but kindly coy ;
Her mirthful laughter rang out blythe and free ;
Fresh was her jest, and clear her brow of cloud ;
Only a drooping of the long-fringed lids,
When Alastair too boldly sought her gaze,
Or a fleet, stealthy, intercepted glance,
By rosed confusion followed, gave his heart
The hope it lived on. So the summer days
Passed blythe for these.
               The hapless Lupola,
Whose sore be-plaguèd life was bare of joy,
Knew but one solace, in the passionate love
She bore her mistress ; and that radiant maid,
Unrecking of a deeper woe than wrought
The poor bemisted vision, did entreat
Her, with a sweet indulgence, now betraying
Some of her heart to one who more divined.

Once on a summer's day, with gathered maids
Round her, Ydonea spun ; while Denys read,
Or hearkened to their singing. She had bidden

Late, he would frame some lilt in Northern mode,
Which now he offered her; all, as his wont,
Limned of the love he lived on.   And she heard,
With less of usual mocking at the theme,
And something of a sigh.   Thus flowed the song:

To My Maid o' the Mountain.

" List to a lay of my Love, who low in the evening
Leaveth her dwelling-place.   Blue is the lift of her glances;
Soft is the glow of her cheek, like the wild-rose that's deepened
      of sunsets;
Gleameth her brow as the mountain-drift snow; and her tresses
Gloom like the storm that o'erhangeth, all heavy in darkness:
Lips, like the ruddiest berry that gladdens the shelters,
Breathe aye the scent of the heather, by-brushed of the bee;
Slight is her form as the saugh that bends low on the waters,
Airy her foot-tread, like hind stepping down to the corrie,
And from its folding the grass-blades spring up, as if wind-swept.
    Come, O my maid, ere the gloaming hath died from the valley!
Come to the hills, to the heights, where the light lieth longer!
Come to my Love that's aloof and eternal as heaven!
    Come, O my queen!"

Hushed was the lute; Ydonea praised and said:
    "She whom this lover sang, had been right fair;"
And sighed, and chid her maidens, and began
A tiny, trifling fancy of a song,
That moved in measure to the whirring wheel:

Spinning Song.

"Many a pickle mak's a muckle
   (Whirr, whirr, my bonnie wheel!);
Lasses, to your labours buckle,
   Strip the staff and wind the reel!

Labour light for eident lasses
   (Whirr, whirr, my canty wheel!);
Swift the yarn betwisted passes
   Through your fingers deft and leal.

Envious plaid that Beauty covers
   (Whirr, whirr, my lightsome wheel!);
Tartans for our lords and lovers,
   Stout to ward a foeman's steel!

Tread, my maidens, shame who lingers!
   (Whirr, whirr, my trusty wheel!);
Sing, to aid your nimble fingers;
   Strip the staff and wind the reel!"

As Denys, with his scroll upon his knee,
Back in the window dreamed, came Randolph there:
  "How now, Ydonea! laverock-lilting, wench?
Rarely thou treat'st thy guardian to a strain!
Where broods thy cousin?"

                "Here, 'mid books, brood I;"
Cried from the window Denys; whereat the Earl,
With laugh that smacked of sneering:

                    "Come away!

I've work for thee ; idle not all the day
With maids and parchments ! Tut, tut ! such a weevil ne'er
Did penetrate dull calf ! Clear thou thy brain
Of books, forsooth !—there's too much prate of books !
Go, read ye men ! Study the brow's spread page,
The deep and dangerous index of the eye,
The lip that smiles to mask, or masks a smile;
    Read ye the meaning of the words that lie,
Sound fair when foulest, sting when seeming sooth :
    Read those that know their ill, and fain conceal it ;
Know those to whom their own soul-depth's unknown ;
    Study thyself, young Denys ; and when learned,
Thou mayst be master of the multitude
For all thy halting person."
                          " Good my lord,
I would command, but not in State nor field ;
Move them that ne'er beheld me, with no voice,
But 'yond our day win through my spirit's travailing
The world to worthiness,—by lettered page.
    For you, methinks, too light hold written lore ;
Life's brief for much of learning ; why should we
Not build on others' foundations ? setting thereon
Hewn stones of self-experience, pain-acquired.
    For men that read may read what men have done ;
And men that read can learn to read mankind
Swifter through scrivener's ink than mere flesh through ;
    Because what has been, shall be,—Human-kind,
Of many moulds, springs from one Master-Mind !
    Grant me my pen, a name ; and Powers of Virtue,—then—
I'll be your heeded minister to Men."
The Earl contemptuous wheeled, and laughed :
                              " Thou art
A blatant stripling ! hence ! Farewell, Sweetheart ! "

LOVE'S DECLARING.

In sylvan glade an olden tale is spoken,
And sweet exchange is made of heart and token.

DENYS departed. Still Ydonea spun
A brief and thoughtful space ; then rising, vowed
The whirring wheel had corded all her brain,
And to unslack it she would breathe the air :
So passed upon her palfrey presently,
With Lupola and Corbred, down the woods.

In bright July, how kind the leafy screen
Of darksome Beeches in their shining green ;
Their deep refreshing green—o'ercanopying
The turf's sparse verdure ; and aflickering down
Their ashen trunks, the sportive light and shade
Plays at pursuing. O thou greenwood Queen !
Meet spouse for royal Oak, thy monarch mate,
When art thou fairest ? In the morning vest
Of Spring's ethereal, palest, tenderest green ?
Thy noontide richness of intense July ?
Or the state robing of an Autumn eve ?—
When not the ore of Ophir, freshly drawn
From Solomon's deep treasure, not the garb

Of a king's daughter, wrought in glowing gold,
Could shame thy sun-kissed glory.
                       Or thy night
Of disrobed Winter, when, bared first to view,
Thy form's pure beauty strikes the woods anew
Each year, with admiration.   Favourite fair!
Best the sweet woodland choirs in song thy praise declare.

Ah! who so happy in the greenwood sweet
As they whose youth hath wakened to its day!
Love's breath to them it is that stirs the leaves;
Love's light o'ershines the sunbeams, and imparts
To the bright verdure his own eternal youth!
  So with Ydonea, 'neath the beechen shade
Dreaming of love upon a summer's hour,—
Pure love, that chiefly doth its giver bless;
Dear love, that like the dew doth e'er return
To enrich wherefrom it riseth; or like stream
Whose sweets, if wasted in a briny main,
Still fertilise their channel's verdant way;
Or maiden carol, like—in dew-bright dawn
Unmarked of any; yet her, her song doth fill
With fuller happiness. Such song would spring
To Ydonea's lips, unbidden; and now she called
To her sad wench to chorus these her strains
Of praise; and cheer, and love her father's north:
Then chid her thoughtless self upon the thought
These glories yielded faint reflections there.
The woman raised her chill and beauteous face
(Light-lacking, as blown drift beneath the shade),
And spake: "O mistress, enter to my heart!
Thy North's no north to me! There is a land
That knows no dark through the brief summer fair,—

Where crimson as thy robe glow wintry heavens;
Where the great pines wrap down the mighty steeps
Of mountain terrors, seamed with raging floods,
That, snow-fed, hurl their madness to the main.
Yond' is my North.   Thy North shows tame to me,
As now would to thy soul forgotten France."

   "Nay, not forgotten," plaintive sued the maid;
"A happy childhood dream, an hour of play,
Too sweet for oblivion; but my perfect life
Forthshone when first I knew how fair a soil
My father's blood made mine."

                "Or haply else,
When first didst find what sort of men they were
Thy father's countrymen?"

                  Ydonea smiled,
Blushed, spake not again; but bending, strove to plait
The waving tresses of Bayoumé's mane,
Whose arching crest, in pretty compliment,
Bowed 'neath a touch that not from butterfly
Could fleece its down.   But silence irked her soon,
And bubbling fancies welled to 'scape her lips:

   "I've heard," she uttered, "grows a malady,
Nor balm nor leech may heal, that to the heart
Clings like that eight-armed monster of the sea,
By suckered limb and foul bird-beak that takes
Life from its victim.   One remede alone
Hath this deep ill!   Bear the sick exile Home,
And health revives!

                Say! would be there thy Joy?"
   "Joy thou, dear Love!   My joy will come to me
When June-flowers bloom in winter; when the Sun
Stoops from his day to wed the pallid Moon;
When Gratitude shall be as frequent flower,

As rose-tipped gowans on a summer sward :
Then, joy shall Lupola ken !—But hearken now !
There's merriment enough a-breaking through
The yonder glades, and never missing mine !"
And woke the woods a man's deep voice in song !

The Hunter's Song.

" Wake the wide woodlands, O song, my song !
       Flee hart and hare,
       Out ferny lair,
       Seek hidden ways,
       Deep in the maze.
          Hollala !
For mine arrow is speedy, my bow is strong,
Mine arm is steady, my sight is long :
      Hollala, hollolu, hollala !

Wake the fair woodlands, O song, my song !
       Swift the bright day
       Passeth away ;
       Night in her walk
       Marksmen will baulk.
          Hollola !
O wild birds, sitting the boughs among,
  Sheltering safe 'neath the leafy dome,
Come down and die, there's a hungry throng
  To feed in the huntsman's home !
          Hollola ! "

" He hath his fill of game " (thus Lupola),
" Else would he ne'er so cheerly warn the woods
Of their life's enemy.   'Tis Comyn Bhan ! "
As thus quo' she, came crashing through the brake
Two hounds of Alastair, whose burst abrupt,
With fluttered riot of the troubled leaves,
Made frolicsome Bayoumé leap and bound,
Half startled, mischievous half ; whereon gave way
Girthings and selle, and but for Alastair's hold,
Ydonea straight had fallen.   Blushing thanks,
Disclaiming fear, she suffered him to lead
Her (trembling natheless) where a fallen trunk
Offered a lichened seat ; and Lupola,
'Sured of her mistress' safety, wandered on
In solitary wont.   .   .   .

When the quaint harness of those elder days
Was fixed and fastened, and the coil repaired,
Ydonea chose the safety of the sward
Till calmed her palfrey's petulance of mood ;
And Alastair, a-twisting round his arm
The rein, moved slowly by his Ladye's side,
Fitting his pace to hers ; while in their rear
Old Corbred, dignified, refused the ken
Of those delinquent hounds that courted play.

He craved excuse for causing her dewray ;
She yielded pardon, granted ere 'twas craved ;
And now, their speech in failing, eloquent,
Let silence fill itself with sweetness.   Soon
He spake again, and in a trance she heard
Tones that surpassed the music of the woods ;
And while they paused beneath the queenly beech
Whose spread down-swept upon her last year's shed

Of winter-wailing tears, whose mothering arms
Enwrapt the lovers in a sylvan clasp,
The Comyn, wooing, won !

Sweep, kindly boughs, in fluttering verdure down,
And veil the rapture of Love's first embrace :
Deep heart to heart, pulsing in passionate beat ;
Warm lip to lip, that draws the exchange of soul,
Sealing each one to each for evermore.

Dance lightly through the woodland, skipping roe !
And, long-eared velvet haunter of the glade,
Deep from thy bracken shade peer forth to know
Whence comes thy safety ?   Cushats on a bough,
Peep over, with your " Curroo, curroo, croo,"
Soft wooing notes, and mark how immortals woo !

Time fled ; they lingered yet.   What hope, what dread,
What latent dreams, what longing fantasies
They cooed upon and conned, 'twere sweet to hear ;
    (So saith the Zephyr hearkening them).
                                        He told
How first within him sprang the conscious life
Of Love ; not soft unfolding, like a flower
In summer's dawning to its new-found sun,
But sudden, as the capsule or seed-shell
Of some rich tropic bloom, ripe bursting, throws
A wealth upon the world, so on her sight
His heart threw forth its passion.
                                And she breathed
How, as the creeping Spring upon the land
Steals, gently waking all to blush and beam,
Till, half surprising, certainty of life

Is on the sense, his hold upon her heart
Itself revealed.

　　　　　　And ever while they spake,
Bayoumé cropped the foliage, or the turf
Impatient pawed, where the o'erbowering shade
Reft the lean herbage of its fostering sun.

Time heartless fled, but was to them no law!
Sweet their harmonious silences ; their speech,
Soft naught to who might hear ; to these, divine.

Now from the kindly warding of her breast
She reft a jewel, and where the gathered plaid
Crost o'er his heart, clasped it ; and bade him note
'Twas the first gift her father gave his bride.

A quaint device it showed of joinèd hearts :
The first, a hot carbuncle, half concealed
Its fellow, of darkest blood-stone ; and the twain
Through piercen were and fixed by shaft of gold,
That cunning artist quaintly so contrived
Should strike the nether heart where carmine showed ;
That stain (mote legends tell) that flecks its face,
Since, blest beyond all stones, it lay beneath
Salvation's cruel Tree.

　　　　　　These double hearts,
Further surmounted by a golden crown,
Bore legend thus :

　　　　　　　" Ane arrowe ; woundis twain."

Smiling she clasped it, and drew back to note
How well he set the gem ; but a quick cry
Brake from her lips : " A blood-spot on thy heart !

O Saints, forfend the omen! Alastair!"
    And lily-pale she grew with dread forebodings!
"Nay, love," he whispered (nor the glad excuse
O'erpassed, thus offered, of a closer embrace),
"'Tis but an emblem of the cherished wound
Thou gav'st my heart, and heal'st this hour self-same.
Or stay! an't please you, set it in my cap
For loftiest honour, love's own beacon-glow!"
    She placed it there, consoled, and murmured, "Now
I crave exchange of token; and, I wis,
Mine is the fairest gold!" Plucking his dirk,
She from his bended head one bright lock severed,
And curled it round her finger-tip, and bound
With living blade of green the dainty coil,
And hid it in her bosom! "Hearken now,
Fair love," she spake: "this golden strand of thee
Shall string my haps of life like jewel-beads.
There's Pearls for Peace (God grant that Peace be mine!);
Onyx mourns sable (oft is mourning blest);
Sapphire's firm Faith in yon blue vault we see;
Joy laughs in rubies; and the Stone that bleeds,
Types mortal suffering, purifying best
The noblest. Last, in lustrous Diamond's shine
Gleams Heavenly Hope, of radiance all divine.
Fair love" (she questioned), "like you my conceit?"
    With wordless lips he praised her fantasie;
And thus the moments melted in sweet signs
And tender toying, and a silence brimmed
With deep enchantment.
                  Now old Corbred rose,
And stretching, gaped; and thrust a chilly nose
In question and reminder 'twixt the pair,
Who marked the shifting shadows.

"See! 'tis late!
Through wears the day.   O graceless Time, avaunt!
Aged out of love, unsympathetic Time,
Art thou, that jealous thievest this our joy."
So plaining, parted.   But to secrecy
Each pledged the other, lest their communings,
So doubly dear, henceforward, should be barred;
For scarce, they felt, would Randolph brook to see
A Comyn bear away the dowered bride
Whose union, fit assorted, might enchance
Her guardian's influence.   And Alastair
Feared lest some rude reverse should break the peace
Of his dear sire, who yet unconscious 'bode
Of their love dalliance.
                    Now, to live anew,
With hearts exchanged, the lovers kissed adieu.

NOTE TO LOVE'S DECLARING.

" *Clings like that eight-armed monster of the sea.*"—P. 101, l. 24.

The octopus.   It is a vulgar superstition that the octopus has the power of sucking blood by its long arms or feelers, of which the suckers are only used for clinging.

Touch me that Lute more gently, lest it jar
Upon my lassitude of jaded sense;
Frame no strung melodies to wake the heed
Into expectance, as aye-recurring Rhyme
Beats the caught ear to fever; but let chords
Fall from thy fingers, as the summer rain
Drips in irregular music from the boughs
Into a pool beneath; or singly breathe
Tones, as of Zephyr on the Æolian harp,
Fitful and tender.

Touch me that Lute more lightly, lest it mar
The train of dreamy fantasies that waft
My spirit down the hills of Long Ago!
Leave me the visions of those vanished hopes:
To call them vain, were to revile the Dead
That promised, not fulfilling ere they died.
I'm weary with what is, and hath to come,
And fain would slumber.

Touch me that Lute no longer; for the stream
Surges insistent with its further tale,
And soughs the promise of the autumn gale,
Minding the happy leaves how fleet is joy.
Give me that toy melodious; would my will
Had strength, like hands that rive these hapless strings,
To silence what must follow!

THE CHAPEL OF ALTYRE.

Shall orison and vigil aught avail,
For one that lies without salvation's pale?

STRANGE 'tis to mark, how lives in daily touch,
In constant sympathy of breathèd air,
Should be in sense and soul dissevered far!
Now pulsed in single beat those lover-hearts
Unread of Denys; nor him rightly reading
Who, hapless, loved, where Love might win no more.
    Earl Moray, in the temple of his soul
Shrining Ambition, ever worshipped there;
And in the desolation of a woe
Unshared, unutterable, and all-unblest,
Lived Lupola, the loneliest of the lone.

Ethereal Luna queens it i' th' sky,
Pale and impassive suzeraine of Night;
Powerful enchantress, who with magic sleep
O'erwhelms the world, and dares Creation show
No beauty but is borrowed from her beams.
    Yet, ah! what tender radiance they have lent;
How wondrous soft on pasture, moor, and main
Falls the translucent sheen; and every shadow,
In sable tracing, woo's the silvern light!

More peaceful lie the sylvan solitudes
Than in their day-dipped gloaming.   Every tree
Stands in his shadowy rest, or with a sound
Of hushing, chides some wanton air that sweeps
In wilfulness athwart his due repose.

O silver Lady of the Night, all hail !
O Shepherdess, by fleecy flocks surrounded !
O floating nymph, on th' impenetrable deep
Of foam-flecked, phosphor-lumined, heavenly seas !
Smile of the Night upon her sleeping child,
The World, that stirs half waking, with a smile
Drowsy responsive :—art thou these, O moon ?
Or a great Soul, in commune fathomless,
Self-merged, amidst of myriad star-bright Minds ?
Or, art the Peace of God, out the Intense
Of dark Time showing ; while the troubled wrack
Vap'rous o'erdrifts, nor touches thee at all ?

.   .   .   .   .   .

Who recks what mystery art ? for thou, O Light,
Art beautiful, exceeding all of praise !

Beneath the Moon, one silver day-in-night,
Where the tall pines crowd closest, and the burn
Of Altyre separates their communioned gloom—
That summer-gurgling, winter-boist'rous burn,
Whose sweet impertinent babbling apes thy flow,
Imperial Findhorn ! when thou cleav'st the land
To roll thy sweeping Majesty along ;—
There, where the woods are deepest, nigh the stream,
A holy, humble chapel through the trees
Peeped eastward with its carven Gothic eye ;
And on the night harmonious numbers brake,
In chorused chant, from out its precincts blest.

Hymn.

Mary ! sweet Mother of the World's Delight,
  Bend thou and heed
From where thou sitt'st, in heavenly garb bedight,
  Our humble meed
Of praise, song-offered ; and in grace requite
  Our ardent longing, our beseeching need.
       Ave Maria !
High Queen of Heaven, we, who dare not near
  The infinite white Throne—
Before whose splendour doth our dust appear
  Helpless and prone—
Plead through thy grace to the aye-listening ear
  Of Him thou lovest, thine Eternal Son.
       Ave Maria !
O martyred Saints and Angels, who may kiss
  Thy vesture's bord,
And live with thee, immaculate, in bliss,
  Anigh our Lord !
Join intercession, and receive for this
  The earth-dulled music of our praises poured.
       Ave Maria !

The holy brethren sang ; but scarce had died
Their latest note, when, startling every sense,
A wail more woful than the Banshee's cry—
More fearsome than the scream of dying steed
That from the slaughter-plain of ruthless war
Haunts a scared hearer long ;—the outer night
Rent ; and each frighted chaunter clutched an arm
Of nighest fellow ; while from amid the rest

Bold brother Odo stepped without the door,
And saw but this—just this, and nothing more :
   Across the silvered land that lay beyond,
Galloped low, lengthily, silent, and swift,
A great grey Wolf, instant evanishing
In the wood's inky shadow, showing therein
Once, where a moon-ray cleft the gloom, and then
Was lost.   Appalled, the shuddering brethren vowed
No earth brute voiced that cry.   Some denizen fiend,
O' the darkling woods, thus turned to fell dismay
Their blessed orisons.
                         Through dragging dark
Invoked those monks, against the wiles of hell,
Anton, and all the saintly calendar—
Till the kind Dawn allowed their home return,
When to the credulous brotherhood they told
Their vigil's misadventure, weird and dread.

The Truant Leaf.

'Twas tossed by the wind to my shoulder—'twas only a little
  brown Leaf,
That sought in my bosom a shelter, or hold in the strays of my
  hair,
To 'scape from the whirl and the whistle, the wailing and wrestling of air,
That hustled its fellows so wildly, out shelter or rest or relief.
                    Poor little brown Leaf!

A moment it lingered, and failing to find a firm hold, it was gone,
And, blent with the rustle and rattle, was hurried from ken and
  from sight,
With its myriad of racing companions, down, down the deep
  mystery of Night:
And why? I can tell not; but certain, I, lonely, felt yet more alone
                    By that little brown Leaf!

I gathered my mantle about me, and set a firm front to the blast,
And skirted the wild-swaying woodland, and passed o'er the dusk-
  bedimmed lawn,
And soon in the glow and the welcome of home, with its draperies
  drawn,
The struggle, the rush, and the raging without was a memory past:
                    And the little brown Leaf?

H

Ah, nay ! in my heart-depth was lying a sense that was scarcely
    a pain—
An echo fantastic of sorrow, a yearning, or conscience of loss—
That crisp little whisper athwart me, that spake by the jerk of the
    toss
Of the Thing that sought shield of my shoulder, and sought it,
    poor atom, in vain !
                    Oh, little brown Leaf !

Ah ! Mothering Instinct of Woman, so holy, intense, and so pure,
Will ye start into life, into loving, at the claim, for the cause, to
    the cure,
                Of a mere withered Leaf ?

'Tis thus ! And when brotherhoods mystic of sorrow make weariful
    moan,
We, traced with such delicate graving, so chorded to exquisite tone,
Shall spring to the succour of anguish made anguish to us through
    our own,
And, linked in that kinship of sorrow, feel never unblest and alone.
                Then thanks, little Leaf,
        For the throe and the thought thou hast shown—
                For the love thou hast known !
            For the love (was it Love ?) thou didst own !

NOTE TO THE CHAPEL OF ALTYRE.

" The Chapel of Altyre."—P. 109.

The church of Altyre is mentioned in ' Registrum Morav,' in 1239.

THE ERN, OR FINDHORN RIVER.

Heedest thou, Stream, the tale sad hearts thee tell,
Of passions that make human life a hell?

LIKE a bold charger from his stall fresh freed,
Whom not a chiding master's hand and voice
Can check in his exuberance of delight,
But with bound, curvet, plunge, and bound again,
Uses less earth than air, and sets more toil
Ten yards to traverse than might pass a mile:
So leaves the Ern her Mona-Liadh bed,
And frets through Dulsie, fumes by Ferness fair;
Now gathering force from Divie's added tide,
Where high Relugas sits, tears Logie by,
Spurns the restraint of Sluie's rock-barred bounds,
Where Darnaway's tall oaks are marshalled bold;
Syne, gently wearied, 'neath the red rock cliffs
Of lovely Altyre calms to steadier flow,
To sweep and swell through bright Cothall, and meads
(St John's yclept) of joust and tournament;
Then down the laughing Laigh into the sea,—
Like the same steed, whose pride, at last bespent,
Calms him to steadier pace and truer speed.

There, where she glided by, at nighest reach
Of Forres' royal borough, Lupola

By the soft stream was wandering pensively;
And in her company the gentle monk,
Confessor to the household, meekly moved—
A good man, and a guileless, much bestirred
To pity for her sorrow, seeking ever
To win confession from her burdened spright.

"Daughter," he urged, "no idly curious vein
Me prompts, but grief to note thy ceaseless care
Thus ever present! Doth impatience move
Thy darkened Being 'gainst the Will Divine?
Or dost in thine affliction recognise
Some Heavenly punishment of sin, concealed
From all but Heaven? Let not longer thus
Dull mysteries, like the rust on iron, eat
Into thy soul; a burden shared becomes
Of easier bearing; and our Church can give
Free absolution to the penitent.
Ah! bid me comfort thee; lay bare thy soul!"

Aye thus he pressed, she answering not at all,
Save with a sigh, scarce patient, or a shift
Of fretted shoulder. At the last she broke
With almost petulant haste upon his phrase:

"Little thou kenn'st what thine urged questioning
May bring for answer! Yet I fain would check
Thy too officious kindness. Therefore now
Say, can thy Church absolve me from my pain? . . .

"There is a burden that I needs must bear.
I cannot bear it! Is thy Church so kind?
Thou'lt tell of painful martyrs—ay, they died
Because they hoped. *I* may not dare to die
Because I hope! Thou riddle me aright!
My heart's so packed with sorrows, that no chink

Might take another one in, but 'twould dispart
The whole asunder.   See! I have no tears!
  I cannot weep, nor pray, nor die; and live
To suffer only!   For my wretched lot
Is of such marvellous and abhorrent dread
That help itself is helpless!   .   .   .

Look! where a light creeps up behind yon bank
Of darksome fir, the cruel eye of Night
Slow openeth; her awaking is my woe!
  O Moon, have mercy! use thy fullest power,
And drive me o'er the waste, all, all bereft
Of reason, that but lights my torturing lot!"
  Some commonplace of soothing filtered through
(From him) her wild beseechment, and she calmed!
  "No sheltering friendship offers me remede;
I seek dull magic's aid, and touch despair!
I wander round the Sanctuary of God,
Moonlit in chilly mocking; and I hear
Of saints and Mary Mother!   Where is peace?
Where is that Vision of the voiceless woods?
That Radiant One, thorn-crowned; for He alone,
I wot, can lift my burden and bestow   .   .   .

  .   .   .   .

Bare thou thy *soul*, saidst thou?   No Soul is mine!
Behold!"—and facing him, she let him know
The horror of her eyes!
  Oh, Heaven forgive him! 'twas a worthy man,
Who well could brook such terrors as might show
Disease of mind or body; but for This
So unprepared—ah! judge him not—was he,
That crying "Anathema," he turned and fled!

Her lips relaxed to something of a smile—
A rayless opening in a dreary sky—
And then she moved, and passing up the stream,
Sought the wood-edge, and sate her down to watch
The wanton zephyr chase the withered leaves.

   " Sport of the gliding Wind,
Oh, wee brown Leaf impelled across the lea,
Rustling in feeble protest! like to me,
   Toy of a Fate; but thine, meseems, is kind—
For brief thy course, and gentle is the death
Thou find'st Findhorn's murmuring flood beneath.

   " I marked thee,. little Leaf !
Anestling in yon hollow 'neath the shade
Of boughs, whereon thine infancy was swayed;
   Then came the wind-waft, whispering a brief
And kind command, when thou didst rise, and hie
Thee swift to yon dark volume rolling by.

   " What utter peace is thine,
Thou soulless, refuse atom of the world !
By lipping wave thy little fold uncurled,
   Perchance borne on to yonder ocean's brine ;
But dead, and lost, and Nothing evermore,
Sense of wild music to my heartis core.

   " Might I not emulate
Thy speeding? and seek rest beneath the tide,
And change for aye this world so chill and wide—
   In bold defying of a threatful fate—
For deep annihilation such as thine,
And pass to nothingness, and leave no sign ! "

Seized with such thoughts, now Lupola arose
And paced anigh the deep and peaceful flow
Of the wide river, sombre with the juice
Of tawny marish, and of ore-dyed spring—
So stilly-seeming, that no sign was shown
Of motion, save by rapid foam-flakes, churned
'Mid rock-beds earlier on the water's way!
    "Take me, O River, to thy cool, soft arms!
Fain would I end this strife, and be at rest:
'Tis but one plunge, and on their placid course
Those foam-flakes checked and dashed, would disappear;
A few wide circles melting swift away,
A rising ripple kissing either bank,
And a few bursting bubbles—nothing more!—
    Then—lip thy reeds, O Water, as before!"

Nigh to the stream she fared, and now her gaze
Lit on a beetle rolling 'mid the leaves,
All-diligent, a tiny clot of soil.
    Idly she watched it, half as in a dream.
Great was the pain the urgent toiler used:
Twigs showed to her vast trunks, and mole-raised mounds
Towered mighty, mountainous; and the pebbles strewn
Along the bord were monstrous boulder blocks,
Giant impediments. Yet on she wore
Her purposed route, still faithful to the task
By love or instinct prompted.
                   Lupola
Almost with interest watched the work at last;
And as she lost it 'neath the heaped decay
Of grass and leafage, crept athwart her mind
A teaching of endurance: "Steadfast thou,
Atom of life, thy purpose to achieve!

Shalt thou outwear me, who have all to win ? "
   She spake, and uttering, sate her gently down,
And watched the water till its dreamy voice,
The fascination of its quietude,
Wrought on her being, and she felt her lids
Droop, and her every nerve relaxed in sleep.

O Sleep, dull mocker of thy sister Death !
Thou incomplete deception, thou balking peace,
Thou promise unfulfilled of vanishment
From self, and from earth anguish !   We pass from Life
So-seeming, to wake stronger for our woe !
   Is this a boon ?   To weaken is t'wards Death ;
And Death—is ease from living.

Across the sky spread Night a drapery dense,
Whose piercen broideries let Heaven through
(Men call these stars); and 'neath the uncertain light—
For Night's full-orbèd Queen had risen and passed—
Trudged a belated shepherd timorous home
With hound at heel, that, pausing sudden, bared
White fangs in a low snarl, and bristled o'er,
And pointed at a tangled maze of reeds
Beside the river.   While his master stayed,
Dreading to venture near, and strove to pierce
With straining eyne the mirk, a rustling thence
Sounded, and, with a mighty leap and rush,
A grizzled Wolf came forth and fled away !

NOTE TO THE ERN, OR FINDHORN RIVER.

" To sweep and swell through bright Cothall."—P. 115, l. 15.

Sir Alexander Penrose Cumming-Gordon (our great-grandfather), with his wife Helen (daughter of Sir Ludovic Grant of Grant and Lady Margaret Ogilvie of Findlater and Seafield), lived for two years after his marriage in a small house at Cothall, down beside the river Findhorn, of which hardly any remains exist, but where he once intended to build a large residence. He also lived at Altyre and Forres House. — *Vide* note "Quaint-structured bower," in Prologue.

IN DARNAWAY.

Where passion's heat makes tinder of desire,
Needs but a little spark to kindle fire.

Now hung about the land, these later days,
A murmuring breath, portentous of discórd
'Twixt Randolph and Dunphail, anent the rights
Of Darnaway's chase Royal, claimed by each
Through kingly writs and deeds.   Such messages,
Such words had been exchanged, as heat the blood
To hasty actions ; and though their hammered wedge
Had split the feeble friendship scarce as yet
Beyond its bark, there were who saw the day
When such a quarrel as would shake the shire
Of Moray, must ensue.
                            It was a morn
On-following hours of balmèd rain, that blest
The gladsome world to fresh fertility,
Giving the cup of every upturned flower
A diamond, and lending every spray
A row of crystals, in whose rainbow sheen
Mirrored a million Suns ; that deeped the moss
To richer tinting in the forest glades,
Wooed the sweet birken's aromatic breath

To blend with odours from each needled pine,
More fragrant than rose-attars of the East.
   Rade through the Royal chase of Darnaway
Earl Moray, and a gaysome hunting-train—
Horse, huntsman, hound, and pricker all agog
To drive a noble quarry to his death
That summer morn so peerless.
                       Nigh the Earl
Bayoumé proudly bore the daintiest maid
In Caledon, her loveliness afire
And glowing with delight of exercise !
   Dear to her soul the palfrey's generous pace,
Cleaving soft airs and swallowing the land
In that far-reaching stretch or maneged bound ;
Spurning each obstacle in pride of pace,
Passing the fallen timbers in his stride,
Sweeping adown the shadowy velvet glades,
Whose branchèd roof showered jewels on his flank,
And gemmed her hair with pearl-drops.
                     Such a glee
In sympathy the steed and mistress shared,
When Randolph chased the Stag in Darnaway.

Roused from his covert by the clangorous horn,
Scarce with cleft hoofs the great Hart skims the turf
In conquering bounds, and seeks a deeper shade,
Brushing the hornèd woodbine draperies,
Whose odours blend with the bruised eglantine
That sheds rose-petals o'er his russet coat.
   Then, sheltering 'mid the bracken, with his head,
His antlered crest, all velour yet, alert ;
He lists, and through his sylvan soul there floats
One bypast memory, when the hunters marked

A mad brute, strengthened by despair, bestem
Yon flood-wrought wave beneath, and scarce their hounds
Restrained from following to a fateful end.
Yet, all-alluring Altyre held no charm
(Though safely reached her fair and favouring shore)
To long detain the exile, and he sought
Again his Darnaway's accustomed home.

But ah! not long to live 'mid those delights,
For true-aimed sped a quivering shaft, and struck
His breast ere dream of peril seized its sense;
And the great hart, with one faint gasp, became
The prey of Alastair's unerring bow.

Then on the silence broke the nearing bay
Of triumphing hounds, and all the gallant rout
Rode to the spot, at fault and wonder-full;
Nor wondered long, for by the fallen king
Stood Comyn, and his henchman Allan Shaw.

"This passeth patience!" wrathful, Moray cried;
"Needs my deep years bow to thy beltless youth
To learn new modes and chivalry in sport?
Good sooth, sir lad, here's lessons twain in one!"
As thus he spake, cold sarcasm replaced
Anger's first flush; but Alastair in haste:
"Lord Earl, mistake not harshly thus mine act,
Nor tax me with such lack of courtesy
As wilful spoiling of your sport! I vow,
By the White Cumin Saint of I-colm-Kil,
The wild-wood lay in silence, and this game
Showed of pursuit no sign; nor could I guess
To-day you rode in the disputed Chase
That rounds the royal seat of Darnaway."

" How now, young braggart ? hast not heard, it takes
Two to make a quarrel—as the steel must strike
A flint to fire ?   So, when my tempered steel
Strikes thy base flint afar and out of ken,
This dull dispute shall die ! "

                              Thus Randolph sneered.
The blood of Comyn stirred so lustily,
That none may tell what provocations rose
To the tongue-tip, had not his darting eye
Caught sign of gathered brows and strainèd lips,
That checked his heat, from pale Ydonea.

    Then, like the height of some imperial Pine
When on its coppered crest in golden flood
The evening sun dwells with a lingering glow,
Reared Alastair his head ; and as that coronal,
Rain-dripping, ray-gilt, breeze-swept, casts abroad
A sheen and sparkle, so he tossed a shower
Of glitter to the wind, and laughed aloud !

    " A threat to blanch a maid or mother's cheek,
And cause the hearkening Corbie whet his beak !
Soothly, Lord Earl !   Come we and you to blows,
Sore will the tussle be, nor victory sure :
Then let our cause of quarrel nobler stand
Than this poor hart, whose crownèd head I'll lay,
Bright Ladye, at your feet, an't please you take
This humble offering for our friendship's sake ;
And Moray shall absolve me in his mind
Of all intent discourteous."

                              Stern the Earl :
    " Our reckoning is to come !   My Ladye ward
Accepts from freebooters no gifts o' grace.
Speed home thy venison ! may it taste as sweet
As the sharp berries of the unripened sloe,

And 'mind thy wasps within their castled byke
Of Randolph's wrath !   Ydonea, hie we home,
I hunt no more this morn in Darnaway."

The train departed ; Alastair home-sped,
Made known to sire and brethren what had chanced
    Grave, the old warrior shook his silver head :
" I would this had not been ; for I am old,
And fain had passed in peace my latest days :
This will breed strife."   Said Alastair, " I fear,
My father, that occasion was desired ;
For though the blood was seething in my veins,
And I, regardless of his numbers, yearned
To brave his insolence with like return,
Yet reined my tongue, and spake the fellow fair,
He did ignore my plea, and snatched offence."

Now when the mid-day meal lay on the board,
Close converse, stirred by this untoward event,
Passed round ; and Alastair would gauge those wells
O' the Past, whose deeps, fresh stirred, their Present made
Turbid once more.
           " Yet once recount the tale
Of Bruce and Comyn feuds, and how it fell
That injury on injury was heaped
By Bruce triumphant, on our clan and name."

" A crown's a golden lure, my son, and gold
To peace and charity hath been a bane
Sin' child-Man's witless eyne its glitter first desired !
But now give heed, and once again shalt hear
How erst the rancour of our foes was born."

NOTES TO DARNAWAY.

"In Darnaway."—P. 122.

THE ancient forest of Tarnawa, or Tarnua, now Darnaway, was a royal possession in 1291, when Edward I. of England directs Alexander Comyn, keeper of the forest, to deliver to the Bishop of Caithness, *oaks*, in payment of masses to be said for the souls of his sister Margaret, and her husband, Alexander, King of Scotland.

In *circa* 1561, Mary Queen of Scots bestowed the earldom of Moray on her natural brother James, the Regent, who was assassinated in Linlithgow. His eldest daughter married Sir James Stuart, Lord Doune, and they succeeded to the earldom. (He was the "bonnie Earl o' Moray," murdered by Lord Huntly, of the ballad.) Thus Darnaway, with other lands of the Moray earldom, came into possession of the Stuarts, in whose name it abides to-day. The *reddendo* required by a charter of Robert II. in 1371, to be given yearly by the keeper of Darnaway, was six broad arrows, yearly delivered on the Feast of St John, at the manor of Darnaway. "The deer of Tarnaway," writes my old friend Charles Edward Stuart (Count d'Albanie), in notes to his 'Lays of the Deer Forest,' "like their cousins of the Monaidhliath, were a mighty race; and their heads, like those of all fine greenwood stags, much stronger and more largely 'summed' than those of the mere mountain herds. Until the last half-century they were numerous in the forest."

He continues, that Pennant, visiting Darnaway in 1772, found the woods near the Findhorn full of red-deer and roe; and that as

late as 1811 a lad fired "into" a plump of twelve stags coming
down the forest, and missed them all ! But the Count d'Albanie
says that dogs were turned loose into the forest to hunt out the
deer for the preservation of young timber, and that when he first
knew it only seven remained, and they were " cunning as old foxes."
In my child days, when I first *realised* the country at all (*circa*
1855-60), I do not remember ever hearing of deer in Darnaway, but
have some vague recollection of a stag appearing on Upper Altyre ;
probably a vanquished and fugitive wooer from the forests above.

" The White Cumin Saint of I-colm-Kil."—P. 124, l. 27.

Cuimine Ailbe (657-669), Abbot of Hy, or Iona, biographer of St
Columba. "His death," says Burton, "was sixty years after that of
the Saint, whom he may have seen and known in his youth."

His work is one of the most valuable extant on the early ecclesiastical history of Scotland aud Ireland. Dr Reeves, the editor of
Adamnan's ' Life of St Columba,' says this abbot was son of Ernans
and of the race of Conall Gulban ; his name is variously written in
Irish MSS. as Cumine, Cumaine, Cumein, &c.

"He was sainted," says the Rev. Thomas MacLauchlin, in his
' Early Scottish Church.' What Comyn or Cumein he was, who
shall say ?

THE UNDOING OF THE COMYN.

For sins all-unassoiled we suffer yet ;
But not our losing shall the world forget.

"When Norway's Babe, the 'Maiden,' queened our land,
Ere her frail arm might bear the sceptre's weight,
Six Regents ruled the Realm, and of these, twain,
John, Badenoch's Lord, and Alexander, Earl
Of wind-swept Buchan ; were the heads and chiefs
Of all the Comyn faction.   Brother he,
This Buchan, to my grandsire—him, ye wot,
That first Red Comyn, whose inheritor
Thou art in truth, my tawny Alastair :
—And John 'the Black' of Badenoch was mine eme.[1]
   This latter, on the death of Norway's maid,
Claimed heirship to the realm, through Donal-Bain,
Our forebear, king of Scots ; but having wived
The Ladye Marjorie Baliol, and in view
Of future possibilities and potencies,
Did yield his claim to brotherly support
Of Baliol and his cause.
                                    I need not speak
Of England's insolence, of Wallace wight,
Of all the bitter days in blood and dule

[1] Uncle.

I

That came and passed; but will recount what most
Ourselves concerns.

                  Mine uncle dead, his son,
'Red John' the second, captive from Dunbar,
Constrained to England, met the Ladye Joan,
Earl Pembroke's sister and co-heritor,
And wed her for his wife. I saw her once;
Sightly, and somewhat cold, she chilled the sense,
Like autumn's rime on summer pastures fallen :·
Yet all our kinsman's heart was hers, that sprang
To flame at her approach; for, Sun-wise, Love
Through Ice itself can strike and kindle fire!
But mark ye, sons!—has been and shall be ever,
That Comyns by their mates are made or marred.
He of our race who makes a prudent choice
Of wise and gracious helpmeet, weareth life
Through in good harmony; but he unblest
In a fair face and fashion, void of soul,
Or trifling, witless woman, self-concerned,
Shall miss the worth of life, and by her lack
Losing his value, touch a bitterest end!

"Now, Baliol's son a minor—Baliol's self
An humbled Monarch, at Montrose discrowned—
Was John of Badenoch Regent of this land,
Like to his kinsman in the 'Maiden's' dawning;
And chief in power and high authority.

He served his country well on Sassenach pride
In Cumberland, and eke on Rosslyn field;
While Bruce had sought to steer him careful courses
'Twixt Edward and leal service to our land.

By all save Bruce and his, was Comyn held
The kingdom's rightful heir; and though the craft

Of Carrick, through submiss and feint of love,
Beguiled the English Edward; yet supreme
(Though by's own actions shorn of English aid,
And reft of Baliol, who in exile pined),
In Scotland Badenoch stood.   .   .   .

Him held the Bruce in dread, and sought to enmesh!

" So factions grew and growled, and swords lay bare,
And all the land seemed like a throbbing ocean,
Whose outmost edge is trimmed of sombre clouds
That herald the piled storm.
                              In winter's prime
It chanced, upon a day, those rivals met.
    I cannot hold that love and·amity
Reigned, each for other, in their several breasts,
As Bruce and Comyn rade from Stirling town;
I cannot deem that either, of generous heart,
Would yield the other his ambition's pride;
For oh! the love of Power doth dwell in man
So inly, that when watching infants play
(Who rules her puppet, or commands his hound),
We sigh in smiling, and do recognise
The promise of their life's maturity.
    But seems, the subject of their nation's woe
These broached, and to our Comyn soothly spake
The Bruce: 'My comrade, make we now resolve
To suit these troubles to our bettering.
I will give aid and set you on the Throne,
To which you deem you rightfully pretend,
So that ensured my hold and tenure be
Of all your present lands and influence;
Or, an it like you better, then assist

My regal claim, and by the Crown I'll swear
You shall sit first and highest after me.'

"Some hold that Comyn deemed the name of King
Then-as, mere form, and like to win the spite
Of factions thus assumed, or ire fourfold
Stir up in Edward.   Others hold that he
Would lull the Bruce, and bide the truer time
Wherein to draw his best occasions forth,
And gathering all his strength, in one effórt
Be rid of Bruce and England by one blow."

"So, from my rumoured knowledge of himself,"
Said Alastair, "I'd read our cousin's mind—
No secondary place could 'suage the lust
Of him who deemed a crown his birthright's due."

"I know not; but in fine, he spake assent
To Bruce's high ambition, and they signed
And sealed a compact that it thus should be.
    This came to knowledge of the English king;
How, none can truly tell.   To me it seems
(My kinsman kenning), that he dropt such words
In spousal dalliance with his lady, Joan,
As gave her clue, which, following out with all
The iced persistence of her English blood,
She touched the secret, and betrayed the same,
Through cowardice of dangers might accrue,
And misbelieving high results to ensue,
E'en through her brother, to his cousin, the king.

"Now, at the English Court great Gloucester's Earl,
Kinsman and friend to Bruce, did catch the wind
Of smouldering wrath; nor daring pen or speech,

Sent spurs and coin to the threatened wight,
Who marked, and fled from London city straight.
    They tell, that lest the snow should Bruce bewray
He caused reverse the shoe-irons of his steed ;
So rode to Scotland."
                Here the heedful loons,
Irreverent brake upon the narrative,
And prayed their sire to dwell not on the going,
But reach the fine of horror !
                   " Hasty lads !
Sooth, sooth ! but, an you will, I'll to Dumfries,
And tell how, ordering justice, Comyn there
To Court had come.
              That tenth of Februar'
Was Nature gently stirring to awaken
From out her wintry slumbers ; but oped her eyne
Upon a deed so black, so foul, so base,
That once again she drew the snowy veil
Athwart their sight, and to oblivion swooned.

    " Our kinsman turned at mid-day to his prayers
Within the shelter of St Francis' Church ;
And thither Bruce repaired, hot haste, to charge
The treachery on his rival.
                 What therein passed
Ken but the stones of that polluted fane :
    The air is charged with ruddy mists of blood,
And in my nostrils hangs the noisome taint
Of battle-fields fresh fought ; and my strained soul
Quivers with craving vengeance on thy race,
O fell Kirkpatrick ! "
                Here in haste arose
The aged knight, striding two turns and fro,

Then swept his hand across his moistened brow,
And standing, spake in passionate tones and low:
  "Without, Kirkpatrick and de Lindsay lingered,
Awaiting Bruce; and some who marked them there,
Noted what haste of tread, what clenching hand,
What bitten nether lip the former showed,
As one whose conscience presaged coming ill.
  His friends assert, no fore-determined plan
Impelled the Bruce, but hasty violent wrath
O'ercame him when he smote! . . .
                       With frantic mien
From out the holy place he rushing came,
And fleeing past the pair, in smothered tones
Called for his horse!
                Kirkpatrick cries: 'What now?
What ails my Lord of Carrick? What hath been
'Twixt thee and Comyn, Bruce?'
                  Who wild replies:
'Delay me not, I doubt he's slain!'
                      'You doubt?'
The murderer scoffs: ''tis I'll mak sicker!' Thus
E'en like a hound who scenting blood must share
And dip his muzzle in't, he makes his way
Right to the very Altar, on whose steps
Lay wounded Badenoch; to whom the assassin dog
Remorseless, dealeth death, and meeting, syne,
Robert de Comyn hasting up the aisle
To his nephew's aid, all bare of arms or fence,
Kirkpatrick speeds the dagger, dripping hot
With kindred life, into a kinsman's heart!

  "So died our own and nearest. Son of mine,
Had then thy being sprung, my vow had lain

Fateful on thy young soul peremptory,
Till on the carcass of that hound of Hell
Thy doubled strokes had struck his funeral knell!"

The greybeard paused; on his young hearer's brow
Upstood the knotted veins in pulsing rage,
And Alastair cursed low and deep; while loud
Beat their strung hearts through quiet of the Hall.
    Their father thus resumed:
                        "This was the knell
Of Comyn hopes and projects; for despair,
And ne'er a chance of grace with Edward more,
Made the Bruce froward all to win or lose;
Who speedy raised the standard of revolt,
And gathered all his partisans for fight.
His crowning followed, by the traitress hand
Of Buchan's crooked Countess; that with stealth
And most disloyal 'haviour thieved the horse,
And did seduce the servants of her lord
To ruin all his race.
                When time had passed,
And wreathed success had crowned the Bruce's hopes,
He for his nephew, Thomas Randolph (sire
Of yonder John), the earldom did erect
Of Moray, and of lands fair appanage
Therewith enriched him. Thus the Bruce's blood
Flowing through Moray's heart, all-predisposed
To wreak us ill, leaps to this dire dispute
Anent our rights of sport in Darnaway—
Rights that no Bruce can give, no Bruce shall take—
Rights ourn by laws no Bruce shall repeal or break!

And yet through dule and danger won we these!

The six-and-twentieth day of ripe July,
In that fell year, twelve hundred ninety-six,
Saw England's Edward ride in Elgin town.
   A Royal sight, i' faith, when Bayard bore
The long-limbed monarch through the wondering streets
(Whose very pavement, rattling, did protest),
Marshalled by banner of that holy John
Of Beverley, and Cuthbert's ensign famed,
That through its carmined wealth of velvet folds
Bore centre-wise [beneath the snowy square
All green and gold begirt of broidery.],
The linen cloth wherewith yon saint had veiled
The Sacred Chalice!   Pendent from a staff
Full fifteen feet, topped with a silvern cross,
This mighty Standard journeyed in the train
Of Durham's warlike Prelate.
                       Followed syne
Stout company of archers, slingers, men
Of crossbow, and the heavy horse, and light,
Clattering and curveting the city down,—
The last, high prancing in uncumbered glee,
Like airy gnats to harass with their stinging
A foe, and flit; their weightier comrades, proud
With chanfron, poitrinal, and croupier charged,
That none repressed their pomp and champing fire
Though the deep air thrilled tremulous around,
And pennons carried by attendant squires
In rearward of their knights, hung heavily,
Unstirred by Æolus, who lay aloft
Breathless with heat.
                'Twas a fair cavalcade,
Primed with a hateful project, e'en to bend
Or crush the Comyn powers within the North!

"Three days the king there sojournèd, and there
He did perforce compel the fealty
Of many knights and men of great degree.
    Such was thy grandsire, prisoner of Dunbar;
Argayle's Macdougall, Alastair of Lorne
(Mine uncle, through his union with the child
Of John, that first Red Comyn); and the famed
Sir Adam Gordon, with a many more,
Who knew that peace, at cost whate'er, alone
Might heal the land's disorder.
                          Then it chanced
We had confirmed to us the keeper's post
Of Darnaway's fair forest, which this Earl
Would seize his own; so finds pretence for feud.
    But all himself is foe, and fiercely fain
To stand the lord of Moray paramount;
Nor will his lust be 'suaged until he sweep
Our holding from the country.   Shall we brook
His proud dominion?"
                          "Nay!" (in chorused shout).
"Then I, the aged, and ye, all young and lusty,
Would tyne our latest drop of Comyn blood
In right and cause of clan and family!"

Now while they fell a-furbishing their arms,
Their bows new-stringing, feathering fresh their shafts,
Held the bright youngsters conclave and discourse
On olden deeds and feats of warriors vanished,
And spake of all each one would do or dare
For Comyn fame and honour.
                          Walter vowed,
In tame Hollandish city he'd set on
A 'prentice garb and badge, with traders mix,

A-learning of their traffic with the world;
So gain him moneys, and enhance the might
And dominance of this their family.
"And I would wander as a Troubadour,"
Brake here young Ian, ere his elder paused,
"In foreign lands, and sing to peasant churls,
Or in fair halls to knights and dainty dames,
Till heavy brain should brighten, jewel eyne
Flash sympathy, and martial bosoms beat
To the heroic numbers of our land;
And I should win the laurel wreath of song,
To swell the honours of our family."

His brethren laughed, sad-witting when he sang
As lief you'd hear a corncrake i' the mow!

Then thoughtful Richard spake:

                "I, brothers all,
Would seek the sacred cloister's hallowed shade,
And in deep abnegation of myself,
Through weighty penance, fasts, and midnight prayers,
Win that high Heaven and all the holy saints
Would prosper your endeavours and intents
To blessing on our clan and family."

The knight laid hand upon the youthful head:
"Nay, son, not mine to doubt but monkish life
Is reverend and holy, and our name
Boasts many a clerk. Hy's abbot, Cumin the Fair,
Wore it with dignity; and well we know
Of William, Scotland's Chancellor, who held
Three years 'gainst Pope and Prelate Durham's See,
At bidding of the Empress-Queen Matilda;
And Odo, Hextild's son: Archbishop John

Of Dublin, envoy to the Holy See
When Beckett vexed King Henry; and others yet.
These, certes, were men of action; but, meseems,
No abjuration of our power of joyaunce,
Our human instincts, pure and heaven-bestowed,
Is God's true service; for the battle-field
Or calm domestic hearth can show His praise
Well, as worn pavement by beseeching knees,
Or life emasculated.
     Something sure
Lacks in humility, when man resigns
God's world, where God has set him, knowing best."

" True, noble sire," duteous his eldest said;
" My soul would brook no cloistering; yet I'd scorn,
For our repute, no task: haggle at trade,
Soil my pure palm with statecraft's turbid ink,
Study and scrawl like any mildewed clerk
Who pores o'er parchment till the cobwebs cling,
(Expelled his brain) among his musty hairs,
That lack heaven's breath to dust them!"
       Loudly laughed
His brethren all: " 'Tis yon would be a sight
To raise our dead a-gibing! At a desk,
Brood free wild Comyns, soiling vellum!—hah!"

" Vaunt not, nor boast this wildness of the race,"
The Chieftain said, with sadness in his smiling;
" Tame ye the Falcon, rather, to employ
Its wilding ways for value and for fame.
See now, set on her perch, yon Haggard bold,
That, bright-eyed, preens her wing like any dove—
Her native savagery by kindly stress

Trained into noble uses !
                  Like to hers,
There is within our blood a certain haste,
Known since our name was spelled, nor slackening speed
In days of Now.
               Be't yours to fitly guide.
What may work nobly, but can eke be base;
Nor deem the wilding free who loves to yield
Masked slavery to the lowest self; but him
Free, truly free, who most is innocent—
Free, who is stark against all tyranny,
Unshackled from all meanness of the mind !

Stand true, O sons, to clan and family !
So, be your boast of lofty things alone :
   What dispositions you may recognise
As of the blood, and native to the race,
Weld and so temper—as an armourer
Converts rough iron to the nobler steel—
Till through the fire of trial, that for all
Who Live, not dully slumbering; doth burn,
Ye may pass shining to the opening glow
Of a fair Future for yourselves and name !

Then my wild Comyns shall be nobly free !
Free, and as fetterless from bonds of crime
As yon sweet laverock, whose untrammelled wing
Scaleth the Heaven where her song upleads ! "

NOTES TO THE UNDOING OF THE COMYN.

"When Norway's Babe, the 'Maiden,' queened our land."—P. 129, l. 1.

ALEXANDER III. of Scotland died in March 1286, leaving as his successor to the throne a granddaughter Margaret, daughter of his daughter Margaret, by Eric, King of Norway. Being only three years old at the date of her grandsire's death, it was needful to form a Government during her minority ; and the Estates of the Kingdom, meeting at Scone on 11th April 1286, appointed six guardians of the State, of whom two were Comyns—Alexander, Earl of Buchan, and John, Lord of Badenoch. For eighteen months this council of Regency ruled with ability and success. Two of their number (the Earls of Buchan and Fife) having died, dissensions arose, and the King of Norway, fearing for his daughter's right, sought counsel from the King of England, who readily offered to use his influence, and thereby pave a way to his own interests. He wished to promote a marriage between the infant Maid of Norway and his own son, Prince Edward, and obtained the Pope's sanction, as the pair were within the prohibited degrees of consanguinity. Matters having been ultimately arranged, commissioners were sent to Norway to bring the child-queen to Scotland for her betrothment. She, being apparently weakly, succumbed to the fatigues of a tempestuous voyage, and having been landed in Orkney, died in September 1290, in her eighth year. She was the last of William the Lion's direct descendants.

" John, Badenoch's Lord."—P. 129, l. 4.

John, styled the Black Comyn, became Lord of Badenoch on the death of his uncle, Walter Comyn, Earl of Menteith, in 1258. He was Regent of Scotland in 1286, competitor for the Crown in 1292, married Marjorie, sister of King John Baliol; died 1299.

" Alexander, Earl of Buchan."—P. 129, l. 4.

Son of the Great Justiciar of Scotland, and brother of John, first Red Comyn;—Earl of Buchan in right of his mother.   Married Elizabeth, second daughter of Roger de Quincey, Earl of Winchester; was Great Justiciar in 1251, and High Constable in 1270, till his death in 1289.   He was twice summoned by Edward I. to perform military service in England, in return for lands he owned there, both by marriage and inheritance (says Dr Taylor).   "De nomine Cumyng erant tres comites, Buchanie, Marre, et Menteith, et simul xxx. milites baltheo accincti" (Exta. e variis Cronicis Scocie, p. 103).   In a clever imitation of an old chronicle, by Mr J. Spence (Ruined Castles in Banff; pub. 1873), occur these lines :—

> " Al saif quhar Comyns haif commauu
> In Baddneuch, Boynef [Banff], and Buthquhan.
>
> .   .   .   .
>
> Frae Ceannguisach ta Peterheid,
> Lyvit nane but dyd the Comyn dreid,
> Fra Carn-a-munt ta Murref se [Moray Firth]
> Thai rulyt wyth ferme auctorite."
>   —Cronyke of Johunes Awchanyowhe, *(circa)* 1400.

"Regnante Alex. Sec., Alexr. Cominius honore Comitio Boghaniæ effloruit qui Rogeri de Quincy, Comitis Wintoniæ in Anglia, filiam et vnam hœredum duxit, &c."—G. Camden's Brita., 1607 (Buchania, p. 713).

The first of these Earls of Buchan was son of Richard Comyn and Hextilda—William Comyn, who first married a granddaughter of

Banquo ; and secondly, the daughter and heiress of " Fergus, the
ancient Earl of Buchan" (who died 1209), and in whose right he
became Earl of Buchan.   He founded the Abbey of Deer, in Aber-
deenshire.   " The Abbey of Deer, which belonged to the Cistercians,
and was founded by W. Cumin, Earl of Buchan," says Camden.
" Obeiit Will. Cumin Comes de Buquhan, Oct. 70, abbatie de Der
fundator" (Chron. de Mailros).   It must have been this Earl who
insulted the famous Rhymer, " True Thomas," according to a tradition mentioned in ' A View of the Diocese of Aberdeen,' written
about 1732.

" On Aiky brae" (in Old Deer parish) are certain stones called
the Cummin's Craig, where it is said one of the Cummins, Earl
of Buchan, by a fall from his horse at hunting, dashed out his
brains.

The prediction goes that this Earl (who lived under Alexander
III.) had called Thomas the Rhymer by the name of Thomas the
Lyer, to show how much he slighted his predictions ; whereupon
that famous fortune-teller denounced his impending fate in these
words, which, it is added, were all literally fulfilled :—

> " Tho' Thomas the Lyer thou callest me,
> A sooth tale I shall tell to thee :
> By Aikyside
> Thy horse shall ride,
> He shall stumble, and thou shalt fa'.
> Thy neck-bane shall break in twa,
> And dogs shall thy banes gnaw,
> And maugre all thy kin and thee,
> Thy own belt thy bier shall be."

" *That first Red Comyn, whose inheritor.*"—P. 129, l. 8.

I am tempted by my present connection with Yorkshire to quote
an anecdote of my turbulent ancestor, John, the first Red Comyn,
from Drake's Antiquities of York.   He (John Comyn) was third son
of William, Earl of Buchan, by his first wife, Matilda Urquhart (de

Montalto), daughter of Cœtisa, daughter of Banquo. He married Mary of Galloway (as elsewhere noted), and owing to the death of both his elder brothers, became head of the Comyn family. He seems to have given much trouble to the kings of the sister kingdoms, for Tytler says "he nearly caused a war" (before 1249) "between Alexander II. and Henry III., by erecting two castles— one in Galloway, another at Hermitage in Liddesdale." He took an active part in the affairs of Scotland during the minority of Alexander III.; but by the influence of the English King he and his brothers, Sir Richard Comyn, and Walter Comyn, Earl of Menteith, were removed from the infant King's councils. However, in 1255 they regained possession of the King and the Queen, and governed the kingdom by the weight of their talents and the influence of their family (says Mrs Cumming-Bruce). According to Drake,—"anno 1268," I read of an account of the origin of a chapel on Ousebridge (York) in the 'Collectanea,' "when there was a peace and agreement made with John Comin, a Scotch nobleman, and the citizens of York (mediantibus regibus Angliæ et Scotiæ), for a fray which had happened upon the bridge, and wherein several of John Comin's servants had been slain. The said lord was to receive three hundred pounds; and the citizens were obliged to build a chapel on the place where the slaughter was made, and to find two priests to celebrate for the souls of the slain for ever. How long they continued to pray for the souls of these Scots . . . I know not."— Eboracum, or the History and Antiquities of the City of York, 1736.

> " Donal-Bain,
> Our forebear, King of Scots; but having wived."—P. 129, l. 13.

Donal-bain, with his brother King Malcolm Ceannmohr, were sons of Duncan, King of Scotland (murdered by Macbeth), by Sybilla, sister of Siward, Earl of Northumberland. He was elected King of Scots in accordance with the ancient law of tanistry, in opposition to his nephew Duncan, son of Malcolm, by his first wife,

Ingioborge.   Donal-bain left an only daughter, Beatrix or Bethoe, who married the Count de St Pol.   Their daughter, Hextilda or Hexilda, Countess of Etheletela, married Richard Cumyn, Justiciar of Scotland, in 1178 to 1189, ancestor of John the "Black" Comyn of Badenoch, first Competitor.   "Why," says Mrs Cumming-Bruce, "Countess of Etheletela, we have not been able to discover ; but Hextilda being of the royal house of Ethel or Athol, probably succeeded to the appanage of her grandfather Donal-bain, who, after his father Crynan (?), appears to have been chief of Athol during the reign of his brother, Malcolm Cænmore.   The Cumyns were ever after nearly connected with Athol."

"*The Ladye Marjorie Baliol, and in view.*"—P. 129, l. 14.

Vide note, p. 151.

"*Of England's insolence, of Wallace wight.*"—P. 129, l. 19.

There seems little doubt that neither Bruce nor Comyn were true friends to Wallace.   Comyn's desertion at the battle of Falkirk would hardly be attributable to panic !   And though he nobly redeemed his fault afterwards, defeating the English at Roslin in three battles in one day, with Wallace and Fraser, and with them was afterwards driven into wilds and fastnesses, where, according to Langtoft, the English historian—

"The Lord of Badenauch, Freselle, and Walais
Lived at thieves law, ever robbing alle wayes."
(Anderson's 'Scot. Na.')—

yet neither of these rivals seems to have been whole-hearted as regards the Scottish patriot.   Buchanan says: "Bruce and Cumin, who, belonging to the blood royal, thought, if they must be subjects, it was more honourable to be so to a great and powerful king, than to an upstart whose dominion would not be less base than danger-

K

ous," &c. And Anderson says that De Brus, father of the king, is described as upbraided by Wallace as the mean hireling of a foreign master, and reduced to tears and to swearing that he would embrace the cause of his oppressed country. This tale, says the 'Scottish Nation,' is a pure myth. "All writers," it says, "seem to think this coalition" (when Bruce and Comyn were associated in the Regency) "had been mainly produced by a desire to crush Wallace, whose patriotism endangered their common pretensions. . . . That the existence, on the part of both, of this feeling is true, . . . we are not prepared to deny."

Mrs Cumming-Bruce avers it was on Wallace realising that the rival parties of Bruce and Comyn were united to oppose him, that he resigned the Governorship of Scotland.

" *Constrained to England, met the Ladye Joan.*"—P. 130, l. 5.

Says Anderson in his 'Scottish Nation,' under head "Cumming": "Besides his [Comyn's] claim to the crown of Scotland, he was also allied by blood to the Royal family of England, having married Joan, sister and co-heir of Aymer de Valence, Earl of Pembroke, whose father was uterine brother of Henry III."

" *An humbled Monarch, at Montrose discrowned.*"—P. 130, l. 23.

"And when he [Edward] had reached Montrose without resistance, Baliol, by the advice of John Cumin of Strathbogie, came and surrendered to him both himself and his crown."—Aikman's Buchanan, p. 399.

" *He served his country well on Sassenach pride.*"—P. 130, l. 27.

"It will be seen from this recapitulation of the principal events in the career of Comyn, that he had done good service to his country, and that he was a more consistent patriot than Bruce, who had, from selfish motives, endeavoured to steer a middle course between his duty to his country and his allegiance to Edward" (and, I would add, his own private interests).—Dr Taylor in 'Edward I. in North of Scotland,' p. 278.

"*'Twixt Edward and leal service to our land.*"—P. 130, l. 30.

Dr. Taylor of Easton, quoting from Sir F. Palgrave's 'Documents,' says that when Bruce, Lord of Annandale, appealed with the " seven Earls," &c., to the King of England, against the tyranny of the regents—John Comyn of Badenoch, and William Fraser, Bishop of St Andrews in 1290-91—there was appended to the petition an anonymous memorandum in Norman-French, which mantained that the Kings of England had the rights of superiority over Scotland, &c.; "the writer intimating, through a confidential agent, that in the event of Edward asserting his right, he would support him with all his friends and adherents." This "treasonable communication" is supposed by Palgrave to be written by Bruce himself. In Fabian's Chronicle (1559), " the seventh parte," p. 147, is this : " In this xxxiii. yeare, Robert le Bruze, *contrary his othe to King Edward before made*, assembled the lordes of Scotlande, and by the counsell of the Abbot of Scone and other that favoured his untrouth, he sent unto Clement the V. for a dispensacion of hys othe before made unto K. Edwarde, and surmised to him that K^{ge} Eddware vexed and greued ye realme of Scotland wrongfully. Whereupon the Pope of Rome wrote unto Kinge Edwarde to leaue of suche doynges. And while this matter was thus complayned on unto the Pope of Rome, the sayde Robert le Bruze made all the labour he might unto the lordes of Scotlande that he were admitted for kynge of y^t region, so that upon the dai of the conception of our lady, on the viii. day of December, a great assembling of the lordes was made at the Abbey of Scone. And upon the day followinge, by the means of the Abbot of that place, manie of the sayde lordes assented to the wyll of the sayde Roberte, excepte Sir Jhon *Comin* [*sic*] onlie. The whiche, in defence of his trouthe and othe, before sworne unto Kinge Edwarde, many reasons and excuses made, and finally sayd that he would not false his othe for no man. For this the sayde Sir J. *Comyn* [*sic*] had greate maugre of Sir Robert le Bruze and manie of ye nobles of Scotland. But he held his opinion so fermely that other began to take his part, that in that counsell rose suche contraritie opinions and reasons, that the sayd counsell was dissolued, and a new set at the Greyfreers of Dunfrize [Dumfries] after Candelmas next ensuyinge. At w^h day of assemble, when ye cause of theyr meting was by Robert le Bruze denounced and shewed, and many of the great lordes of the lande had granted to him their aydes and assistence, the forenamed Sir J. Comin and other sat still and sayde no worde." The chronicler goes on to say, in his long-winded fashion, that Robert Bruce expostulating with Comyn, the latter replies that for the weal of the land he would stand to uttermost of his power. "But 'for I se y^t ye entende rather subuercion than the weale thereof, I will therefore ye know I shall nother ayde you w^h counsel nor yet w^h strength." Others "admitted his sad and trew answere."

So the "cronikler" goes on to tell how Bruce followed Comyn into the church of "ye freers" (the Greyfriars), and wounded him to death with his "sweard," "and after slew *Sir Roger his brother*, which would have defended the foresayd Sir John." Here Fabian falls into error, as the other victim was *Sir Robert*, UNCLE to the Red Comyn. (*Vide* note, Sir R. Comyn, p. 73.) Buchanan calls him rightly Robert.

In a beautiful MSS. illuminated Polychronicon, of date 1387, in possession of Lord Middleton, this occurs : "Robt. le bruz toke wrongfulliche ye kingdom of Scotland, and about Est [Easter] he slouz [slew] John le comyn at dumfrees in ye cherche of frer menours, for he wolde noght assent to hym in y^t treasoun. But ye kyng of Engelond came and chased yis Robt., and heng ye sleers [slayers] of yis John."

Stowe says in his 'Annales of England,' 1592, p. 315 : "Robt. Bruse, an Englishman, presuming by the right of his wife to usurpe the kingdome of Scotland, called a Parliament of the nobles of Scotlande WITHIN [*sic*] the church of the Friers Minors in Domfries, where hee slewe John Comin because he would not agree to the treason," &c.

And Camden (under "Nidisdale," pp. 1197, 1198, Gibson's English edition, 1722) hath : "Dumfreys.—The town is . . . remarkable for the murder of John Commin, a person exceeding all others in interest amongst the Scots—whom Robert Brus, lest he should oppose his coming to the crown, ran through in the church, and easily got a pardon from the Pope for a murther committed in a sacred place."

"*I cannot hold that love and amity.*"—P. 131, l. 13.

"The conduct of de Brus at this juncture [after 1296], as throughout the entire period prior to his assumption of the crown, not being understood, has excited the wonder and regret of posterity. Supple, dextrous, and accommodating, now in arms for his country, and then leagued with her oppressors, now swearing fealty to the English king, and again accepting the guardianship of Scotland in the name of Baliol, it seems to require all the energy, perseverance, and consummate prudence and valour of after years to redeem his character from the charge of apparent and culpable weakness.

"De Brus the guardian of Scotland in the name of Baliol! says Lord Hailes, is one of those historical phenomena which are inexplicable. . . . His grandfather, after vainly endeavouring to establish his pretensions to the throne of Scotland, had quietly acquiesced in the elevation of Baliol. His father . . . had submitted uniformly and implicitly to the superior ascendancy of the English monarch. Bruce, therefore, though convinced of his right to the Scottish throne, and determined to assert it, could not in the meantime, with decency or a hope of success, urge the claim in his own person. In doing so he would have had to contend with a rival who was at that time one of the most powerful men in the kingdom, . . . the Red Comyn, who was allied to many of the noblest families in England and Scotland, and who by the decision of Edward possessed in succession a clear

right to the Scottish crown.   Between the families of Bruce and
Comyn there had existed for many years all the jealousy and hatred
which rival and irreconcilable interests could create." . . . After
1300 de Brus "made his peace with Edward by surrendering himself
to the English Warden of the Western Marches.   During the three
successive campaigns which took place previous to the final subjugation of Scotland, and the submission of the Comyns in 1304, de Brus
continued faithful to Edward. . . .   The murder of John Comyn,
younger of Badenoch, 10th February 1305-6, is one of those passages
in the obscure history of that period which has exercised the patience
and tried the candour of historians.   The contradictory and most
improbable details of this event given by our Scottish historians,—
written as they were long after the event took place—can only be
regarded as the embodiment and embellishment of national traditions;
and unfortunately the contemporary writers of England are silent as
to nearly all but the fact itself, and the accounts of later ones are as
difficult to reconcile with probability as those of the Scottish. . . .

   "The whole antecedents would appear to be prepared under the
inventive powers of tradition, to account for the murder of Comyn
as an act contemplated beforehand, whereas it is most evident that
it was as unexpected on the part of Bruce as on that of his victim.
It was a hasty quarrel between two proud-spirited rivals.

   "De Brus had made no preparation to assert his right to the crown.
. . .   Amidst a mass of contradictory improbabilities, one genuine
public contemporary document is worth a hundred conjectures!

   "In his first public instrument after the slaughter of Comyn, King
Edward expressly says that he reposed entire confidence in De Brus
(Fœd. 11, 938).   It is not easy to see how he could do so, if he were
possessed of written evidence to prove that the intentions of De Brus
were hostile. . . .   On meeting Comyn, therefore, de Bruce de-
manded a private interview and an explanation.   In their conversation some hot words took place, and de Bruce struck Comyn with
his dagger.

   "The impetuous zeal of his followers aggravated the crime, and

gave the whole transaction the appearance of premeditated assassi-
nation.

"Such is the conclusion at which we have been compelled to arrive,
after a careful consideration of all the circumstances."—Anderson's
'Scottish Nation,' under head "Bruce."

The whole of this article is worth reading, to any one interested in
the history of Scotland. I have given the more or less popular version of the story in the poem itself.

" The Throne,
To which you deem you rightfully pretend."—P. 131, l. 28 ; and
" Wived the Ladye Marjorie Baliol."—P. 129, l. 14.

"The connection Comyn claimed with the Royal line . . . was
as being descended from Donaldbane, brother of Malcolm Ceanmore,
not as a descendant of David, Earl of Huntingdon," says Mrs Cumming-Bruce, p. 125 (History, Bruces and Cummings). Of this David,
Earl of Huntingdon, Buchanan says he "was brother of King
William of Scotland, and granduncle of Alexander III., and married
in England Matilda or Maude, daughter of the Earl of Chester, by
whom he had three daughters. *Margaret,* the eldest of these, was
married to Allan of Galloway, a powerful chieftain among the Scots ;
the second to Robert Bruce, an Englishman, &c. . . . ; the third
to Henry Hastings, &c. . . . Allan of Galloway, who married
Margaret, had by her three daughters, of whom 1. *Dornagilla* or
Devergel, married John Baliol, father of the competitor. 2. *Isabella*
or Isobel, married Robert Bruce (great-grandfather of King Robert,
seventh Robert in family) ; and 3. *Mary,* married John Cumin." And
Buchanan also says (p. 391 of vol. i., Aikman's)—"Baliol, by his
mother, possessed the whole extensive county of Galloway, and had
allied himself to the Cumins, the most powerful family in Scotland
next the king, by means of John Cumin, who had married Mary
the sister of Dornagilla."

Hollinshed says in his 'Chronicles of Scotland' (quotes Mrs

Cumming-Bruce)—"John Cuming had by Mary his wife, sister of Devorgoile, only one daughter, Dornagilla, married to Archibald Douglas, the Regent, killed at Halidon, 1333." In 'History of the Houses of Douglas and Angus,' by Mr David Hume, printed 1648, is written—"The time and order of the History [of the Douglases] requireth that we speake of Archibald Douglas, Lord of Galloway, and Governor of Scotland ; . . . he married Dornagilla, daughter to Red John Cummin, *whom King Robert slew at Dumfrees* [*sic*].

"This [?] John Cummin was stiled Lord of Galloway, having married a daughter of Allane, Lord of Galloway, called Mary, whose elder sister, Dornagilla, John Baliol had married, and therefore he is also stiled Lord of Galloway. There was also a third of these daughters married (as our writers say) to the Earl of Albemarle : it seemeth the lands of Galloway (Lord Allan dying without heirs male) have been divided among the three sisters ; as for his third, wee finde nothing else of her. This Archibald having married John Cummin's daughter, the inheritrix of the lands of Galloway, . . . hee obtains the lands of Galloway. . . . Some alledge that Red John Cummin did not marry the Lord of Gallowaye's daughter, Marie, but a daughter of John Baliol of Harcourt in Normandy, called Adama, whom he begot on his wife, Dornagilla, who was daughter to Allane, Lord of Galloway ; but how came Red John to stile himself Lord of Galloway, seeing his wife was Adama Balliol, who had brothers, at least one, to wit, John Balliol, that was competitor with Bruce ?"

David Hume and Hollinshed have both muddled. It was Red John Comyn *the first* who married Mary of Galloway. His son, John the Black Comyn, Lord of Badenoch, Regent and competitor, married Marjorie, sister to King John Baliol ; *their* daughter, Dornagilla Douglas, must have been named after her grandmother, Dornagilla of Galloway, wife to the elder Baliol. The Douglases laid a claim to the crown through this marriage in 1370. In 'Scala Chronica' (121) we find, quotes Mrs Cumming-Bruce—

" Johan de Balliol avoit lii sœurs :
La primer fut Margaret Dame de Gilliesland ;
La second fut Dame de Cousey ;
La tierce avoit Johan Comyn à mari
Père celui Robert Bruis tua à Dumfries. "

We know the second Red John Comyn, murdered by Bruce,
married Joan or Johanna de Valence, first cousin to Edward I. of
England. Their daughters were—*Joan*, wife to the Earl of Athole,
and *Elizabeth*, wife to Richard, Lord Talbot, from whom the Talbots
quarter the three garbs or, on field azure, of the Comyns. Wynton
names the four daughters of his (second Red John's) grandfather, the
first Red Comyn, as wives to Ric de Seward, Godfrey de Mowbray,
Alexander of Argyll, and Walter de Moravia. John the Black
Comyn of Badenoch is called by Thomas Crawford in his 'Officers
of State,' Sir John Comyn of Cumbernauld and Lord of Galloway,
in right of his wife Marjorie, after the fall of her brother Baliol.

" Some hold that Comyn deemed the name of King," &c.—P. 132, l. 3.

I have endeavoured in my rendering of this historical event to be
impartial, and show, as was likely the case, that self-interest as well
as patriotism stirred in the breasts of both rivals. But Comyn's
position was a very difficult one : his sworn allegiance to and personal connection with the English king, his patriotism, and his
natural desire to profit by the judgment of his nation, whose
majority acknowledged his right to the crown, must have caused
a turmoil of spirit likely to show itself in any inconsistencies of
behaviour. I have no doubt that had Comyn got rid of Bruce instead of the reverse, those modern writers and novelists to whom
Bruce is a noble hero and Comyn much the opposite, would have
written on another tack. " Nothing succeeds like success ! "

" She touched the secret, and betrayed the same."—P. 132, l. 24.

" Blind Harry," from whom I gathered this idea, is not a very reliable " cronikler," yet the hypothesis that the Lady Joan divulged the paction (if it were such) between her lord and Bruce, is quite plausible.

" Now, at the English Court great Gloucester's Earl."—P. 132, l. 28.

According to Buchanan, it was the Earl of Montgomery who warned Bruce.

" O fell Kirkpatrick!"—P. 133, l. 30.

We used to hear that the Empress Eugenie, wife of Napoleon III. of France, was descended from this Kirkpatrick, the murderer of our forebear, Robert de Comyn.   How well I remember my brother William, the present head and chief of Comyn, declaring as a child, when we and the Elgin boys used to play together, that he had two feudal enemies—your second brother, Robert Bruce (a boy rather younger than himself), and the young Prince Imperial of France !

Then, how strangely sad seemed his account, when in later years he was one of those to receive into camp the corpse of the most illustrious victim of the Zulu war, when he cut locks of hair from the young head to send to his friends in France, and counted the seventeen assegai-wounds, *all* in front, that brought the brave lad his early end.   Perhaps his death saved many lives, and himself much woe.

" Robert de Comyn hasting up the aisle."—P. 134, l. 27.

Sir Robert Comyn was the fourth and last surviving son of the first John Comyn (Red).   From him is descended the Altyre family.   He died defending his nephew, Red John the second, from Kirkpatrick, &c., at Dumfries, 10th February 1305-6.

Robert, second son of the murdered man Sir Robert, entered the
Polish service, where he rose to considerable rank. He married
Beatrix Ross of Rarrichies (ancestors of Balnagowan), and had three
sons—Angus, Gilbert, and Donald. Angus, the eldest, married a
daughter of Mackintosh, Captain of Clan Chattan, and had three
sons—Thomas, his heir ; Lachlan, killed at Inverlochy (and surely
the chieftain mentioned in the tradition that gave birth to this poem),
and Angus, who died in foreign service—both *s. p.* Sir Thomas—who
succeeded his father, and married, first, Helen of Aberbuthnot, and
second, a Macgregor of Macgregor—was a man of great property, and
obtained (says Mrs Cumming-Bruce) from the Bishop of Moray,
circa 1350, a lease of the lands of Rothiemurchus. He was killed
by the Shaws in a skirmish over this property, the head of that sept
having been previously slain in fight for the same cause.—*Vide* also
note, " Had marked his step beside it," p. 91.

" *And ne'er a chance of grace with Edward more.*"—P. 135, l. 11.

"The news of the murder of Comyn reached Edward while residing with his Court at Winchester. . . . He immediately nomi-
nated the Earl of Pembroke Governor of Scotland, ordered a new
levy of troops, and proceeding to London, held a solemn entertainment,
in which . . . the Prince of Wales, with three hundred youths
of the best families in England, received the honour of knighthood,
and with the King made a vow instantly to depart for Scotland,
and take no rest till the death of Comyn was avenged on Bruce."
—Anderson's ' Scottish Nation,' under head " Bruce."

Dr Taylor describes (from Tytler, &c.) the magnificence of the
pageant on this occasion : " The young knights and their retinue
pitching their tents in the Temple Gardens, whose trees were cut
down to give space ; their receiving from the Royal wardrobe the
red and white garments and embroidered belts for the vigil in the
Temple Church ; and next day receiving swords and spurs at the
high altar in Westminster.

"At the banquet which followed were two white swans covered with network and bells of gold, and on these, as well as to his God, King Edward vowed his vengeance for Comyn's murder."

" *Of Buchan's crooked Countess; that with stealth.*"—P. 135, l. 16.

"She [Countess of Buchan, wife to Comyn, Earl of Buchan, and daughter of Earl of Fife] stol fro her lord alle his grete hors, and with swech men as sche trosted cam to that same abbay" (Scone) —Cappgrave's Chronicle, p. 173.

This is the lady whom King Edward imprisoned for four years in a lattice cage, and hung up to public scorn in a turret on Berwick walls. It is the fashion among story-writers to make a heroine of this Countess of Buchan. Considering that she betrayed and robbed her own husband, I think she got her deserts.

> " *The Earldom did erect*
> *Of Moray, and of lands fair appanage.*"—P. 135, l. 23.

The charter of erection of this earldom, Mrs Cumming-Bruce says, is still extant. "From Fochabers on the Spey, to Glengarry and Glenelg, to the boundaries of Argyll and the Earldom of Ross."

" *Of Durham's warlike Prelate.*"—P. 136, l. 16.

Anthony Beck, Bishop of Durham, says Dr Taylor, joined Edward I. on the Scottish side of the Tweed. "Along with the 1000 foot and 500 horse which this warlike Prelate brought with him, he had a retinue of 26 standard-bearers of his own household, and 140 knights from the Palatinate of Durham, in immediate attendance on himself," &c.

His niece and heiress, Alice, was the progenitress of the Willoughbys [d'Eresby].

" Of Darnaway's fair forest, which this Earl."—P. 137, l. 13.

About the year 1370, *circa* 24 years after John Randolph's death, Sir Richard Comyn receives from David II. a grant of the lands of Devally (now Dunphail), with office of Forester of Tarnawa, previously held by Sir Alexander Comyn, and once by Robert Bruce himself.—*Vide* previous note.

" Of William, Scotland's Chancellor, who held," &c.—P. 138, l. 28.

William Comyn was second son to the Earl of Northumberland, killed at Durham, 28th January 1068-69. (*Vide* second part of this note.) "He was bred a clerk by Gaufrid or Geoffry, Bishop of Durham, and was chancellor of King David I. of Scotland, 1142. After the capture of King Stephen at Lincoln, David I., on joining his niece the Empress Queen, left his chancellor, William Comyn, at Durham, with instructions to hold that important bishopric in her name and with the hope that he would be elected to the vacant see. On the death of Bishop Geoffry, his friends, wishing to further the views of Comyn, kept the event a profound secret." The chapter alone refusing consent, they escape from Durham, and choose William de St Barbara, Dean of York, to be bishop, but found the chancellor a determined opponent. "In vain the Pope deprived him of the Archdeaconry of Worcester, and launched an anathema at his head.

"In vain the newly appointed Bishop endeavoured to enter the episcopality by force of arms. Comyn set at naught the anger of the distant Pope, and drove out the monks who attempted to give secret admission to his rival; and, converting their monastery into a fortress, filled it with men-at-arms, and for three years kept the Bishop at bay, &c. . . . The death, however, of a favourite nephew, William Cumyn, induced him to . . . compromise, and on the Bishop again seeking admission in 1144, Cumyn received him in the garb of a penitent at the gates, and consented to his enjoying the undisputed possession of his bishopric, whilst a grant of the castle and honours of Northallerton were bestowed on the chancellor's nephew, Richard Cumyn."—Mrs Cumming-Bruce.

In Camden (Gibson's trans.) we find under head Yorks, *Northalverton* (p. 914): "William Comin, who forcibly possessed himself of the see of Durham, built the castle here, and gave it to his nephew, which is now almost quite gone."

"*And Odo, Hextild's Son.*"—P. 138, l. 31.

Odo, third son of Richard Cumyn, High Justiciar 1178-89. He was witness, with his mother, Hextilda, Countess of Etheletela, of a grant to Kelso, in the Glasgow Chartulary.—Mrs Cumming-Bruce.

"*Archbishop John Of Dublin, envoy to the Holy See.*"—P. 138, l. 31.

John Comyn was consecrated Archbishop of Dublin 1182, when Roderick O'Connor was King of Connaught. He is mentioned as a Commissioner from the English Bishops to the Pope in 1167, in reference to King Henry's dispute with Beckett. In Gibson's ' Camden,' under " Dublin," p. 1367, is mentioned " a stately church dedicated to St Patrick." . . . Afterwards it was much enlarged by King John, and made a church of prebendaries by John Comyn, Archbishop of Dublin, which was confirmed by Pope Celestine III. in the year 1191. The curious thing is, that I find no mention of this Archbishop Comyn in Mrs Cumming-Bruce's work, though he must have been a man of some note. Señor Comyn, the Spanish Ambassador in London (about 1874-75), claimed descent from Gilbert Comyn, who married Juggy Mulreinn, only daughter of Dudley Mulreinn, standard-bearer and one of the generals of Roderick O'Connor, King of Ireland. (This from a letter written by his widow, the Señora Dolores de Comyn, in my possession.) It is not improbable that John Comyn may have been accompanied by relatives when he went to his Irish see,

and that this Gilbert may have been one of them. The pedigree
of Robert, Earl of Northumberland, following, gives Archbishop
John of Dublin, as brother to Richard, husband of Hextilda. At
Nostell Priory, Wakefield, Yorkshire, I noticed, while Lord St
Oswald was showing me his church there, a window in which a
priest was depicted kneeling in his robes, and on further examina-
tion found he was a Cumyn, Prior of Nostell.

Lady St Oswald writes : " I have copied the remarks I came
across, about ten days ago, in a little book on some of the villages
about here. Ackton is three miles from here, and in old times was
part of the large possessions of the Priors of Nostell. This sentence
does not say much, it only confirms your impression that Alured
Cumyn was probably belonging to your old House. . . . It does
not appear to be known where or when he died or was buried :
1535 is the date on the window in our church, on which he is
represented kneeling in his robes.' (She quotes the passage.) " In
the east window of Ackton Church may be discovered a device of
the letters A. and C., connected with a ribbon looped, and beneath
them a wheat sheaf all in gold on an azure ground. This is the
device of Alured Cumyn, one of the latest in the series of Priors of
Nostell—the wheat sheaf indicating that he claimed some connection
with the great House of Comyn in Scotland, who used the three wheat
sheaves for their arms. The area of Prior Cumyn begins in 1524,
and extends to the very eve of the dissolution of his house." I
should like to find more matter anent this Prior Alured Cumyn, who
held office in the Church so long after the old knight of Dunphail
spoke of his kinsmen marked in ecclesiastical history. Referring to
the mention of Robert de Comyn, Earl of Northumberland, the first
British ancestor of the Cumming family, I quote a passage from
Stowe's 'Annales of England' (1592) : " Lib. Dunelm, 1069, page
140.—King William gave to Robert, surnamed Cumin, the Earldome
of Northumberland. Of whose comming thither, when the men of
that country heard, they made themselves ready to forsake their
houses, and to shift for themselves abroad ; but sodainly there fell

such abundance of snow and roughnes of weather, that they could
not in any wise flie; wherefore they took a device [advice?], and
concluded either to flie the realme or else to die altogether for the
liberty of the countrie.   The which thing when the Bishop of
Durham understoode, hee went out to meete the Earle, and exhorted
him to turn back again; but he suffering his souldiours to robbe
and spoyle, would not hear any counsail of health, but he forthwith
entred Durham with seven hundred men, spoyling like enemies
through the house of Durham everywhere what they lifted for the
time, which lasted not long, for on the next morning early the
men of Northumberland being gathered together, burst open the
gates, and running up and downe, slaye all that they found in that
citie, that tooke part with the Earle, whereby all the streetes were
filled with blood and dead bodies.   Some there were that defended
the entrie of the house wherein the Earle was, and had thought to
have saved himselfe; but the other by fire endeavoured to burne
the house with all that were therein, whereby the west tower of the
church was burnt, but through the wind that then blew out of the
east, the church escaped burning; notwithstanding—the house yet
burning as it began—some of them that were within were burnt,
and other some, whilest they burst out to save themselves, were
immediately slaine, so that the Earle himselfe was dispatched, and
all his souldiours saving one that hardly escaped, being wounded.

   " King William taking great displeasure with these doings of the
Northumbers, directed a certain Duke with an army to revenge the
slaughter of Earle Robert; but when they were come to Alverton,
and was in the next morning setting out towardes Durham, there
arose such a darkenesse of weather, through thicknesse of clouds, that
they could unneth see one another, so that they wuld not find their
way; whereupon they returned, and so it came to passe, God
having pitie upon them, that they heard of the departure of their
enemies before they heard of their comming towards them." (How
little these old "croniklers" practised terseness of style!) And
again, p. 146: "And after King William deprived Gospatricke of

DAGOBERT, descended from the Royal line

GENEBALDUS, Chief of the Franks (A

DAGOBERT, Chief of the Fra

CLODŒUS, Chief of the Franks (or I

MARCOMERUS, Chief of the Fr

PHARAMOND, first King of the F

CLODION.

MEROVEUS I.

CHILDERIC I.

CLOVIS I. = St Clotilda, daughter of Dul

CLOTAIRE I. = Jugonda.

CHILPERIC I. = Fredegonde

CLOTAIRE II.

BLITHILDE, BLYTHILDA, or SICHILDA = Asopert, Au

ARNOLD, Marquis of Antwe

ST ARNULPH, Bishop of Metz, Marquis of Antwerp, and first of h

ANSCHISE, or ANSECISE, Mayor of the Palace, Marquis of Antwerp

PEPIN D'HERISTAL or LE GROS, Mayor of the Palace, Marquis of Antwer

CAROLUS SUDISES or MARTEL, Mayor of the Palac

PEPIN, the Short, King of France = Bertha.

768.   THE EMPEROR CHARLEMAGNE (of Gern

CHARLES DUC D'INGELHEIM, 5t

GODFREY.

BALDWIN.[1]

JOHN COUNT DE COMYN, and Baron

EUSTACE,
Baron de Topsburg.

HARLOWEN DE (

COUNT ROBERT DE COMYN
or CUMIN,
Earl of Northumberland.

ODO,
Bishop of Bayeux,
and Earl of Kent.

ROBER
and

JOHN CUMIN.

WILLIAM CUMIN,
Chancellor to David I.
King of Scotland.

WILLIAM DE MO
Earl of Cornw

WILLIAM CUMIN.

ADELM DE 1

WILLIAM CUMIN,
killed 1144.

RICHARD CUMIN, = Hextilda, grand-
died 1189.   daughter of King
                  Donaldbane.

JOHN CUMIN,
Archbishop of
Dublin,
died 1212.

WM. FIT
Gover

Stemma, showing the lineal descent of the noble family of COMYN, CUMIN, or CUMING;

1 Baldwin was son of another Baldwin, son of (

f Burgundy.　　　　　Aldiger, last King of the Boiarians (A.D. 456).

Theodoric, 1st Duke of Bavaria.

Utilo, Marquis of Antwerp = Clotilde, daughter of Theodoric, King of Metz.

Hugopert, Marquis of Antwerp.

rt, or Osbert—Marquis of Antwerp.

amily who was Mayor of the Palace.

eated Duke of Brabant by Dagobert I.

nd Duke of Brabant = Albieda, the Concubine.

nd Duke of Austrasia.

r), King of France.　　814.

on.

onsburg.

EVILLE or DE BURG = Arlotta of Falaise, mother of William the Conqueror.

ount de Mortagne = MATILDA DE MONTGOMERY.　　MARGARET DE BURG = Richard d'Avranches.
rl of Cornwall.

NE,　　　　　　　　　　　　　　　　　HUGH LUPOR,　　MAUD = Ralph de Bohun.
　　　　　　　　　　　　　　　　　　Earl of Chester.

).　　　　　　　　JOHN DE BURG.

ELM DE BURG, = Isabel, natural　　HUBERT DE BURG, = Isabella of Gloucester.
of Ireland.　　daughter of　　　　Earl of Kent.　　= Margaret.
　　　　　　King Richard I.

the Merovingian and Carlovingian Kings of France, and from the Royal House of the Boii.

his Earldome, laying unto his charge, that hee had consulted with them that slewe the Earle Roberte Comen [*sic*] of Durham," &c. A genealogical tree of this same Earl Robert de Comyn is here appended, as sent to me (and similar to another sent from a different quarter, to Mrs Cumming-Bruce, after her work was published). She therein gives a part of it, with two more generations between Duc d'Ingelheim and Baldwin, as due. I merely give this for what it is worth, disclaiming any responsibility for its errors.

PLOTTING.

One man's ambition works the world dismay :
For lighter lunes are maniacs hid away.

A STATELY chamber was the Castle Hall
Of Forres, though in fashion of the time
Its fair proportions knew nor stone nor clay.
Built of great oaks from wooded Darnaway,
Pine-planked and plastered o'er in goodly guise,
It showed, for prince or peer, a seemly dwelling.

Earl Moray, by the meal-displenished board,
Sate in this hall, late lingering, racked of mind.
His household noted that the wonted calm
Of his impassive visage showed a change—
A shade of thought, perhaps not wholly ire,
Stirred by that morn's encounter ; but a tinge,
Somewhat of exultation blent therewith,
At such good cause for discord proffered there.

Up in the rampant, chainless North, that bore
All-unsubdued the shocks of these rude times,
Would Randolph reign alone, unchallenged lord ;
And while the falling race (but forceful yet)
Of Comyn there abode, he might not hope

To roar the forest, as the manèd king
Of burning Africk sends defiance forth,
That none dare question, counter, or constrain.

"Dispute? I'faith!" he thought—and thought aloud—
"Young whelp, thou yappest over-lustily!
Saint Andrew! will these Comyns alway rise
Like wood in water?—must the axe be left
Stuck in the cloven beam to force it sink?
Learn't they no lessons from the Bruce's hands,
Were they not stripped of holdings, spoiled, pursued,
Till a man scarce had sense of self and reason?
And still they hold their crownless heads as high,
Clutching the mantle of their former pride,
As if they yet ruled Scotland, and compelled
Care-bred respect from England!
    Ah! Morayland! art small, so small, too small
For mine ambition's sharing! See, proud race,
I'll serve me heir herein to Bruce, mine eme!
I'll be that iron axe that sinks the wood:
I'll drive thy sons to death or exile, seize
Thy maids for serfs, and tramp thine arrogant head
In mire, as I would foul those yellow locks
That tossed defiance late in Darnaway!
    Where then thy pride? Where then thy proverbed guile?
I'd·leave thee scarce a cavern for a home;
And for a tomb, only the barren moor,
That bears thy grey badge-willow!"
                                        He uprose,
To stride with bitter laughter through the hall!

"About mine ears there blows, out o'er the land,
A blast of broil and bicker from the West:

I sent a fellow spying out the cause.
He tells, Lochaber's landless chieftain there
Seeks to regain his forfeit holding, to whom
Comyn of Raites with pick of following
Conjoins, and leaves his own with scanty guard.
    Kin here! Clan there! You fillip at a wasp,
And bring the buzzing byke about your head!
    Dunphail disfriended, *all* shall dub me foe!

" I feign attack on Raites, and spur that foe
I' the West, through hope of mine alliance, to oppose
Raites and Lochaber; Raites, so rumour lauds,
Bound nobly by his pledgèd aid, will trust
To others, as Dunphail, his home's defending;
When by a counter movement I can turn
And siege Dunphail, disgarrisoned and weak.
    Thus, thus, ye subtle Comyns, strategy
Shall baulk your warring guile!"
                                This in raised tones
He said, and struck the board with clenchèd hand;
And, as the thud made horn and platter ring,
A heavy targe, loose-hung upon the wall,
Crashed down, and reeling, rolled to Moray's feet!
    Aside he dashed it with impatient stroke:
" I hail the omen! 'twas a Highland targe."
He spake, and passed; and summoned forth his Knights,
Asked not advice, but laid before their heed
His plans mature, that showed their duty's deed.

NOTES TO PLOTTING.

" A stately chamber was the Castle Hall
Of Forres."—P. 162, l. 1.

THE buildings for family use in those early days, within the sterner stone structure of the castles, whether royal or noble, were much built of wood.

In the Castle of Inverness, about the year 1263, there was built for Alexander III. a wardrobe-room with a double wooden roof; and a new hall, which, as it cost only 48s., must also have been of wood, was erected in the Castle of Invery. Tytler describes a hall of this description as framed in strong oak, which was covered with a planking of fir, overlaid with plaster, painted and gilt; and large oak pillars supporting the building were embedded at base in mason-work. The walls, if not decorated, were hung with tapestry. Such a hall must have been that in which Earl Moray and his knights ate and sate in Forres Castle.

" And while the falling race (but forceful yet)
Of Comyn."—P. 162, l. 18.

Among the many letters received by Mrs Cumming-Bruce, after the publication of her large work on the Bruces and Comyns, is a letter which may amuse those of the family who had not been shown it by the authoress herself, which proves that even in these late times the race is believed to be still "force-full," and that "there is life in the old dog yet"!

"STRANRAER, *October 6th*, '70.

"MADAM,—I have lately read your interesting and valuable 'Family Records of the Bruces and the Cumyns.' Such a work can only be fully appreciated by those who may have paid a little attention to the subject of ethnology and physiology, and the hereditary transmission of strong physical and mental characteristics from remarkable progenitors. The physiognomy, the physiology, and the cerebral organisation of some of the more marked members of the Cumming race [*Cumming race !*—is this a pun or a prophecy ? —E. M. M.] that I have seen and known in this locality are singularly corroborative of your records respecting it. You mention the case of Robert Cumming, . . . whose stature was six feet six inches. There died not many years ago a female collateral, whom I knew well, whose height was six feet four inches. She was well-formed, had handsome features, and was a very intelligent woman. A gentleman died here lately about eighty-four years of age . . . rich. . . . He was without doubt the best practical business-man in the county, and did what probably no other man in Scotland could have done at the age of eighty, and was a remarkable instance of the strength and beauty of his race. His father died in 1858, aged ninety-six years.

"In 1834 I attended the funeral of a female, who died at 102 years of age, and who retained all her faculties up to the last. *She* was tall ; I have never forgotten her face, above 100 years old, so fresh, and having that peculiar radiation, that glow of prescient intuition [*sic !*], that is one of the peculiar transmitted hereditary characteristics of the Cumming race ! *Her* mother lived to 103 years of age. There is a marked peculiarity in some of the Cummings that I have seen, that is only found in extreme development in the organisation of those who have been able to 'leave their footprints on the sands of time,' and must have been possessed by, and

transmitted down from, the first distinguished progenitors, to the
existing race, by that unerring law of hereditary descent, of strongly
marked physical and mental characteristics. Such recurrent instances of longevity [we have given up the habit of longevity, I
think !—perhaps the gods have begun to love us !—E. M. M.], great
stature, physical strength and beauty, show beyond all doubt that
they must have been transmitted down from a very remarkable type
of progenitor. I must in conclusion beg to thank you for the interesting information and corroborative satisfaction I have derived
from the perusal of your valuable publication.—I am, &c.,

"CUMMING T——N."

"*Clutching the mantle of their former pride.*"—P. 163, l. 13.

"The Cumins," says Mr Riddel, "were certainly the most illustrious of our Scottish families, and their blood at this day circulates
through all that is noble in the sister kingdom, including even the
numerous and Royal descendants of King Henry IV."—(Reply
to the misstatements of Dr Hamilton of Bardowie, in his late
'Memoirs of the House of Hamilton Corrected,' p. 7 : Edinburgh,
1828.)

The Earl of Dunbar and March writes to King Henry IV. : "18th
daie of Feverer, anno 1400, . . . and, excellent Prince, syn that I
claym to be of kyn tyl yhow, and it peraventour nocht knawen on
yhour pairt, I schaw it to your Lordship be this my lettre, that gif
Dame Alice the Bewmont was yhour graunde dame, Dame Marjory Comyne, hyrr full sistre, was my graunde dame on the t'other
side ; sa that I am bot of the feirde degre of kyn tyll yhow, the
qwhilk in alde tyme was callit neir," &c.

These ladies were daughters and co-heiresses of Alexander Comyn,
fourth Earl of Buchan.

In 'Registrum Moraviensi' appears also, . . . "I, Henry of Lan-
castre, chalangis this realme and the crowne, . . . as I, that am
descendit be the richt line of the blude Cummyn fra the gude King

Henry the Thyrd, and throch that richt that Goddys grace has send me, with help of my frendys, to recover it, the quhilk realme was in poynt to be tint [lost] and undone be fault of guvernance, and for undoing of the gude lawys." (See also the Black Book of Scone.)

Fordun also tells us that *Henry IV. of England*, replying to a Monkish petition, says : "Ego inquit sum semi Scotus, *de sanguine Cominiensium generatus*," or, "Sanguine Cominiensi ex parte matris generatus." (These are quoted by Mrs Cumming-Bruce.)

" The original agitators of the country, comprising almost all the principal families of the Cumins,—Walter, Earl of Menteith ; Alexander, Earl of Buchan ; John, Earl of Athole ; and William, Earl of Mar ; together with several gentlemen of rank of the same faction,— having refused to obey the summons . . ." And again—"The whole power was nearly engrossed by the Cumin faction, who treated the public revenue as their private patrimony ; they oppressed the people, and rather commanded than obeyed the King."—Buchanan (Aikman), p. 378.

> " *Where then thy pride ?   Where then thy proverbed guile ?* "
> —P. 163, l. 24.

Sir Walter Scott in 'Waverley' quotes the old Gaelic proverb, " While there's a leaf in the forest, there's guile in a Comyn." J. F. Campbell of Islay used to give it to me in Gaelic as "*tree*," not "*leaf* ": "Fad 's a bhi 's *craoibh* 's a choill bi 'ch foill 's a Chuimeinach," arguing that the trees are leafless in winter. Yet the feudal enemy whose confusion and undoing he ascribed to the subtle strategy of his Comyn foe, rather than to lack of wits or daring on his own part, was doubtless best acquainted with the evergreen needles of the Scottish fir.

> " *He tells, Lochaber's landless chieftain there.*"—P. 164, l. 2.

This must have been Lachlan (brother to Sir Thomas Comyn, and great-great-grandson of John, the first Red Comyn), who is given as having been killed in a skirmish at Inverlochy. (*Vide* note, "Had marked his step," &c., p. 91.)

Lochaber came into possession of the Comyns (says Dr Taylor in a letter to myself) early in the thirteenth century. John Comyn is mentioned as a party to an insurrection against Government of Edward I. in 1297.

It is stated in Stevenson's 'Hist. Doct.,' vol. ii. p. 190, that he had two large galleys anchored near his castle (" quod juxta castrum Johannes Cumin in Lochaber, duæ magnæ galæ fuerunt"), between 1286 and 1306.

I do not feel sure whether this John Cumin was Red No. 2, Bruce's victim, or his father John, the "Black" lord of Badenoch.

In Gregory's ' History of the Western Highlands and Isles,' at p. 20, it is mentioned—" The Lordship of Lochaber, forfeited by one of the powerful family of Comyn, seems to have been divided between Angus Oich and Roderick,—the former, junior of Isla ; latter, Ruari Mac Alan, the bastard brother and leader of the vassals of Christina, daughter and heiress of Alan Mac Ruari of the North Isles."—It is pretty certain that the forfeiture thus made by Robert I. (Bruce) was cancelled when David Cumyn, Earl of Athole, was fighting in the interests of Edward Baliol, and that Sir Robert Comyn, son of Sir Robert, killed with his nephew, Red John Comyn, at Dumfries in 1306, was reinstated in the lands of Lochaber as heir to his mother, the daughter of *William* Comyn of that Ilk. (Who this William Comyn was exactly, I do not find.) Sir Robert was one of his kinsman of Athole's principal supporters, and doubtless welcomed the latter when he fled to Lochaber, pursued by Earl Randolph (of Moray). He is said to have been killed at Kildrummie with Athole.

I do not think Mrs Cumming-Bruce mentions this. Hollinshed says, in his version of ' Bellenden's History of Scotland' : "At this bickering were slain two of the Comyns, Robert and William," &c.

It is not stated who held Lochaber after the death of Sir Robert Comyn (at Kildrummie in 1335). It likely reverted to Angus

Oich, the former Brucean proprietor, and that Lachlan Comyn was fighting with him to regain possession when he was killed.

In 1344 Lochaber was given to John, Lord of the Isles, in whose family it remained till 1372, when it was granted by Robert II. to John Dunbar, Earl of Moray, and his wife, the Princess Marjory. Mrs Cumming-Bruce quotes from 'Origines Parles. Scotiæ': "Of Inverlochy all that we know is that it was the chief castle of the *Cumyns of Lochaber*, and that Sir Robert Comyn, first of the Altyre line, married Egidia, one of the three co-heiresses of *William Cumyn of Lochaber*. . . . At the mouth of the river Lochy in Lochaber stand ruins of Inverlochy Castle, consisting of four round towers thirty feet high, &c. . . . The largest of these towers, the western, is known as the Comyn's tower, and has walls ten feet thick," &c. Most of the above is given in my note on "Inverlochy."

"Comyn of Raites with pick of following."—P. 164, l. 4.

Who this Comyn of Rait, Raites, or Retz was, is not easily defined. Dr Taylor gives Raite, near Nairn, to the Comyns, *tempus* Edward I., and Mrs Cumming-Bruce (Bruces and Cumyns) has followed him, and also Sir Thomas Dick Lauder, in what Dr Taylor was afterwards convinced is error. The ancient castle of Rait, on whose site the modern house of Belleville, near Kingussie, now stands, was a Comyn stronghold (as also the Castle of Ruthven, a little farther south, at Kingussie itself). It was the scene of a tragic episode in the traditions of Cumming and Macintosh feuds (*vide* "Run-rig" in "Ballads; by the Lady Middleton"), and was a place of greater importance than Raite, near Nairn. It seems, therefore, certain that the Raites in Badenoch was the one of this tradition. But who the hero (for the tradition so treats him) really was, or what his connection with the head branch of the family, I have as yet failed to trace. The feuds of the Highland clans and many great Scottish families make research on such points as this harassing and often futile. If private papers existed, they were carried off by feudal foes or destroyed by fire ; nor did the custom of making abbeys and cathedrals keeping-places for deeds and documents ensure their safety, as the burning of Elgin Cathedral and its treasures by the Wolfe of Badenoch in 1390 proves. Such ancient families as those of Cameron of Lochiel, Fraser of Lovat, &c., possess few or no old papers of value, from these and like causes.

Mrs Cumming-Bruce conjectures that Alexander, son of Sir Thomas Cumyn and his second wife, daughter of Macgregor of that Ilk, may have been the fiery Laird of Raites, "who is said to have been a man of slender abilities, but being the wealthiest and most powerful of his name in the district, was looked up to by the Comyns of Moray as their leader." Alexander would have been far too young for this hypothesis ; he was son of a second marriage, and yet by the tradition should have been old enough to have nearly grown-up children. (Sir Thomas died about 1365.) It was more likely his (Alexander's) great-uncle *Gilbert*, second son of Robert, son of Sir Robert, murdered at Dumfries by his wife, Egidia Comyn of Lochaber. Gilbert married a daughter of Macdonald of Clanronald (Lord of the Isles), and must have been a man of consequence : he "made a considerable figure in the family feuds of those days," says Mrs Cumming-Bruce. She says he was succeeded by his nephew David, which looks as if he had no son, as mentioned in the tradition of the Raites hero, whose "claymore was ground by his son" ; but the son may have died, perhaps, fighting by his father's side. Or there is Donald, younger brother of this Angus, who also likely shared in their grandmother Egidia's lands of Lochaber, which, it is said, included Urquhart Castle in Inverness-shire, Lochindorbh in Moray, and Lochaneilan in Rothiemurchus. If the chieftain of Raites was either of these two, he would be *uncle* to Lachlan, slain at Inverlochy in the same contest between the Cumyns and Randolph.

Nature in Autumn.

THE bracken is brown on the steep,
The leaf is forsaking the tree,
The hills are asleep, and asleep
  Is the storm-weary Sea.
      If loving is losing; and living, long dying,—
      Breathe deep the bright moments, that flying
                  Are crying:
      " O Life, is thy promise all lying ? "

Hoarse brags the dark deer from the hill;
Adrift lies the boat on the wave;
All Nature in sweetness wears still
  T'wards the hush of her grave.
      If loving be losing, if Life is refusing
      The fruits of its promise on fields of our choosing,
                  Sad musing
      We mourn: " Love and Life is all losing ! "

The pulse of her passion beats dull;
The doom of her dying draws near;
And the winds cease their wailing, and lull
  To the hush by a bier.

If Love be but loss, and our Life but slow dying,
Taste, taste not of joys ever lying,
                As flying
They pass, with their laughter like sighing !

What recks she of passion or power ?
How touches her tiredness or pain,
In us, the dim dreams of an hour,
   Fainting sobs of a strain ?
      When loving is losing, and Life a dull drifting
      To Death through decay, on the sands ever shifting
                What lifting
      Shall ken the dark cloud-banks, unrifting ?

Ah ! why, t'wards her fashion or mood
Should our spirits for sympathy pine ?
She, e'en from her birth, death-endued ;
   We, in measure, Divine !
      True Love never loseth ; true Life bridgeth dying
      To the Shores of the ceasing of sighing,
                And lying—
      To the stilling of fears and of crying.

LOCH ROMACH.

Fair is pure Love, and foul its mock, I wis :
Worship or insult proves alike—a kiss !

As o'er thy North, O Caledon the Fair !
October soareth now, her lustrous hair
Wreathed berry-bright, and scarlet poppy, born
Thus late, to enhance the glow of orient corn ;
With Tyrian mantle broidered all of gold,
Saffron, gules, emerald, woven through each fold
In outspread hands, as waiting Heaven's sign,
To cast upon the Land that gift divine :
So poised the Dame, five centuries ago,
O'er wood and plain, and hills fresh capped with Snow !
    Marvelled the high peaks o' the blue dream-built range,
How ear' was spread for them that silvery veil ;
For ambient Nature breathed no frosty change,
Nor winter winds had 'gun to carp and wail.
    But, when the victims famèd are, and fair,
How due a bier of beauty to prepare :
When vast the richness of the sacrifice,
The 'rounding scene should, gorgeous, charm the eyes.
    So spake October : " There the sign I read,
And o'er sweet Moray this my gift I spread ;

For all-imperfect would its decking be,
Had lacked the aid, O Snow, I gain by thee!"
　She cast the Mantle, and the glowing Earth
Rose, all-triumphant at her fresh-won worth,
Unrecking that the gift did herald day,
Of sure, of swift, though glorious decay:
　As moved the Hindoo widow to her doom,
In jewelled pomp, and mockery of Death,
By pageant passage to an ashen tomb,
While awed beholders checked the labouring breath.

　In such October-time of fair decay,
Oh, meet me 'mong the birkens, lover mine!
What bower for love more witchingly arrayed?
And while thy voice sighs music in mine ear,
Let me look up those dainty, argent stems,
Into the golden deluges o'erhead,
Through whose rich filigree appears the dream
Of Heaven's sapphire, deepening into dusk!
　There will we wander on a halcyon eve,
When the soft gloaming makes mysterious
The vivid glowing colours of the day,
And gaze on distance melting down to gloom,
From silver-columned Halls, enarched with gold!
　Fair lies the delicate landscape there beneath,
Like a sweet maid in loveliness reposing;
Wendeth yon gleaming river through the land,
Peaceful, as distance veils each throb and throe;
And dream-like woodlands, ebbing, billowed deep
To where pale seas reflect the latest sheen
Of sun-kissed vapours, 'gainst whose fading sweet
The mountain-ranges stand out, solemn, clear.

.　　　.　　　.　　　.　　　.　　　.

In suchlike scenes the lovers of this lay
Met (and in harsher scenes, to them as fair);
For never since that fateful Hart had died
In Darnaway, Earl Moray and Dunphail
Had feigned the hollow amity of the past,
And Randolph blazoned loudly through the land:
"Should a presumptuous Comyn dare a pace
On his domain, the penalty were Death."

   .   .   .   .

So met Ydonea and Alastair
In stolen maskèd modes that Love might teach;
And, as beneath the shelter of a rock,
In dank unwholesome corners, lives and thrives
Some dainty bloom, so in their hearts, 'neath shade
Of trouble, and 'mid threatening breath of feuds,
Blossomed Love's sacred bud, that aye shall bear
Adversity's drear test, if worth be truly there.

   .   .   .   .

The henchman Shaw, the handmaid Lupola,
Would meet, Love's messengers; and some pretext
Was made why should Ydonea here or there
Şeek exercise or sport, at such good times
As led the Earl afar, or Denys knew
Deep in his studies.

   .   .   .   .

                Up amid the hills,
Where fair Loch Romach, like Ferrara blade,
Lay, velvet-bedded in the deep green pines,
Ydonea and her maids, one dulcet day,
Weary with hunting, halted, after noon;
And while Sieur Denys rode in further chase,
The bright girl-bevy waited by the Loch
His promised return ere even: th' adventurous few

Bathed in those quiet waters, while the rest
Chorused their laughter, pelting them with cones
Or tiny pebbles of the gravelly brink,—
What time their Ladye passed with Lupola,
And faithful-following Corbred, up the braes,
Where in a brush-bound hollow, screened from view,
Stayed Alastair, expectant!

                He forth sprang
Right joyously, to greet his heart's delight:
The waiting-woman moved from sight and sound,
And left the lovers twain to blended joy.

   Passed their first meeting's tenderness, (and oh!
How long, eventless, dim, had shown the days
Of th' unblest se'nnight since they met), was told
A tale by him unto his list'ning love
Of warlike rumours from the West, where sought
Lochaber to regain his ancient rights
O'er Inverlochy, reft by Brucean powers
From Comyn hold.

           She said: "Thou goest not yonder?"
He answered: "Nay, till Randolph should declare
Upon that question late uprisen—his sword
In scabbard or unsheathed—it were not wise
Dunphail should void or thin her garrison!"

.   .   .   .

   As showed yon Lochan's face, that bore the cloud,
Or the sun's gladding, each by each in turn,
So, sad and hopeful in alternate moods,
These gracious lovers sped the snatchèd hours.

   She spake of Hope, nor deemed for so slight cause
Randolph could long be rancorous, and prayed
Her love would smooth his sire to mend the breach.

   He spake of Honour, and declared the Knight

M

Would court a siege e'er yet would yield his right;
And gloomily forespake of future days
Blank of his bride—days like the sterile course
Of a once river on an arid plain.

    Then, as she soothed, and strove his mood to curb
He, like a fretted steed too long restrained,
Burst forth in passionate guise, erst capturing
The gentle hands that softly gestured peace.

.   .   .   .

    " I am no scholar, Love, that I should seek
To borrow parlance from some buried sage;
Or like gay troubadours of these our times,
With carven sentences and counted sighings,
With modelled looks, and action well commanded,
Recite my pictured passion, courteouslie.
    Day of my Soul, when far I fare from thee
The night winds of my being hold their sway,
And drive me wandering 'mong the gloomy pines
That threatful stand, with nought of sympathy,
Above my frenzy. Then this heart distraught
Throws out wild arms to grasp a phantom Thee:
And oh! the maddening fire in heart and brain,
The wild desire, the absence, and the void!
'Come then, O Love! to me, to me,' I cry;
Burdened the air is, and the woods are dumb,
But sound tumultuous rends my bursting brain:
One touch, one glimpse of Thee, would lull the storm.
I cannot bear it! 'Come, Ydonea! come!'"

.   .   .   .   .   .

The small palm fluttered, but his grasp forbade.

.   .   .   .   .   .

" Haply expectant, then, I raise my head
And look around, and hearken for thy feet,—
As had my plaint by magic brought thee nigh;

As if along the orange mosses swept
Thy raiment's cramoisie; or glinting rays
Athwart the boughs lit thy dusk locks delight!
   But oh! thou comest not, thou art not there;
The stern woods scorn my bitter agony
When I resume myself; and sibilant mock
The breezes, and the strung sense slacks; while dull
Despair is tenant of this barren heart:
Then on the earth, exhausted, prone I fall,
Whose chilly breast repels me back to life!

.   .   .   .   .   .

What! wouldst thou leave me? have I frayed my sweet?
Forgive the intemperate speech, and let me dream
While thus I hold thee pressed against my heart,
Those hours, the bantlings of disordered sleep!"

.   .   .   .

But she from out his strong detaining clasp
Slipping her hands, unwound his prisoning arm,
And rose, and stept a pace beyond their seat,
And gaily spake; but with a tremor soft,
That half belied the hardiesse of her mien:
   "Fair sir, my lover! wildest Alastair
Of all your most untamed and turbulent race,
You do forget this weakling frame of mine
Is no proud war-shaft, clutched from wrestling foe,
But a light willow wand crushed readily,
And these rough transports please me not at all:
—My fingers' smart resents that powerful grasp.
I'll tell thee now, in most romantic guise,
How truly doth my presence touch thy soul."

.   .   .   .

Then in a bantering tone that quavered yet:

.   .   .   .

"As to the parchèd wanderer's craving sight

Glows the rich garnet of the beading cup,
Or shows to tirèd steed the homely stall ;
As to the winter-watching sentry's frame
Appeals the guard-room fire in glow and gleam——"

   .   .   .   .

  Deep mortified, her love no more would hear.
  " Fie ! stay !" cried Alastair, and on her gloomed ;
"It hath been said, that jests ill-timed do jar
As joyous music on a mournful mind !
I laid not bare, thus to provoke thy mirth,
My soul's disorder !   Doth thy colder mood
Thus bear to quip and mock in my despite,
So may it ; but at least I can abjure
The pain of heark'ning !"
                 Now he moved, and made
As if, half sullen, he would wend away :
She, gently chiding, sought again his side.
"Why chill me, Maiden, with thy kindly cold ?
I would the fervour of my speech could fire
Thy gentle bosom with responsive glow !
  I wot thou lov'st me true, else wherefore here ?
But, as the pale dim Lily to the sight
Of one who craves for colour, or the fall
Of gelid flakes on Nature's shuddering life,
Thou seemest mostly."
             Smiled Ydonea then,
Yet touched his hand with supplicating gest :
  "Impetuous Sweetheart, I am but a Maid.
We may not speak our love in guardless modes,
Nor phrase all-uncontrolled our heart's outflowing :
A Maiden may enjoy, or must endure,
Love's bliss or pain to secret self alone,
Chiefly, methinks ; that her sweet reticence

May right your balance, breed in you respect,
And be her own true safeguard and your succour.

   .   .   .   .

Call me not cold: the warmth is surer there,
That even Thou, who first and lone didst light
Love's altar-fire to glow within my breast,
Shouldst find it chary of flaming." Then her eyes
Uplift, had changed their planet, and the Sun
Of Love flashed forth where Luna late had ruled;
  And he, half-startled, heard :

                             "Deep is my love,
Believe, O Alastair! if charely spoken :
Mark! the cool Lily hath a golden soul;
And though the snows be purely blank and chill,
Yet 'neath their mask the heart o' the world's afire !"

   .   .   .   .

"O Lily love, unveil thy sunbright soul !
O World of worth, bare thy warm heart to me,
Else, shivering like a fevered wight, I burn,
Nor bless my Leech for cheerless comforting !"

   .   .   .   .

  "And that hath reached its limit for the nonce,"
She said: "I go! my cousin returns; my maids
Will weary. Corbred, hence !"

                   He breathed: "One word,
Where next to meet?" She, smiling, waved farewell.

   .   .   .   .

A glint of crimson through the trees, and he
Was left alone, and turned him home, and thought :
"My Love, my dearest Ladye, did I scare
My gentle cushat with a falcon swoop?

Let me in iron fetters set my heart,
And rule my speech to order—hope and wait!"
.   .   .   .   .   .
.   .   .   .   .   .

While thus the lovers sweet communion held,
The waiting-woman wandered up the brae,
Shunning, in customed fashion, all the cheer
That reached her, ringing from the Loch below.
Ere long, sharp-crackling on the brittle twigs
And barren sheddings of the spinous fir,
A rearward footfall made her look around
And face the henchman Shaw, who in a trice
Beside her came.   Much love or kind inclining
Felt she towards no man, haply least for him;
And some instinctive prompting ever made
Her errands with him brief ones.

       'Twas a man,
You'd call him red or yellow, and insult
Each colour; low of brow, and cold of eye
That nothing ever softened or surprised
Into expression!   .   .   .
  An ever-ready rascal 'twas, with tongue
Smooth as a kestrel's beak, and full as keen
To wound you, when it liked him.   Saxon speech
Was meagre with him, though enough for all
Of converse deigned by Lupola.   Most suave
And douce was he to her—too suave, too soft;
A something of the gentleness that dwells
In cats or tigers, purring till they show
Their sudden claws; and aye conceding her
The deference that oft is surest springe
To catch unwary woman hearts on wing.

She never greeted him, but moved along.

. . . .

　"Sweet mistress" (and a something in his tone
Bade her look towards him, liking him the less):
"Good company commendeth not contempt!
Prithee, step slower, while I speak with thee.
Hark! how the wood-doves coo on yonder pine!
So coo our lover-lords beneath the hill;
Rough is my speech, and words with me be few,
But fewest words know fittest how to woo."
　Beyond its wonted flow, his speech was glib,
But to her ear in utterance thicker grew.

. . . .

Then proud the woman: "Of your courtesy
I would crave solitude. Man, let me be!"
　Quoth Allan: "Coy and modest, sweeter she!
Fair Madam, hold my hand; for pretty feet
Strike no considering out these laidly stones.
Wilt not? Then art thou cross-grained. Hearken now!
I'll tell thee thou art fairer than thy Ladye;
I love her not, she looketh askance at me—
Thy modest Ladye, loving stealthy-wise,
Tendering right cheek to who would kiss the left."

　Then Lupola flashed forth: "Thou scoffing fool!
Would I were man, to force thee swallow lie,
And tongue that spake it! Hence with thy lie, and thee!"
　He only laughed, and staggered in his gait.
"Step slower, prithee, lest I pluck thy robe!
Thou'rt fairer, said I, than thy Ladye's self;
The ripple of a thousand streams is shown
On hair, whose every wave reflects the sun!

Thy form than hers is nobler—as a birk
Shows by burn willow; ruddier is thy mouth,
Ruddy and ripe,—I fain would taste its sweetness."

.   .   .   .

" Leave me, thou shameless Gael !" she panted, scared
At such unwonted ways.
                              " Nay, halt and hear.
I'll tell thee that thine eyes are none so blind ;
I mark their glitter now, and e'en will view
Their bandaged beauties."
                              Insolent, essayed
Allan to strip the hood from off her head !
Aside she sprang, and struck his arm away,
And mastered by her terror, as a flame
Speeds on parched moor wrathful before the blast,
She down the brae, disordered, voiceless, sped ;
Nor could her meeting Ladye gather sense
From her first speech ; but what she after learnt
Acquainted Alastair, with cautioning words,
Part culled from Lupola in latter times,
And part from self-foreboding consciousness.

    The Comyn dealt to Shaw no measured wrath,
Who marvelled such light error as proffered kiss
To maid unwilling should be thus condemned.

    His mind was base ; and this deserved reproof,
Rankling, did fester there ; and Lupola
With her fair mistress double-barbed the shaft
That wrought the sore.
                              This Allan was a sprout
Of an unfriendly sept, and Alastair

Had friended him because he lacked a friend,
And liked the fellow for no worthier cause.
  Such sense of debt towards a higher spirit
To Allan's warped and cankered soul was gall;
Who bided but his day to throw the score
Of obligations in his master's face:
  For why? The man was base; no subtler cause!

NOTES TO LOCH ROMACH.

" Loch Romach."—P. 174.

"ROMACH" is the Gaelic word for "shaggy" or "hairy," and is the name of a romantic loch some miles above Altyre, and about nine from Forres.

I describe it as it now shows, though the young pine-wood on its craggy sides was planted by my grandfather, the late Sir William G. G. Cumming; and some say he dammed the burn running through the ravine into the lake that now lies there. However this may be, there is no doubt that once a chain of lakelets lay through those gullies; and probably at the time of my traditions their sides were a mass of wood as to-day, only more varied in character—oak, birch, and alder mingling with the sterner pine. Hence, no doubt, the name of the spot, "hairy" or "shaggy" with rough timber.

" With Tyrian mantle broidered all of gold," &c.—P. 174, l. 5.

The wonderful beauty of these October days in Morayshire is indescribable. The melting of autumn into winter, the blending, as it were, of the glories of both, each kind to the other,—when the remnants of often late harvest, rich on the golden earth, seem waiting to greet the first silver snow-crowns wherewith winter makes kings of the mountains, north and west; when the sweeping woodlands glow in tints vying with those of an American "fall"; when the summer flowers still linger in an air almost balmy, that makes one look in vague surprise over the azure Firth to the snowy peaks beyond, as on a picture in which one has no living part.

The Tyrian broidered mantle of autumn is perhaps the fairest

vesting our fair land of Moray knows. And yet, who that saw it
will forget, in that year of 1888, the admiring surprise of the abnor-
mal snowfall in June ! Before the vanishing of its transient splen-
dours, we stood on the heights above the river Findhorn, that rolled
full, but not drumlie, its sardonyx-hued waters far below ; looking
on the tardy developing foliage that showed in tints, less intense
but more tender, almost the variety of autumn. There glowed
ruddy the rich young leafage of oaks, the copper youth of the poplar ;
there shimmered that indescribable green of the birch in spring, by
the nearly as vivid but varied tone of the larches ; in strong contrast gloomed the glaucous colouring of the solemn Scotch fir, and
more mellowed verdure of spruce, with here and there a gean or
bird-cherry in full white blossom ;—all this glory of foliage massing
the banks above and below, to the plains, and shores of the Moray
Firth, on whose bord that strange line of piled and undulating
sand-heaps, marking the grave of buried Culbin estate ; gleamed
like the brightest gold. Beyond smiled the soft blue Firth, then—
wonderful to see !—the glittering silver snow on the whole range of
mountains from Inverness-shire to Caithness, heaped their bases of
transparent seeming sapphire. This, under a sky such as one sees
in the Riviera, in an air whose geniality mocked the unseasonable
visitor and made the snow vanish all too soon, and in an atmos-
phere we Northerners know—when a limner would need to liquefy
all the strange and out-of-way treasures of a jewel-store, and fuse
them with opals, golden and other, ere his brush could render the
colouring on his canvas ! What is the magic of the Moray air ?
Oh, my land ! my home-land ! in these days of change and fritter-
ing varieties, when it is reckoned almost a shame to feel deeply,
and when expression of feeling is mocked at as " gush " ; when reverence is sneered at, when patriotism is drooping, and all that can be
done to slacken the clasp of heart and hand over the haunts and
holdings of one's forebears and one's people is being achieved ;—shrine
thyself in the few souls that cling to thee still for thine own dear
sake, in worshipful reverence—as does mine.

DENYS.

Of one who sought to win a prize at length ;
And losing, proved him stronger than his strength.

OH ! words that were conned long ago
  (How old are the sweet days departed !),
Are ye his, for his life's dreary morrow ?
  Doth his soul feel the words that he read,
With his sense ?
             " There is no deeper woe,
Than to think on the Past of thy joy,
  In thy Present of sorrow ! "

An Eben Song.

" Sweet, when the day delayeth to decline,
  And pale delicious evening paints the sky
With primrose, opaline, and silver shine—
  Soft evanescent lights that dim and die ;

Stand in the Pleasaunce with me, fond and fain,
  When argent Lys do yield their faint perfume,
And Roses drip with the late genial rain,
  And Myosotis greys for lack of lume ;

And ilka bird is bedded on her bough,
  And the great moth makes tapers of thine eyes
In heavy hovering anear their lowe;
  And one cold star peers envious from the skies.

Thou art so beautiful, pale mystic Queen!
  With dying day upon thy soothful face;
Love, wayward wight, in awed and reverent mien
  Gazes and sighs, and scarce takes heart o' grace.

For Love lies languorous where thou art the Light;
  All glitter's garish; passion there, profane;
The jealous Sun retireth at thy sight,
  But Day to view thee, loitereth on the wane.

Stand in the Pleasaunce with me, ere the Night
  For thee contesteth with this fading Day;
Ah! sweet, my Queen! ah! fair, my heart's delight!
  Lean to my lips, list, list their whispering lay."

.   . .   .

  Thus Denys sang and ceased, and straightway mazed
In moods of tangled thought, passed slowly down
The Pleasaunce path, all leaf-strown by the hand
Of careless autumn: not the fair lilies shone
In silver radiance, yellow-hearted, now!
The summer flowers were dead, yet in his breast
The summer hopes to fruitage ripened fast.
It seemed as if a graver mould of mind
Ydonea late betrayed—as had the year,
In softly passing season, laid its touch
Upon her buoyant spirit, and awoke
A sympathy of tenderness therein.

A rarer, deeper smile upon her lip,
Lay like the autumnal richness on the land ;
A gentler beam dwelt in her melting eye,
Like the soft harvest moon in kindly shine ;
And something in her voice disturbed the soul
With sadness that was sweet, as doth the wind
Woo through the woods in deep October even.

    .   .   .   .   .

So Denys deeply pondered, for his love
Wild cried within him, like the petulant child
Cajoled to sleep's tranquillity, and will not.
    Culling dropped ears from fair forsaken fields,
He, gleaner-like, upon kind Memory's plain
Gathered new hopes and fed his hungering heart :
Buried in books, in harmonies absorbed,
He followed none Earl Moray's grim advice—
To con his fellow-man, and learn his kind.
If their wry moving thrust his World awry,
He sought the lettered page, or bade his lute
Lament, and sighed, and straight forgot the whole :
Thus read Ydonea not, nor Alastair.

    .   .   .   .   .

Yet here the stake so vast bade caution live,
Lest the sweet maiden heart, as yet unstirred,
Like some bright wilding, sylvan-sought, should quail ;
So warily (as he recked) was culled and conned
Each sign, that seemed to note her dormant soul
Stirred to his love-lyre tones.
                      But here, as wont,
The blind God balked his wile : he saw no more
(O cunning liar-Love ! O dear deceit !)
Than fed his hopes, nor dreamed of Alastair !

    .   .   .

Now fell he back on memoried days of France,
When he would watch the Maiden, as they came
One after one, the lovers bold or bland!
She, that a moment syne had shown as free
As wild white rose upon its swaying spray—
Laughing in open innocence to the world,
Would, on their proffered homage, coldly turn—
Proud and self-stayed as any virgin Lys,
Whose modest earthward bells do all ignore
Of woodland adoration!

                       "But when I,"
He mused, "make shy approach of uttered love,
How doth she laugh, sweet girl! so blithely laugh,
No summer rill hath half the rippling joy;
Right well persuaded that I jest, or garb
Her in some Poet-Ideal for the nonce;
Bidding me set my bashful words to song,
Or rhyme them featly in an ordered guise:
  So must I still, and laugh, and meet her mood,
As aye her childhood's playmate!"

                          When the wind
Stirred now the whisp'rous flooring, Denys stood
And made low melody with an ancient air
To zephyr's luting.

A Réveillé.

Awake, O maid! why sleep beyond the dawn?
Awake, arise, to love and ecstasy!
The draping mists of doubt are all withdrawn,
  And Love is free!

                And Love is free!

Ah! Love, enclasped in frail and shattered form,
Scarce mote aspire to worth and beauty blent;
And the poor bark lies tossed of wave and storm
   Till Hope is spent!
                     Till Hope is spent!

Oil thou the waves, kind Reason, and assure,
The captive Love in this poor barque of mine,
That yon sweet Port of waters calm and pure
   He shall not tyne!
                     He shall not tyne!

For may thy gifts, great Heaven, of Soul and Song,
Ne'er plead my cause with Her, whom I adore?
My best, mine all, to Her doth whole belong—
   What lacketh more?
                     What lacketh more?

Love lacketh—Love, imprisoned from her ken;
Out, captive, out, and teach thine ecstasy!
Rouse thee, dear heart, to slumber ne'er again;
   For Love is free!
                     For Love is free!

.   .   .   .   .   .

"I have not wooed thee, dear, as others woo;
Sworn no fond oaths, profaning Heaven with vows,
Nor dinned my sorrows on thy shrinking sense:
But when I sang of birds, I aped thy song,
And when I hymned the flowers, thou wert my flower,
And when I praised my God, thou wert the way
To faith, and Heaven, and Him!

Life of my love, that, mothered, sprang from thee;
Love of my life, that death were, but for thee;
Hope's truest pledge, and memory's cherished light:
The bright streams murmuring on their gentle way,
The wafting wind, the billowy-bosomed cloud,
And all thy sisterhood of beauty,—say!
Have they not whispered thee, of *how* I love?"

He stept the path now like a conqueror,
The love-light shining in his fervid eyes;
Then stood with clasping hands and brow upraised:

"Shall, buoyant Hope, thy soaring wing convey
Me to the bosom of attainment sweet?
Or, where Despair's dull Dragon waits his prey
In black abyss, shall I fall strengthless, foiled?
It cannot be! My Ladye, and my love,
I'll venture all, nor tarry yet an hour;
Mine are the chances, mine be victory!
Ydonea! Love and Denys hie to thee!"

.   .   .   .

.   .   .   .

But now she met him, now she hurried on,
Eyne all dilated, wild locks, snood befreed,
Confusion in her gait, and after her
Hound Corbred, trotting sagely, slow, and wide.

"Oh, Denys! oh, my play-fellow, my friend!
Aid thou thy cousin in her sore distress;—
I am too wae to weep, and where to turn
For help and good advising may not find."
He laid aside his purpose new conceived
To soothe her, and with brother's kindly care

N

Led to their summer seat (where redly brown
Their fruit replaced the embowering roses' snow)
The maid, and gently questioned her, who strove
To still her bosom's throbbing, and reveal
Why mantling blushes dried th' all-willing tear.

    She hid her face deep in her tremulous hands;
She dropped the hands, and turned her face away;
Then strove to speak, then gasped, and uttered nought;
At length forth-burst:
                "Oh, brother of my youth!
Have I then erred in hiding long from thee
The dearest secret of a woman's soul;
And is my chastisement this present pain?"

    Why did he start?   Oh, panting breast, be still!
What meant this trouble, this confusèd mien,
In his sweet Worship?   Could it be that Love,
Love for himself, should turn his world to light,
By those dear lips and maiden shame betrayed?

    O'erwhelmed with torturing hope, he only clasped
Her hand in his hand, waiting for the rest.

.   .   .   .   .

Alas! alas! the fulgent autumn day,
That had some moments syne pervaded all
His sense with radiant glory of delight,
For one brief instant blanked to utmost dark;
And then!—the whole bright, vast, encircling world
Was grey, to him therein, for evermore!

.   .   .   .   .   .

    To her the golden day did but recall
A golden head, and golden hours of love,
And golden hopes in peril; and she wept.
His clasp was no less tender to her sense,
She marked no fading of the deep dark eyes,

She never felt each blood-drop in his heart
Froze as if Death, whom he would, after, woo,
Had prescience of his prayer—and did respond.
   But now—nor power, nor passion; scarcely pain!
For, like a deadening drug, such shocks can show
The Mercy that All-rules; an instant draught
Of kind Nepenthe; 'during scarce a sigh,
Yet, through its charity, suspended force,
Resting, reviveth, strengthened to Endure.

But powerless—though the mind resumed its sway—
Were lips for speech: Ydonea's sobs brake free,
   Till low he forced:
                     "You love him—Comyn Bán?
I never knew it: tell me all your pain."
   She thought his agonised constraint of speech,
So cold in utterance, chided her distress;
Calmed with strong effort, and spake of times when passed
Their dear love-meetings, 'neath his viewless eyne.
   Then further said, her handmaid Lupola,
That stealthy-footed Mystery, had heard,
Unseen of them, Earl Moray and his knights,
Hold warlike conclave on the vexèd theme
Of Comyn subjugation; Alastair
Was foremost marked for ruin, and Dunphail
Doomed now to fall by force or strategy.
   She told.   He heark'd, as in a painful dream.
He shivered; had the day grown late and chill?
While she, too sad to marvel at his mien,
Spake further of Western war, where strove the Lord
Of reft Lochaber to regain his due.
   Raites to his succour gone, on lands of Raites
The Earl designed a false attack should draw
Alastair forth, to guard his clansman's hearth;

Which bald, half-fencèd moment for Dunphail
Randolph would seize, and make the fortress sure.
　　'Not that dispute alone in Darnaway
Inflames his breast, but mischief's purpose dire,
That like a dammed-up flood doth thinly ooze
Through the small rift of a minute offence,
Bursting its bound at last, to 'whelm the vale.
　　They must be warned—oh, Denys, they must know
That theirs is but to bide, and shield their home !
But who can warn ? and how ?   The Earl commands
A rigid ward ; and none may pass the gates
This night, ohn leave of him.   Me he commands
Attend him, shortly ; nor I excuse may find,
E'en might be braved the route afoot, alone ;
And Lupola, whose leech denies the breath
Of vap'rous night to those poor blighted eyne,
Would, absent, cause suspicion !   Counsel me !'"

　　His soul resumed her sway, and now his breast
Beat with pain's wild assertion.   Solitude
Must, must be sought, else in unlicensed mode
Would break the knowledge that she ne'er must know
Upon Ydonea.   But his brain rang round
Half-witless words :
　　　　　　　　"Must know, must know to-night !
And who shall tell ?   What if they be not told ?"

　　He raised himself, unbent his icy limbs,
And stood on leaden feet, like one who lives,
But as despite him : having willed to die,
And so embraced his doom—that like the wretch
Who, sudden freed from durance dark and long,
Craved to return, and 'scape the blinding day—
Life vexed him, as a burden fresh resumed.

She covered all her face to mask the tears
That natheless trickled wilful into sight,
And never thought of Denys.
                    Sudden he forced
A muttered word : " I'll seek thee presently,"
And fled as fast as might his halting limbs,
Into his chamber. . . .

Brothers ! oh, pry not here ! Our human anguishing,
Our feeble shadow of Gethsemane,
Is warded well by One Who heeds our cry :
" Wilt *Thou* not watch with me, this torture hour ? "

Drop we the veil ; leave him, for earth, alone.

Alone ! Poor victim of the tyrant Love,
The world's tormentor (else, her brightest bliss) !
Alone, with all the passion, gloom, despair,
The piteous pain, the painful tenderness ;
The baffled hope, that dared to live no more ;
Wrestling with self, crying out upon her name,
And all but cursing his :—came worthier thoughts,
Now devil-promptings ; then half-uttered prayer,
Its certain answer, and the mastery
Won thereby over self : a tale to gloss
Unlingering o'er,—past power of graven words.

  Enough ! He rose, resolved and fortified ;
Threw off the man, and clad the Angel on :
For her to dare ? his life was all her own !
For her to die ? what left grey life to him
Of joy or gaining ?
                  Ay ! He would, sad, alone,
Drag his poor limbs, unstrung, those weary miles,

To warn the menacèd Dunphail, and seal
By his own deed the warrant of his doom !

We borrow from our Immortality
The might to do such deeds, when mortal strength
Of will and flesh forsake us.   O ye men
Applauding acts whose outward show reveals
What toil and torture wrought accomplishment,
Who see the strife but through its vast results,
And crown the expended hero—give his meed
Of praise to Denys ; 'vest in Martyr's weed !

And if the wild winds' Temperer, to this
Shorn weakling of His flock, in grace had sent
Comyn unconscious towards ; sparing thereby
To him some weariness ; wherethrough his soul
Might better brook his now kenned rival's sight,
And in few'st words his mission speak, and part—
What if this chanced ?.
                    Was fainter praise his due ?

But not e'en thus-wise did he miss the joy
Of suffering for her sake : when late at eve,
Nearing the burgh, on slow and trailing feet,
He chanced upon the Earl !
                    Randolph, surprised
At such unwonted vigour there displayed,
Questioned, suspected ; and without ado :
   " Young Sir, an' if it like you to partake,
With bats and owls, the sweets of evening air,
Methinks you'll scarce refuse a pleasant ride
Towards my poor house in Elgin, there to bide
Such time as suits my pleasure."

In an hour,
Erst catching speech of Lupola, who bore
His tidings to her Ladye; Denys passed
Through the mirk night to Elgin.

.   .   .   .

Sore missed the maid her mild harmonious friend;
Nor mote she vent her grateful heart of praise
For that which made him exile; nor entreat
Her guardian for his freedom and return.
   For, with concern and care Randolph appeared
Laden these passing days; and her cold heart
Gathered from signs (slight signs, by caution veiled),
That brooding strife would soon in tempest break.
   Ere long, sad-hearing that her cousin lay
At Elgin, sick; by reason of the stress
Her needs had placed upon him (and his love—
But that was dark to her); she took up heart,
And craved the Earl to send her thither, where
Might she attend and minister to him
Whose balm, leech, cordial, she alone could be.
   Thus reft of sight and sound of Alastair,
She, helpless for his weal, with many a prayer
Did leave her love to God.

.   .   .   .

——— ——— —— ———

NOTE TO DENYS.

"*There is no deeper woe*," &c.—P. 188, l. 6.

From Dante: "Nessun maggior dolore," &c.

THE FIERY CROSS.

The Raven War round Inverlochy flies ;
Then wings, half-gorged, his way to Northern skies.

It fell about this time that Alastair,
With Shaw, in search of game to spread their board,
Was passing up the land.
                         Low on the land
Peace lay : such peace reigns on a sullen shore
When silent seas recede, and draw, and gather
Up in one long heaped ridge of volumed wrath,
Rearing, to turn and thunder on the strand.

  Since those first threats of tempest in the west
No tidings neared Dunphail ; nor mote they spare
One spy from out their slender garrison
Till Randolph's purposes for peace or war
Should be declared.
                    But on this quest they met
One, travel-marred, exhausted ; whose aspéct
Proved haste and dire disorder. Him they learned,
A Comyn from Lochaber, charged with news
Of fearsome import ; but so weary he,
So grief- and way-worn, that they bore him home
Unquestioned, and with careful ministering
Of most immediate needs, unlocked his speech,
And learned the full fresh horror of his tale :

"Ochone! my clansmen, ne'er November blast
Did herald such a winter of sore storm
As mine appearing a distress of news:
The fight hath been at Inverlochy; all
Was fatal loss—Lochaber's self is slain!"
A gasp! a crush upon the reed-strewn floor,
As every hearer in that startled hall
Close to the speaker trod; and then a hush—
So deep, that the down-fluttering of a bird
By-past the window, through the quiet noon,
Brake it, alarming; then one chorused—

                       "Slain?"

And low the messenger: "'Tis sooth I tell;
And night and day I speeded with the tidings,
For, haply, worse will follow.

                    With us warred
The gallant Raites; but on the eve of fight
One came in haste, with news that Moray's Earl
Menaced that chieftain's holding. Proudly he:
'So help the God of battles, I will fight
Cause for my cousin first, and syne for me!'
We fought; but not with us those Hero Ghosts
That gave Lochaber to his foeman's arm!
We fought, and hurled defiances at Fate;
But Fate, defied, revengeful mocked our strife.
  So, when the sad day died, and trembling stars
Crept forth, like widows pale; our stricken lave,
Outnumbered, from their craggy refuge crawled
Upon that scene of death, and blood, and dule,
To cry the Coronach and plan revenge!

  "Ah me! what woe was there! what carnage drear!
What scattered foliage from our noblest trees,

Sons of my clan, tossed on the ravaged heath !
  Not as the autumn leaves, in due decaying,
Float meek to Earth through azure moveless air,
Peaceful to fade the ancestral boughs beneath,
Death their desire, dust their accepted doom :
  But, as thou'st known that fierce September fall,
When the wild North incites the dreamy West
To rise and wrestle o'er the 'frighted land ;
Who, roused, and strong from seasons of repose,
Gathers his mighty limbs and bounds to meet !—
  Ah, then ! what centuries avail the Oak ?
What mighty trunk of Pine can thole the brunt ?
But splintered corpses, boughs all wildly hurled,
And roots, earth-bound, up-wrenched and flung in air,
Mark the fierce vigour of the mad affray ;
While the poor leaves, in all their verdure torn
With ruthless haste from nursing twig or stem,
Lie in green eddy, heap, or whirlèd wave,
And show, in weird confusion of their fall,
The sad surprise of such unripe decay !

.   .   .   .   .   .

So did they lie, the brethren of our name !
Ah, God ! I paced 'mid the familiar dead,
And marked with eyeballs dim, and seared, and dry,
How like the summer leaves hastened to dust,
Low lay the young and fair, the fresh and bright !
And tore my hair with gnarled and eld-stiff fingers,
And hurled a curse to heeding Heaven or Hell—
So dread a curse, that the grim skulking wolf,
Prowling upon the outskirts of the moor,
The corbie glooming on the naked bough
Of some time-withered, tempest-bleachen pine,
Heard ; and lest they, as sharing in the blood,

Might share the malediction I invoked,
Heard, and forbore to taste.
                              A-many there,
Bright loons, had learnt their warring lore from me,
And I could mark the measure of their blows
On fallen foemen round.   But now I came
To one who knelt and bowed him, as were praying,
But knelt to Death, and bowed 'neath strucken blow—
Young Hamish of the glen !   O dear my son !
That curlèd head, now from its trunk half severed,
Tyned one brown lock, that bound with silken thread
Lies in the plaid-wrapped bosom of my child.
Ochone ! ochone ! the darling of my hearth,
Unwed but widowed, who shall comfort thee ? "

     .   .   .   .   .   .

His head the veteran veiled ; nor one disturbed
The pregnant silence, till a dull step without
Caused all give heed to the unclosing door.

There-through into the chamber passed a man
Bearing a wondrous burden, which he laid
On the dark board, and back, a pace, withdrew.
    'Twas an exceeding rude-constructed cross,
Fashioned as if in dire imperious haste.
Two broken shafts, bound with a marlèd shred
Torn from the plaid of some departed Gael,
Were cross-wise lashed upon a battle-axe,
And smouldered from a flame but scarce extinguished ;
While gore, congealed alike on haft and iron,
Red, recent, thrilled each shuddering onlooker !

     .   .   .   .

    Then reverent did Sir Alexander raise
The awful symbol, and inquiring looked

To the dark messenger, who, harshly chanting,
Gave the grim summons in a measured tone.

"The Summons."

"The blood of the Comyn fresh tainteth the gale !
The cheeks of his women are haggard and pale !
And hills of Lochaber ring loud to their wail !

Past, past is the battle; but seek not repose;
The clan looks around it to number its foes,
When lo ! what dark cloud from the Northland down blows ?

The chief of Clan Allan hath armed for the fight,
The shrouds of the mountain lie heavy and white,
Hoarse croaketh the corbie from gloaming till light.

The brow of the chieftain is gathered in gloom,
His spirit is sunk in a chasm of doom ;
He calleth his clansmen to conquest or tomb !

Oh, rouse ye, Clan Comyn, from mountain and moor !
Out wood and by water ! forth cavern or door !
No shelter is trusty, no homestead is sure !

Raites' daughter hath burnished his armour of steel,
His claymore is ground by his son on the wheel ;
Now dare, ye false foemen, for mercy appeal !

That Cross with the blood of Lochaber is dyed ;
'Twas dipped in the torrent that welled from his side,
And loudly for vengeance his spirit hath cried.

Oh, rouse ye, Clan Comyn! the muster of war
Is cried from the summit of chill, grey Cairn-Bar:
There gather,—come morrow,—from nigh and from far."

Grave spake the Chieftain: "We obey!" and gave
The fateful sign to yon dark messenger,
Who forth on his grim errand passed from sight.

Now chief confusion reigned throughout Dunphail,
All fraught with preparation. Alastair
Should head the little force that lent its aid
To 'leaguered Raites; and in their careless youth
His brothers joyed to polish and adorn
War-gear and arms, light recking of the chance
That might undo their hero and their toil.

So passed that day and next, at whose gloam hour
Came the young Roof-tree of the home, all war-
Bedight and harnessed, to his sire, and told
Low on his knee the story of his love.
"And if," he said " (for hap and chance is war),
I see thee, Father, see her, nevermore,
Convey her, with thy blessing, my farewell!"
Betwixt them, much of converse thereanent
Made the time flee; and counsel wise and true
The Chieftain gave, until the tidings came
That men and moment summoned. Then the Sire,
Upstanding to his martial height, so spake:
.   " Glory not 'longs to Dread, to Mercy more;
Honour not thrives by Blood, but Principle;
Fame is a fickle friend,—an enemy
Most dire,—ill-worn. Be not a serf to these,

But Justice love, and Gentleness (when mayst),
That sits as fair upon a warrior
As on a woman.   Love thou thy Duty first ;
Thy comrade next ; thyself—why, not at all !
But yield thyself respect; and merit it,
Winning the same from others, all-ungrudged."

   " Father, farewell ; I crave thy benison."
" My blessing on thee, eldest-born, and best;
That I must spare thee, wae's my heart to-day ;
God sain and save thee, God thine arms invest
With favoured David's strength against the foe,
That on thy Clan, and Home, and Heart would prey !
   Ay ! God's best blessing : in His keeping go
Forth from the bield where thou art light and joy,
There, where our honour call thee, go, my boy.'

—

NOTE TO THE FIERY CROSS.

" *The chief of Clan Allan hath armed for the fight.*"—P. 204, l. 9.

Randolph, Earl of Moray, was so styled (*vide* note, p. 73.)

THE WAR.

Oh ! wreck, and ruth, and ruin ; earth and skies
In jangling discord each with other vies.

It was the hour, when bright from every hill
The beacons mocked a few unwilling stars
That quivered 'mid the obscurity of Heaven.
    Fiercely those war-fires glared, and at their 'hest
The Comyn bands on Cairn-Bar's burning height
Mustered, and waited for the fateful dawn.

The frigid Moon, with sickly halo 'rounded,
Cast on the scene a pale and niggard light,
Discouraging ; and threatened wrath and storm
By her unwholesome aspect.
                                    Jealous-sick
Art thou, dull orb, of that young shining head,
Crowned godlike with its casque in golden gleaming ?
Deem'st thou the Sun-god comes to baulk thy shine,
Stealing thine hour, anticipating day ?

.   .   .   .   .   .

In silence and apart stood Alastair ;
For not his mood might brook companioning :
Wandered his spirit in Immortal realms ;
Lost in the Infinite, he stood alone.
    Oh, fair to see, as poet-sculptor's dream,

That lonely form !—in tender moonlight shades
And silvern beams invest ; all statue-still
He stood ; a pure, harmonious, moveless, mute,—
Ensculptured hero ; marble-memoried.

As thus entranced he bode, anigh the blaze
Of the great beacon fed to wrathful flare
The early comers lingered, for the warmth
Lent to their waiting limbs ; those last arrived,
Warmed yet of motion, stood or sate without,
In converse joined, or slumbering ; and apart,
   Their leaders plotted, waiting for the dawn.

Dawn ! Northern Dawn ! cold, in thy fairest seeming ;
Too young for ruth ; untried for sympathy :
Rather give me, O North ! thy mellowed gloam,
Whose tender consolations salve the sense,
Day-worn, and weary with the glare of noon.

Now rose, from hollow purples of her couch,
The Morn, who, unrefreshed, reluctant parts
Cloud-curtain drapery ; where-through the Wind,
Her Herald, blew so shrill ; that, petulant,
The Dame in shrouding mists her fairness veiled ;
And swept now, 'thwart the dull and gleamless Heaven,
Grey, cumb'rous threats of most congenial storm.
   When man 'gainst man in wrath bestirs, when burns
His soul with hate and vengeance ; and the fiend
Exults within him : how yon lurid sky,
Banked in black cloud on heavy horizon piled,
Concerts his mood ! while the advancing Storm
Calls in vague moanings to the doomèd leaves,
By no wind stirred, yet quivering all with dread.

Know'st thou that shudder of the forest trees
Before the rain-breath? when the heavy pines
Quake, and the Larch weeps golden woe, and spreads
Lithe arms in vain appealing to the blasts
That strip her bare for Winter!

                  At the Dawn
Such tempest threats chill the unrested soul,
And every haggard sleep-lorn warriour
Gazed, in the dusky day, on's neighbour's face;
Anon, around him, on the opening scene.

    The mist-wreaths rose from every shrouded hill
With slow delaying, as if loath to leave
Their tops defenceless to the increasing blast:
On dark Bareven's height the flame had died,
No light lit up the Gorm, or other mount
Late signal-crested; but the whole appeared
As if that day had dawned as other days,
And should wear by like other kindred days,
That knew the wrestling of an Autumn storm,
And passed, full tired.

               O fair and wide expanse,
Viewed from thy height, Cairnbar, of soil and sea!
Fair, with the storm-wrack gathering o'er the sky,
And not a gleam to illume those hilly heights
Bending to sombre hollows. Fairer yet
In gladsome May-time, when the glowing broom
And balmy gorse drapes every slope in gold;
When birk-shaws glisten in their maiden green
With sparkling laughter to the sunny sheen,
And through yet lifeless heather peeps the star
Of silvern " Wintergreen." 'Tis then those piles
Of heapen sapphire show their true-worn name—

o

"Cairngorms"—snow-seamed and distant. Then, the Firth
Lies calmly pale, and hills to North and West
Smile, with soft mystery, across its span
To little Nairn, set on her sandy plain!
    Fair-vestured World! in azure, green, and gold
Harmoniously arrayed!
                    Banish the dream—
Such memories banish; for, O May! with thee,
The maidenhood of the year, the tender prime
Of bloom and beauty, these have naught to do;
But, waning season of the Earth's decay,
October, at thine ending, is their hour.
          Float, dying leaves—but lovely in your death—
          Soft, lovely leaves, down to your endless death;
          But from your drear decay what tenderlings
          Shall spring! and all the treading of the woods,
          Those million, million, tiny perfect things
          That give Him glory, Who created all!
            "Call me not sad," saith Autumn at her end;
          "I type the Death that maketh many lives!"

Now rose each Comyn at his Chieftain's call,
Knotted the brog-thong, shook the dewy plaid,
Grasped firm his claymore, slung the fending targe;
Then, while their leaders counselled, turned him once
To his Home's airt with all its treasure-store;
Clasping dear memories to his hungry heart,
With painful yearning or with wild farewell.
    Now moved the little host adown the hill,
And crossed the wild t'wards Darnaway; nor marked
Or life or sound on all their desolate way,
Save Hoodies twain, gorging their matin meal;
Save Curlew's cry, or Stonechat's monotone.

Raites led the van; anon marched brave Drumynd;
And last, the little levy of Dunphail
Assumed the rearward post, lest some surprise
Should be designed by an all-trait'rous foe.

The foremost act of Randolph for offence
Had been to seize the guardless hunting-seat
Sylvaned in Darnaway; and thitherwards
The Comyn leaders led—in reasoning thought
That none would guess their first attack could be
On what, late won, should stand in ward secure.

Where erst, in bygone ages of the world,
Some lochan slept, or deep inciding flood
Wore its dark home, hung Boggan-geal's ravine:
This passed they by, not recking there to find
Fresh need for caution; but, with clash and cry
Of battle, ringing through the stunted wood
That topped the brae; on their appallèd force
Rushed strong array of Randolph's men-at-arms.

Like some frayed flock in wild confusion heaped,
Hustling, 'fore wolfish onslaught; so, mad, blind,
The amazèd band, of wild surprise alone
Conscious, brake free from all control, and fled.
Now darker grew the Heaven with nearing storm,
And deeped the wild distraction. Vainly strove
Their frantic leaders to restrain or guide;
Was Panic, fell and foul, to out-general these?
Not so! Reason revived 'mid gathering gloom;
The leechcraft rude of Saxon steel restored
By blooding, and the Highland courage sprang!
Each leader claimed his men; and gathering now

Into some show of serried ranks and firm,
Back upon Clune retired, where, making stand,
They hoped a space to breathe, and check the foe.
    Sudden grew murmurs : " Where ? the Chieftain Raites ?
Not now with us ! nor living, with the foe !
Could he, that knew but conquest heretofore,
Brook twice defeat, and live ? "

    Sound high the Coronach ! and curse the hand
That loosed thy spirit into other spheres,
O noble Raites ! nay, rather be our arms
Nerved by the Ghost of Vengeance to the fray !
    Glow fresh, O faded purple of the moor,
Dyed with the flood from such a glorious heart !
But for each bloom so dyed, a widow's tear
For foe shall fall, embittering Ranlach's ground,
Till from its briny soil shall spring no joy !
    Prone lies thy corpse, O peerless Chief of men,
Upon the shore of this rock-roughened world—
An empty shell, lone and untenanted !
For among Hero-spirits reigneth thine
In blissful calm : our lot, to mourn—and war !

    Nor time nor woman was, to wail the dead :
Sternly the battle called ; and pressed the foe
So hotly, that despairing long to hold
A post all-doubtful, Alastair resolved
To hew a path and push his bold retreat
Beyond the river.
              High his claymore waving,
He cried : " Who fears not Death can follow me ! "
And desperate carved his way, fighting each foot
Of ground with vantage through the fierce surprise

Of onslaught; till the Rhait Cuik of the Ern
Was won, and at their feet the torrent rolled.

Where Findhorn's stream is born, the Heavens had wept,
And swelled her flood amain; whose turbid tide,
Lashing its banks, impetuous hurried on
To void its brimming volume.   Up aloft
The cloud battalions drove athwart the sky
Before wild winds, that now continuous
From every airt o' the World tore sweeping on,
Nor gave distracted vapours time for tears.
Steep were the braes that Rannoch's pool o'erhung,
Where raging rapids seethed, and rudely whirled
A Foam-witch in her cornered gloom; the crags
Of hemming granite grey, veined as with gore,
Bore the showered gold of faëry birkens, bending
Sweetly to charm and still the violent flood;
And nigh their grace, harsh clung a weird, dead Pine,
Like skeleton whose dying clutch decay
Had failed to slacken, still to the careless stone,
Amid whose haggard holdings woodbine strayed.

Here came the Comyns; big each heart with hope,
And bold resolve the ford to win, and gain
Kind sylvan shades beyond—when lo! a cry
Brake from those first, and echoed through the ranks,
Ringing wild change on horror and dismay;
For on the far side stood, in horsed array,
Himself commanding, Randolph's armoured crew.

Ruin and death, no less!   Pressed from the rear,
In front prevented, hope denied; yet rose
Fresh courage, bred of shame at late defeat,

And with one desperate rush they took the wave
To gain that steep, beglazed of dead fir-spines,
Whence their mere fury of onslaught might dislodge
Those waiting horsemen from their proudful stand.

Alas ! alas ! yon flood should melt the rock,
Or woodbine wrench therefrom the dead pine's hold,
Ere flesh could break or pierce those ranks of steel.

Fierce raged the fight on earth ; and fierce in air
The storm, long lowering, brake ; and, rattling, crashed
Opposing clouds, whose thunder-wrack o'erspreads
The indignant Heavens. Now the levin gleams,
And thousand eyeballs wild reflect its glare,
Fraught with deep hate or purpose furyful !
    Flash not the dulled claymores ; but, blood-bedimmed,
They shake red rain athwart the battling airs,
That hurtle, cleft by multitudinous shafts
From twanging bow-strings sped !
                                The whinnying steeds
Chime mad war-music from their jangling bits,
Drum the dull soil, or, clattering, fire the rocks ;
While loud the wind outroars the slogan cries,
Or whirls the shriek of slaughter to the hills,
That, echoing, hurl it back. And high above,
The Raven, sable vulture of the North,
Wears his dark watch, and croaks a hungry joy.

Worn by the day's long toil, with 'minished force,
Scarce Alastair and his could 'fend the rear,
And shield Drumynd from his sore-pressing foe.
    And now, its bearer slain, his Standard falls ;
Low lies its azure field with golden garbs,

Tramped, on the river's brink; but seizing straight,
The Comyn hurled those torn, ensanguined folds,
Wrapped round their staff, across the drumlie wave,
Midst of the surging, swaying rout beyond,
And with a shout above the din, he bade
  "The bravest grasp, and keep it!"

                             Then a plunge,
A wild sharp struggle with the deepening flood,
Whose fury checked the following of the foe,
And he and his were in the fiercest whirl
Of the confronted battle. .   .   .

  Ah! what avail 'gainst a relentless might?
'Gainst war-steed, mailèd men, and Saxon spear?

  The weary Highlandmen, drenched, wounded, worn,
Fell like the husks and sheaths of blown Spring buds
Tossed on the wave!

                      Now from the tattered skies
Fell some great tears, yet more, and faster, more;
And then the cloud-dams rent, and on the scene
Wept all the pitiful Heavens.   Alastair,
As yet unmaimed, sprang free from stone to stone—
Aid, or avenger—and vainly strove to front
Randolph in single encounter. He, from the brae
Bytimes down dashed, to seal some clansman's doom,
Who, by fall'n steed, with slight advantage, fought
Its rider, mailed. "No quarter!" was his shout
That bade his spearmen thrust beneath the wave
Each upturned visage, panting yet for life;
And stab at agonised hands that clutched the crags
Out from the maddened river!

                      All was lost!
Drowned these, pierced those: by wave or weapon slain,
Slipping from glazèd steep, writhing 'mid rocks,

On every side a foeman's steel they found,
And nowhere mercy—nowhere aught but doom!

Ah! what avails, when Hope's dismasted barque,
Surge-swamped, is 'gulphed within a pitiless main—
    The last wild stretching of vain hands, the last
Imploring cry, the latest labouring gasp
Of failing forces—ere the o'erwhelming waves
Silence and still; ah! travailers, what avails
When Doom speaks thund'rous out down-drooping skies,
And Cormorant Death glides darkling o'er the foam?

What needs more tell? the unequal fight is o'er,
And Ern, red-rolling to the expectant sea,
Bore on her tale of lives to speak their dule;
Bidding the sad salt waves raise crested heads
In surging reprobation.
                        From the scene,
Surfeit with slaughter, leaving prostrate there
Some dead, and all their wounded with them borne,
The victors and their leader passed away.

    Died the spent wind; but still a leaden lift
Dissolved in sorrow on the weary land;
While the few 'scapen Comyns stole apart
Into the woods; Drumynd, death-struck, was ta'en
By his poor rest of following to their home,
Through hidden careful paths; and Alastair,
Not daring to Dunphail (whither with haste
Had, doubtless, Randolph and his soldiers fared
To siege the fortress), hied him to the haunt
In well-concealed Slaginnan, there to bide,

Waiting the issues of this fateful day :
   And fell the Autumn evening, grim and grey.

   Oh, mirk and din of war ! oh, waste of blood !
How long wilt foul the fairness of the world ?
   So long as Man's proud heart and lustful flesh
Clog and encrust his Soul !

   The drenching rain had ceased ; the elements,
Worn weary, stilled ; and now the loosened leaves
Won peace, unhurried by those blustering threats,
To drop in quiet to their dank repose.
   Float, dying leaves, and gild the sodden loam :
Death here is rife ; oh, hide his ruthless tread !
Lie soft and fair ! a pall for these that lie,
A bier for those who wait their turn to die.

NOTES TO THE WAR.

" O fair and wide expanse ! "—P. 209, l. 21.

I HAVE described the country as it now appears. Then, in all probability, most of the scene was shrouded in vast forest. Sir Thomas Dick Lauder in his 'Highland Rambles' speaks of the comparatively recent destruction of the forests thereabouts, and gives the tale of a man who said that in his youth, early in the eighteenth century, he would enter the shade of the forest of Dulnain near Grantown, and hardly see the sun till he emerged from the forest below Cawdor Castle, near Nairn.

" Save Curlew's cry, or Stonechat's monotone."—P. 210, l. 32.

An old Morayshire saw, referring to the edible value of the curlew, says—

" Be she white, or be she black,
She carries twal [twelve] pence on her back."

" Raites led the van ; anon marched brave Drumynd." [1]—P. 211, l. 1.

Drummine or Drumynd was the name of a great forest, extending from Lochindorbh, and included that Stronkaltere (which may be the present Stronivaich of Altyre, just above the house and policies) mentioned by Wynton in his Chronicle, book viii. :—

[1] Pronounce Drum*meine.*

"Schyre Andrew of Murrawe than lay,
With the Menyhe that wyth him were
In the wode of Stronkaltere," &c.

About a mile from this wood of the Stronivaich, just where the
lands of Altyre and Logie join, a small bit of land is still called
Drummine. Shaw's History of Moray hath : "On the point where
Avon and Livat (rivers) join, stands the castle of Drummin, which
was the seat of the Barons of Strathavon," &c. And it is mentioned
in Sir Robert Sibald's 'Account of the Countrey of Strathspey'
(*circa* A.D. 1680): "Glenlivet, . . . where are the castles of
Blairphine and Drummine."

Though it seems impossible to certify who this "Drumynd" of
the tradition was, there can be little doubt that he, like Raites, was
a member of Clan Comyn ; and that Sir Thomas Dick Lauder
calls him so justifiably. Mrs Cumming-Bruce (History, Bruces
and Cumyns) hath, that in 1614 James Cuming of Altyre gives a
wadset of Outlawell, Sluie, and *Drummyne*, to John Cuming, Outlawell ; and also in 1669, "The town and lands of Drummyne—
now a part of the estate of Logie, belonging to Robert Cuming,
second of Altyre — were wadset by him to John Cuming his
brother, for three thousand merks."

" *Wore its dark home, hung Boggan-geal's ravine.*"—P. 211, l. 13.

Literally, *white bog*—nowadays, "Whitemire."

" *For foe shall fall, embittering Ranlach's ground.*"—P. 212, l. 15.

Randolph was called Ranlach by the Highlanders.

" *In blissful calm : our lot, to mourn—and war !*"—P. 212, l. 21.

Tradition says that when, after the defeat of the Comyns, Randolph
buried Raites on the field of fight, he exclaimed, " I have there buried

the plague of Moray!" The people believed after this that the
disease was buried there, and that it would come forth if the ground
were disturbed.

"*Of onslaught; till the Rhait Cuik of the Ern.*"—P. 213, l. 1.

The "Strait Road," or narrow pass, a passage between rocks on
the Findhorn. In Wyntoun's 'Cronykil,' book viii. and about chap.
32, this pass is mentioned as having been the means of saving Sir
Andrew Murray (of Bothwell) when retreating before the army of
King Edward III. of England in 1336.

> "Thai had with thaim ane
> That kennyd hame a by-way,
> That ewyn down betwixt craggys lay :
> Throw that *strayte Rode* that I dewys,
> Thai gat well frae thare innymys," &c.

And then Wyntoun goes on to say—

> "The Kyng" [Edward] " being baulked in pursuit,
> Northwartis [northward] on his gate can ga.
> He come to *Blare*, and thare thai lay," &c.

Blare is Blairs of Altyre, that home-farm where Mr Robert Walker
now rears (for Sir William G. Gordon Cumming) the celebrated black
polled cattle. How surprised King Edward would have been to
fall on a herd of these ! Mrs Cumming-Bruce, who knew the
country well, does not believe horsemen could have crossed the
"Rhait Cuack," but believes rather Sir Andrew took a ford near
Sluie, below Altyre, "little known or used," which is in a direct
line with the "hame, . . . whether Darnawa' or Pettie (Sir
Andrew's paternal property)." There is a spirited description in
Stuart's 'Lays of the Deer Forest' (p. 281 of vol. ii.) of passing
the ford of Craig-Darach, near Logie-Cuming, at much risk of
life, which proves that a Findhorn ford was ofttimes a risky
crossing.

" Low lies its azure field with golden garbs."—P. 214, l. 30.

It would be curious to trace whether the successors of Hugh Lupus in the earldom of Chester wore the three garbs or (or topaz) on field azure, in right of the Comyns. They are also the arms of Chester city. Hugh was "sister's sonne to William the Conquisitater;" and, as can be seen in the Tree of Robert de Comyn, previously given, about fourth in descent from John, Count de Comyn. I leave this to a better herald than myself. "Randulph, Earl of Chester, the first of that name, relinquished the coat armour, which John, Earl of Cumberland, his father, did beare, [Topageon three barres of the Ruby], and assumed B three garbs or. The field is blew, which coulour representeth the aire, the greatest favourer of life. The three garbs signifying in armes, wheat sheafes, be very properly given in gold. Randulph signified to all men by his coat armour his nature inclining to peace," &c.—Lacie's Nobilitie, p. 48, in Ferne's 'Blazon of Gentrie,' published 1586.

Lacy's statement is in contradiction to a pedigree in possession of the Duke of Westminster, which gives to that Randulph, sixth earl, a lion ; and to Hugh Cyveliod, fifth earl, the six (or three) garbs or. Many families wear these garbs from Comyn descent.

ALLAN SHAW.

Caught like a carrion fowl at horrid food,
On traitorie doth a chidden traitor brood.

A WILD-CAT, warden of the fern-draped gloom,
Fled with her breed of brindled tigerlings
(Low chattering growls of wrath, full impotent;)
From their deep wonning in Slaginnan's dell,
To find another home.
                              There, where the rocks
Brake through the land, and tumbling down its steep,
Vexed with their chaos the ravine's descent—
Half hid by matted verdure, and by crags
Jutting, o'ershadowed—gloomed a sombre Cave.
   From entrance strait, that barely might admit
One burly wight; in gradual decline
The dark den widened, till its last profound
Might house perchance a score, with scanty room;
More seemly dwelling for that Madam Puss
Than for humanity; but Alastair
Had marked for service in a time of ill
This rock-bound den, and thither came he now
With certain followers, (hapless residue
Of his poor band, all bare of sheltering bield)—
With certain followers,—and Allan Shaw.

And Randolph, with his soldiers, sieged Dunphail.

Now followed threatful days, when chill suspense
Pillowed their scanty rest; and when their toil
Lay in hard-seeking meagre sustenance,
Or hovering Moray's outposts nigh, to mark
If, by whatever mortal means or risk,
Some food might reach the affamished garrison.
   Gloaming had scarce her soothful brow declined
Twice o'er that scene of fight, when Alastair
Thither repaired, to note if some bereaved
Mourned o'er his dead, or gave them sepulchre.
   Nearing the fatal spot, he seemed to spy,
Bending above a body lying prone,
The figure of a man! A further look
Brought to his consciousness th' abhorrent fact,
That here no mourner plained him o'er his kin,
But some depraved and brutish peasant churl
Rifled the dead—perchance the scarce yet dead!
   He stayed and watched, to certify his sense,
Lest dusk and distance should his gaze defraud;
And then stole gently forward. . . .
   So wrapped the creature was in his attempt
To pluck the garnish from his prostrate prey,
Or so the river's rushing dulled his ear,
That ne'er he marked th' approach of Alastair,
Who on the crouching thief sprang sudden, sure,
And with a sword-stroke flat upon his pate,
Felled him to earth!
           "What, Allan! Allan Shaw!
Mine henchman caught in such a dastard deed—
The mate of gleds and corbies! Why, here's blood,
Fresh blood! Assassin, do'st thou murder here?"

He struck him with his foot, and half benumbed
By the rough shock of Comyn's lightning blow,
Allan growled sullen :

                  " Stern your judgment seems !
Yon fellow is a foeman, and my dirk
Ended the work your own perchance began ! "
    " Hence ! from my sight ! the craven who would kill
A wight defenceless, whatsoe'er he be,
To pillage from him dead, is foulest cur !
And, Allan, mark me ! shouldst thou prove again
Guilty of such an act, I'll mirror none
Thy crown on claymore's flat, but cause its edge
Speak my abhorrence of thy devil's deed !
Begone ! show in thy future, penitence ! "

    Upgathering of himself in sullen shame
(Or what within his breast, all conscience-void,
Held lieu of shame), slunk the cowed thief away ;
But left his lord by dark disquietings
Vaguely impressed ; who much misliked the scowl
Of ominous spite on Shaw's malignant face,
That showed with startling sense of matter new
To's lord's discovery !
                  But from his wrought brain
Full soon momentous musings drove away
All alien thoughts ; and Allan passed from heed ;
Who nathless conned and brooded o'er revenge.

    How wore the doleful days, me lists o'er-pass,
Lest patience fail my hearkeners (eke, and time) ;
How Alastair, from out his cave would fathom
The fading woods, and seek some joyless roof,
Where lurked few sad survivors of their force,

Whose bankrupt hearts, cowed, desolate, he essayed
To stir for vengeance; or 'gainst the compassers
Of that doomed fortress where their Chieftain lay,
And prove him Help and Hope not wholly passed
Into their sealèd tombs.   .   .   .

    Me lists not tell—save just at tip of tongue—
(Lie by, thou Lyre! sing softly, wind and tide!)—
How certain carles, rude men, and rough of speech—
Men of a further North, they told, who came
A-buying hides from Moray's flock-strewn Laigh—
Sought a night's warding from Earl Randolph's host.

    The leader of these wanderers, (they were three)—
A man misshapen, bent, of swarthy face,
And bandaged poll;—craved that the laden sleds
Bearing their wares, might pass ythrough the ranks,
For greater surety.
                    How within the night
The startled soldiery were roused to know
A sally from the Castle had secured
Meal-sacks, low-lurking 'neath those piled-up hides,
From off the o'erturned sleds; and through the mirk,
Each on a draught-horse mounted, had escaped
The wily owners.   Not the punishing
Of those unwary sentries then could baulk
The fresh-fed garrison, that still withstood.

    But Randolph waxed impatient, till the fiends
Sent his desire towards his ruthless hand.

There's no true joy in Memory, for she
Within her very essence holdeth Death.
    What is, is what has been; so, part in Death!

P

What may be, may be never : thus, unborn,
Is better than the dream of sad regret
Our dearest memories bring us—being past.

Whilk is the woe of life ?—the " Might have been,"
The sad " Has been," or rueful " Might have done " ?
    I wot this last—our lack.   God ruleth all,
But gave to Man Free-will !   .   .   .

THE TRAGEDY.

Ah ! fickle fairness, why so swift to fade ?
Fair hope, fair life, fair nature, lowly laid !

Low in the folding of the dim-draped eve
A little wind lay sighing out its life,
And passed, and was not.   Then a dolorous Owl,
Fluffed on an ancient fir, deridingly
Hooted the faintness of the weary World.

Later, an hour, and 'neath his perch there passed
The stealthy tread of evil-purposed feet,
And a dull light, by guarded lanthorn thrown.

He rose, the solemn fowl ; in floundering flight,
Beat with light plumes of down the quiet air,
And skimming nigh the intruders on his hour,
Moved, dazed and wroth, to seek a farther bower.

Onward the feet trode, and the bended twigs
And withering ferns, released, each to its place
Returned with tiny cracks, and whispered plaints
Behind them ; and a trail of silence lay
On the hushed forest.
                        Down within the gorge
Of caved Slaginnan, Alastair, and those
Who shared his woe and wandering, slept ; the while
One of their number kept a careful ward.

Where dips the land towards Slaginnan's deep,
Those wary feet, more slow and careful grown,
Made pause ; and now, fell whispers on the night
Of moulded mischief hung !   Then onward yet,
And downward now, the careful treading moved,
Keeping to front the murmur of the stream ;
And when the feeble lanthorn light revealed
Dark Divie's flow beneath them, did the men
Whose were those footfalls, wait, and one, their Chief,
Spoke to another, unto whom all seemed
To look for guidance.

         " Art thou sure they sleep ? "
" My lord, 'twas mine to watch, and theirs to slumber ! "
" Go, and spy out their attitude ; we pause,
Lest, entering the glen, some ambush lurk ! "

    And as the bidden passed, as bidder bade,
A second of his following moved towards
Their leader.

        " Trust we wisely thus, Lord Earl,
This unkempt traitor ? fear you ne'er a springe
Set 'yond for us ? "

         " Ay, Adam ! I might fear,
Not Mercy ; haply clumsiness in planning,
Had he for greed alone betrayed his master :
But I discern the promptings of a hate—
Hate, such his like can foster, sharpening all
His will and wit—and know him surely ours."

Now, like a blasted thing of evil Night,
Along the tangled going Allan Shaw
Writhed like a slimy adder.   Chill was the night,
And dark, and very dank, and full of fear.

Sighed a soft leaflet down; he started! Now
A drowsy puddock flopped aside, and forced
Cold beadings from his brow! Too nigh he brushed
A rocky ledge, and scared a restful bat
To leathery flutterings; then stumbled he,
Short panting, gripped of horror, daft with fear,
Fast through Slaginnan to the rock-heaped earth
Near by its Cave; and when his bounding heart
Gave his lips grace, toned he a curlew-call
Low through the air; whereto in answering,
An owl high-hooted—and a Comyn showed,
Forth peering from the opening.
       " Whence art thou,
Allan ? " he asked; " lately I signalled ! came
No answer to my signal ! Did ye nap ?
'Twere well for thee our leader slept, and sound,
An it were so ! "
       " Nay ! nay ! I did but move
Farther afield to note the neighbourage clear.
They sleep, thou saidst ? 'tis well; sleep thou ! I watch ! "
  And forth he went again, and came to them,
That armoured band by Divie's side, to whom
He told his absence' finding. These delayed
A little while, till all of Alastair,
To Allan trusting, should be merged in sleep;
And then Earl Moray bade him lead the way !

Those that within the cave, their weary heads,
And almost hope-lorn hearts, with slumber dulled,
Leaped into consciousness, as on their sense
Crept low an alien sound, a clank of iron,
And nigher murmuring than Divie's tide,
That grew to clash and tramping as they hearked.

Then, on their wakened eyes a lurid light
Brake, fitful—flickering; and Comyn Bān
Forth-spying, saw what sent an icy tide
Through the brave heart that ne'er had flinchcd before!

A score of men, with gait assured of those
No longer questing, wotting that their prey
Lay by their hand—men armoured, shielded, armed—
Came the Ravine along, by three and three;
And each alternate man to right and left
Bore high a flaming torch, that 'mazed the rocks
Into a fiendish splendour—visage-wrought,
Curled into mockery; and writhed the trees
To forms that, imp-like, pointed gibing claws
In threatening, all toward the cave.
                                        At front,
With step less confident, one walked alone—
One who seemed willing in a cowering way
To blend him with the others, and be lost;
But to precedence yet appeared compelled,
Honourless, undesired; and led the way.
   As nearer fared the troop, marked Alastair
One man brought up the rear, and time by time
Voiced some command.   Slowly they marched and sure,
Until the level of the ground was left,
And the slope breasted to the upward cave.

Then Alastair him turned unto the few
Who waited: " Clansmen, treachery's on the crawl!
Its semblance cometh yonder—Allan Shaw ! "

They clung against the rocks, they clomb to spy,
And as each left the opening, low he swore,

And cast about him, groping i' the dark
For some avenging weapon.
                              " Clansmen all "
(And stern the accents sounded), " we must die !
And I would less lament it, could I find
One shaft within my clutch to cleave the skull
Of him who hath undone us ! "   Alastair
So spake, and grim they waited !
                              Now without,
The dell's invaders halted, and the Earl,
Late last, came forward, and surveyed the ground ;
While Allan sheltered him amid the men,
As if their hostile presence lent defence ;
For every stone or gnarlèd trunk of tree
Burned with his Master's eyne !

.   .   .   .

" Alastair Comyn ! thou whom men style Fair,"
   (The 'rounding rocks in echo moaned " despair ! "),
" Fallen is thy pride ; mine hour of reckoning nigh ! "
   (Dim distance bade the doomed prepare to " die ").
" The foe thou'st dared too long, seals here thy doom."
   (Hollow that mocking echo voiced " thy tomb ").

   " An it be sealed, Lord Earl, I meet it here !
Meseems you choose fit tools for your employ :
A traitor henchman leads you to my lair,
When all your armoury fails you ! "
                              " Parley now,"
Randolph returned ; " I'll lend to thee thy life
To drag in durance with thy captured kin
In some deep Fortress of my Earldom's bounding ;
Thou'st braved too long and overtly my power
For doucer dealings !   Wilt thou parley thus ? "

But silence long and weighty was alone.
Once yet he called, then came the answer:

        " No ! "

" Now may the devils deserve me, if I brook
Thy braz'd defiance longer ! "

         And he turned,
And to the waiting men-at-arms he called,
Bidding them pile upon the cavern's mouth .
Branches, and grass, and leafage.   Furthermore,
Bade hew damp heather with their swords, that, heaped
These over, covered every aperture.

  Then forward stepped two soldiers, furnished each
With flaming brand, and thrust it in the mass,
And stood aback, and waited.   .   .   .

  There is a Glory in the awe of Fire,
Fierce beauty, savage grace, that overpowers
The senses' horror, and compels the soul
To homage of the Terrible in strength.

  But, sickening breath of fever, pent and choked,
Thou chill-struck malady that moulders slow,
Smoke !
What fairness can thy poisonous being show ?
Writhing, O bastard progeny of heat and damp,
Creep where the lawful flame, the child of Air,
Disdains to show !
Smoke !
Leaden and grey, and crawling adder-like
Out chink and crevice, writhing on the ground,
It oozed, it grovelled, shamed to face the dusk
(Dusk that was darkness), and daring not to rise,
It stole apart, and hid in corners—lay
'Low rocks and hung about the fading ferns

Like a night thief; and in a guarded nook,
Where Allan, gnawing at his hands, low sate,
Swathed him, and caused him gasp!

      Now on the ears
Of those who waited fell a dreary sound
Like a long sobbing curse, and then a gleam
As of a dirk-point stabbed up through the smoke,
And syne a choking scream: . . .

     "Dog! let me forth,
To die as Comyns wont!"

     "Nay! like a fox
In dark dens sneaking, die!"

      John Randolph, stern
And pitiless, replied. And then no more!
 But still they waited, and the fume-snakes crawled.

And now a joyous flash and sprout of flame—
A triumph-signal of the work well done—
Lit up the scene, and woke the sullen cliffs,
Striking the casques and armour all to gold,
As the damp heather, dried, flared into life,
To vivid triumphant being, for a space;
Then sank, expended.

     When the lingering breaths
In heavy swathes rolled off, and showed the place
A blackened ruin, gave the Earl command
To bring the dead above.

     They found them set
Each with his head close shrouded in his plaid;
And Alastair yet grasped his bootless brand!
 Moray commanded, and they took his head,
His golden head, from off him; and he lay,
What once was Alastair, a thing of Earth,

'Mid earthy desolation !

             Wrap, thou Night,
Thy raiment yet about the wakening World,
Lest horrored madness seize her; for the Dawn,
Her saffron-locked and rose-browed love, no more
Shall kiss her greeting; thread her meadows' dew;
Wake her songed reveil : prone he lieth, here !

Now led the Earl his troop from out the glen,
Of Allan all unmindful, who remained
Rooted within his corner, gnawing yet
His traitor hands, and hugging his revenge.

As through the deeper wood these slayers moved,
A soldier hurled his torch (all needless now,
For dawn the dull East tinted) into the dense
Beyond him, and a comrade queried " Why ? "
    " Marry ! meseems a catamount or wolf
Watched us thereout; I gave him hint to leap ! "

Ere Time, with limp and nerveless hand, had stripped
The dusk of two dim hours from off the Day—
Since first the trembling light had dared to peep
Into that shamèd dell—rushed Lupola
Upon her Ladye's heed in breathless guise :
    " Madam, away ! Ydonea, 'tis no time
For sleep, when danger menaceth our love :
I know (it recks not how), was one who saw,
Earl Moray and his men about the Dawn
Pass from Slaginnan t'wards Dunphail, and heard
Purpose of final siege, and speech that showed
Alastair Comyn captured !   Thou must ride !
    I bribed the warders; bade thy palfrey stand

Down by the gate, and filched thy cousin's garb.
   Disguise thee speedily; I am with thee straight:
Quick! haste! thou yet mayst save!"
                            In 'wilderment,
In grief and fear; not pausing to inquire
Further, or learn what brought the fateful news,
At Lupola's wild words Ydonea rose,
Garbed, mounted, rade from Elgin.   And the while
Sieur Denys slept, unconscious!   .   .   .

THE FALL.

Such deeds have been, such acts again may show :
He only, ordering, doth the wherefore know.

SUN! that in Heaven's high portal seem'st the gaze
Of the Unseen, show forth, lest sightless man,
Himself dim-visioned, deem this act unmarked
Of One to Whom, adown thy slanting rays,
Each mote hath destinies, each film a fate.
   Now the unveilèd Orb a searching flood
Of Radiance poured on yon grim Tragedy
In deep Slaginnan! Ah! what scene was there
Of trampled sod, and floral ravaging,
And man's destroying, and of Autumn death—
Its summer past in desolation laid,
Its peace of tender fading all defiled.
   Wild Divie moaned and plained beneath her bank,
Autumnal flooded from the storm-washed hills;
And in the o'ershadowed corners of the dell,
On chill and dank and death-corrupted air,
Heavy with dying Nature's fainting breath;
The smoke hung, pall-like, impotent to rise.

Prone on the moss, near by the Cavern's mouth,
Cushioned on crimson, lay the crownless corse

Of what was Alastair !   .   .   .   .   .

On his cold breast he lay, with arms outspread ;
And a great feathering, bent, compassionate fern,
A tawny bracken, threw its dying fronds
Across the severed neck, where once had waved
Those locks all-golden !
                                        Not the pitying Sun
Would long o'erlook such woe, but hid him soon
Behind deep-rolling clouds ; and the few leaves
That hastening winter spared, shivered o'erhead,
And dropped with sound of sighing.
                                        Came a man,
And stood amid the ruin silently,
But like no mourner,—it was Allan Shaw.

He knoweth not mankind who dwells to seek
A mighty motive for a monstrous crime :
As thorn-prick, rankling in unwholesome flesh,
Will work a deeper ill than thrust of spear
In purer principle ; so in some minds
Light injuries work, or mean offendings fester,
To ill results, all-disproportionèd.

Thou modern Cain, can the desirèd grasp
Of that mere dross have prompted e'en to blood ?
Or thou, vain coward, patientless of blame,
In whom the chiding of a tyrant King
(Child-petulant upon the lightest lack)
Bred purpose of a war—achieved, that sent
Thousands to bootless graves—art thou belied ?
Oh, of earth, earthy ! through what petty paths
We crawl to being very Kings in crime !
A slip from conscience ; then, refusing shame,

We plant a hardness in us, and astound
Hell, with our second action !
                                  So with him,
The traitor Allan, o'er whose cankered heart
Triumph reigned wholly, as he stood and gazed
At his once kindly master, lying there.

    Sudden, brisk feet came down the rocks, and one
Of Randolph's soldiery approached, and cried :
    " Why, Shaw ! what doest thou here ? "
" I watch ! "
                  " What watchest ? "
" Why, nothing ! for a dead man's naught ; and one
Without his head—that classed him 'mid his kind—
Is even less !   So I watch—nothing ! "
                                  " Stay ! "
Gravely that other in a warning tone.
" Speak the Monks sooth, the Soul is yet alive :
And, prithee, what ? if from some rended cloud
It may be glowering at thee ? for in truth
Art thou a scurrilous, unfaithful Knave !
And, but thou'st served our purpose, I would slay thee ! "
    Allan looked up and round, and on the earth,
And shuddering, while he poorly aped a laugh,
Growled ; " Tush ! a sorry jest !   Why art thou here ? "
    " My lord hath lost a weapon, and I seek it."
" Red work up there ? "
                                  " Ay, marry, very red !
Red autumn leaves showering the sullen ground ;
Red flames that, waving, wrap the walls around ;
Red blood enough to quench them.   Look aloft !
The over-floating clouds in lurid glow
Do mock a sunset, though the day is ear' ;

But many Suns of life this day are set,
And Randolph hath no foes!"

          "Then all are slain—
His people, that lies there?"

          "Ay, every one!"
"Hell hold them!" through his teeth the traitor hissed:
"I hate them, dead, for his dead sake that died
To glut my vengeance!"

          "Glut thy venom, toad!
I hate thee, fellow, whose cold glittering eye,
Ere now, would glisten with a well of tears,
Wert less than Monster!"

          "Adam, thou art bold!"
And Allan gripped his dirk, half menacing:
"What! am I God, that I should ill forgive?
Use fairer words then, or, by the Heaven, I'll swear . . ."

  "How now!—take heed; there's in thy heart no Heaven,
And fiends would grudge it empty!"

          "Prithee, truce;
Cease thy base gibing, that like rock-shed rill
Falls courseless, to no end! How fared ye hence?."

  Then Adam spake the tragedy:

          "From here
The Earl passed to Dunphail, upon thy news
Of sore distressment in provision-store.
Arrived beneath the rock-walls that so well
Mocked our manœuvring late, and scorned our siege,
Randolph caused sound a parley, and desired
One to confer withal, and bear the Knight
A private message for his single heed!
  No answer gat we, long! Amid the woods,
When came the end, we found three fellows hid,

Escapen 'mid the hurly of the last
That gave no willing quarter.   Questioned, these
Say the old Comyn feared a stratagem;
But by his sons (who, curious half, and half
In nameless dread) o'erruled, gave grudged consent
That a slight cord, dependent from the cliff,
Might haul the message, penned, before the eyes
Of one, his son, some skilled in clerkly guise."

    "Ay, ay! young Richard clerked it, from the monks
Winning such needless lore!"
                            "Needless indeed!"
Adam rejoined; "for sure no six-years' brat
But mote Earl Randolph's message read full plain;
For to the cord, a meal-sack firm attached
Enwrapped—thy Master's head!
                            'Twas swift up-drawn;
And one amid our throng cried lusty loud,
With more methought of wit than courtesy:
"There's beef unto your bannocks, Comyns all!"[1]

  .   .   .   .

We heard their cry! we marked the stillness syne;
And then five forms of Comyn's brethren showed
A moment on the height, and on our ears
Poured maledictions that should vex the ghost
Of Randolph's mother, an she loved her son!
    But in an instant, as a cawing band
Of rooks would scatter if the eyrie's King
Swooped in their midst, the youngsters fell aback;
And lone and grand upon the outmost wall
His father stood!

---

[1] "Beef to your bannocks, like the Comyn's head,"—passed into a local proverb.

We saw him plain, and saw
That in his hands the head of Alastair,
High borne, commixt its flood of sunlit gold
With breeze-blown silver of his hoary hairs—
Like vapourous breaths that, rising eastward, blend
With the first beams of morning.　.　.　.

　We marked him kiss again, and once again,
That relic of his Lost; and then we heard
(And not a man of us but hushed to hear):

　"Thy morsel's bitter, Moray—bitter-sweet!
My love, my hope, my life was centred here,
And not a hair upon this curlèd head
But twined my heart around!
　　　　　　　　　　Yet mark me now!
I'd gnaw this morsel to its very bone
(If hunger so out-natured quality),
Before one stick, or stone, or sod of our'n
To thee would I surrender!"　.　.　.

　There was no man of us but hushed to hear;
There was no soul of ours, that in those tones,
Clear through the distance, caught the merest trace
Of age or weakness.　I happed nigh our lord,
And marked his visage.　Saints! but the man is stone,
And seemed it!　.　.　.
　　　　　　　　I have bonnie sons mysel',
And felt　.　.　.　Methinks a bone choked me last meal,
And pricks my gullet yet, watering my sight!
A murrain on the ox that grew the bone!
　But, Allan, thou art a devil—which I knew
When I this heard, and saw it!"
　　　　　　　　　　"Devil thou!

Q

That art so fine a judge of devildom :
My devil's none thy gendering !   On with thy tale ! "

" Those captured late, our prisoners, say the Knight
Fell from his high composure, and our view ;
And then within the fortress such a scene
Showed, as left no eye tearless !   .   .   .
   Only the Ancient never shed a tear,
But paced the earth, and beat upon his breast,
Kissing the Head, and looking on't so long,
As might his gaze absorb it from decay ;
   And while his younglings wailed like girls, he'd cry
Such miserable words :
              ' Oh, Alastair !
Oh, dull ! oh, cold ! oh, sunless, sightless wreck !
Here is my front of woe, mine end of joy !
No more this dear brow's dawning shall arise
Upon the gloom of my befrosted night ;
Not now the song-cheer of thy lip shall wake
Mine agèd sense to tender memories
Of her, whose primal bliss wert thou !
                    Sweet wife !
I've imaged oft, when in the Visioned Land
We twain should meet ; how I would tell of him,
How he ne'er failed me ; not in word or work
Lacked he of love, of reverence, of delight.
   Now, dost thou greet himself ?
                 Praise Heaven, mine years
Promise brief severance ; and we meet again,
Three hearts, not twain.'   .   .   .
            Long, long, they say, he raved—
Thus wild raved he ; and sore his sons bewailed !
   At length one neared him, and with tear-roughed cheeks

Cried for revenge, and speedy. 'Sir,' he said,
'Was scarce a gowpen [1] of the girnel's [2] meal
Left, and dull famine clutched, with griping claw,
On the bare garrison.' His Sons sprang next
From the abasement of their grief, and prayed—
Wrought with mad ire, and reckless in their ruth:
'Command a sally!'

                  Over-long's my tale!
I'll shorten it! Forth to a man they came;
Nor long the struggle 'gainst their weakness proved,—
Though fury and despair be mighty arms!
Right well they warred. But soon the encumbered hearth
Of their Dunphail bore Sire and son alike,
Heaped in opposing barrier to the foe
So long, so well prevented.

                One was there,
A fair-haired stripling of some fifteen springs,
Who battled like his betters, ere he fell!

   Wae's me! who owns a master, needs obey him;
And soldiers cannot question; but I cared
That this sight piteous bore no mark of mine:
   I slunk aloof, and aimed my strokes at air!

When none were left to slay, and naught to find,
They fired whate'er would flame; dispersing next
To seek for fugitives, nor found but three;
   And then, stern-ordering that his victims' heads
Should fray, from portals of the Earldom burghs,
John Randolph rade aback to Forres town."

   "What of the captured ones?"

                       "He set them free!"

[1] Handful.   [2] Meal-chest.

"Free?"   "Ay! they served no purpose, in destroying!
Our master kills not, save for gain!"

        "Of gold?"

"Of gold! thou grasping Judas! nay, of power!"

 "Judas me none!   How may thy sorry soul
Dream of the sweets of Vengeance?   Love can pall,
Ambition pale, and pelf will scarce assuage
The needs itself createth!   But Revenge
Makes its own life so wholly, 'twere enough
To thirst, to quaff, to die!"   .   .   .

 The soldier heard, wide-eyed; and then, with wrath:
"Villain!" he cried, "I am no customed Seer;
But something breathes me, as thou bidest there,
That if God mark in Heaven, thou shalt scarce
This day go scathless hence!"

        He only scowled,
And cursed uneasy oaths; and Adam passed,
Forgetful of his errand, out the glen,
As if some presence foul defiled the spot.

 And Allan stayed, regardant, as before.

NOTES TO THE FALL.

" Or thou, vain coward, patientless of blame."—P. 237, l. 24.

IT is recorded by Duc de St Simon in his memoirs how Louvois, minister of war, and also superintendent of buildings to Louis XIV. of France, having been publicly reproved by that king for a crooked window in the Trianon, then in course of erection ; was so piqued in pride and wounded at the Monarch's apparent oblivion of his services, that he actually brought about a war to make himself necessary, and divert the mind of that pettiest of tyrants, Louis " le Grand."

" Of rooks would scatter if the eyrie's King."—P. 240, l. 26.

I saw once a curious encounter between an eagle and rooks. Fishing one day at the river's mouth in Applecross, Ross-shire, I was startled out of a dreamy mood by a rush and flap, and great wind, close to my head. Looking up in alarm, I saw a great eagle, which had evidently swooped at the scarlet cap I wore, soaring upwards, not a fishing-rod length above me. In a few seconds he was mobbed by squadrons of rooks, who came as if by magic from the woods over the river, and who seemed bent on driving him from their neighbourhood. Up he sailed, making little dips at them now and then, when they wheeled and scattered, like curs faced by a mastiff—till the whole vanished from sight against the blue heavens. I remember one of our stalkers telling me he had been swooped at by an eagle as he slept on a hillside in Skye. He wore a scarlet neckcloth.

" His father stood ! "—P. 240, l. 29.

There is known to have existed a poem or dirge in Gaelic called "The Lament of Shennan Paul Glas to his people on the rock," which was the supposed utterance of the old Comyn in his grief and despair ; but like many another, it is lost and forgotten. What the real spelling of "Shennan Paul Glas" can be, I can only conjecture: "Shean-an-mhol-glas," "The old bare grey one"—*i.e.,* "the bereaved greybeard."

RETRIBUTION.

Trait'rie avenged and tyranny proved vain,
The Were-wolf winneth Life, and parts from pain.

WHY speed so fast, thou steed, upon the lea?
Bearing thy light boy-burthen, as the breeze
Bears the light petal of a bloom dissolved
In tears for her own fading.
      Not thy task
To hunt the wedded Hart from forest joys;
Or, when the falcon flies through greying airs
Of nigh November, emulate on Earth
Her speed in Ether! Mayst not, joyous now,
To the clear melody of maiden's laughter
Throw out thy hoofs in sportive capriole
At Corbred, barking to thy shaken rein.
 Bayoumé, of assurèd feet, oh fail!
This once—oh fail, and foul thee in the dust,
If haply she might find a gentler end,
Who rides unto such anguish!
      But he sped
As true as heretofore; and all too soon
His boy-garbed mistress reached the stony shaw
That lies before Slaginnan, where she came
Unreasoning, as impelled by wayward Fates

To where she earliest met him.

　　　　　　　　　　　Once again
She tied Bayoumé to a hazel bough,
And clomb adown the stones—and saw him lie !

She gave no cry, she never made a moan,
But stood with eyes that strained, with severed lips,
And passed a hand across her misted gaze,
Unconscious.　Then, as some light water-sedge
Sways 'fore the whelm of swift down-driving wave
A moment, ere it bends to rise no more ;
So swayed her form—then sank an insensate heap,
Lifeless, upon the Dead.

　　　　　　　　　　And Allan came,
And dared, a callous hound, to touch her hand,
And felt it chilling, chilling ; and he said
To his vile self aloud, " She too is dead ! "

What holds thee, Allan, Allan, lingering here ?
What keeps thee, traitor, by the double bier ?
Oh tool, fiend-wrought, of those thy work hath slain,
Begone !　Thou canst not go ! for on the wane
Thy Star is, paling in its sanguined sky,
And o'er thine unblest tomb the wave rolls high !

She came, that woman, mystic Lupola,
With step as stealthy-rapid as of yore ;
And Allan turned him t'wards her with a jeer,
But 'neath his breath, for even he not dared
To rouse the echoes of Slaginnan's dell :
　" The gallant lovers, are they wed in death ?
Mark the kind priest that wrought the union !
The one would strike me—ay, and earned his doom !

The one would flout me, 'plain of me, and warn
My Master (faugh ! the word !) to trust me none :
And so, she got her doom ; and lieth there !
D'ye mark me, woman !—ay, and lieth there !
    Poor Allan Shaw is mighty for revenge—
Poor Allan ! fed and kept for Charity,
By the cursed Comyns ; struck, and slurred, and blown
By a traducing tongue : but hand that struck,
And tongue that vilified, lie here all cold ;
And Allan is content !
                I leave to thee
My watch and ward, in worthy company !' "
    He moved away ; but pausing, loitered yet
For one last gloating look : and saw the Dead,
And noted Lupola, entrancèd, stand
Where first her foot was checked upon their sight ;
    And then he made as, passing her, would go !

    She turned, and reft the bandage from her eyes,
And all the horrid Animal glared out
In wild expansion of ungoverned rage !
    His gaze, enchained, could not escape, nor free
Its spell-bound terror ; but the mind in him
Sought abject flight ; and back he stepped, and back,
She following, creeping, holding him, as doth
A snake her victim. And his grim visage paled,
And his dank hair got life, and stood erect
In fierce amaze ; and dropped his heavy jaw :
And back he stepped, she followed ; back he trod,
She following, with her body crouched to spring ;
And seemed as if the very stones made way,
For never faltered Allan's backward tread ;
And out the glen, and out into the day,

And near the roar of Divie raging down
In foaming spate: so, back and back he stepped.

Sudden the Woman made her spring, and stood
With arms thrown up, straight to a watching sky!
On the rock-edge, fixed, rigid, firm, she stayed,
As struck (a statued Nemesis) to stone,
And looked at Something whirled adown the wave
With tense unchanging face: then, as the flood
Raged on, and rolled the traitor out of sight,
And out of life, and out of all but Doom,
Her arms drooped slowly, and she sighed "Amen!"

Back Lupola her heavy steps retraced
Into Slaginnan; but when paces few
Traversed its depth, she paused, beholding there,
His face turned from her, standing by the Dead,
Randolph of Moray : and her rended soul
Rose up to curse him; but he spake aloud,
And she, as in a trance of anguish, heard:

"And is it thus, ah! poor, my gentle Ward?
Randolph is seldom wont to be thus moved!
Still dost thou lie! in death, Ydonea?
    What! hath some vengeful Comyn done the deed?
Or didst thou love, and self-inflict thy fate?
    I dare not near thee; 'tis a sickly sight:
But rise, my wench, and leave that headless foe.
    What is't retards my firm advance? Ah, speak!
I'll find thee lovers! maidens soon forget!

"No word! no answer!—ay, 'tis death! What blood!
What rivers! pools!—or is't thy mantle's glow

Deceives my war-used eye? Thou, Moray! fie!
Girling it thus; a wench self-pricked, and puling
At sight of gore! I dare not go anear!
I have no strength; I would this were undone!

   Nay, recreant! nay! kenn'st well there was no room
For Randolph and for Comyn in the land:
The weird was rede; and I will ne'er repent!

   "Yet he was fair and very brave, Ydonea!
An thou wilt rise, we'll lay in fitting grave,
With cairns of honour o'er him, thy bright love;
We'll friend it with his kin!

                   Dear God! my brain
Is clouding, surely. Have I not seen the hair
Of his own Father lying on their hearth,
Drenched in the blood of those five bonnie sons
Scattered around him: five, I said,—and I
Hold heirless honours!

                Say, is this a dream?
I will awake! I cannot! . . .
         . . . Hell! what's here?"

   She stood before him with uncovered gaze,
Fresh from her Retribution; and the spell
So seized him that he muttered:
                "This is part,
Oh! part of visioned horrors!"
                And he stood
Dazed, and half faint. She with a haggard finger
Pointed the blood-steeped Earth between them spread;
And thus they stayed, while Time might count threescore;
And then her pallid lips unclosed, and forth
Rushed a pent volume of denouncing words!

" Ah ! thou mayst look in wonder on thy work :
Canst not undo it now, whate'er thy will !

   Man, didst thou deem thy fell ambition cleft
A clean and even course to lead its road ?
Didst hope to choose the victims of thy will—
Sweep on the stones that checked thy torrent course,
Nor harm the leafage dipping by the tide ?
Mow the fair grain, nor cut the mingling flowers ?
Rend the strong oak, nor tear the ivy twine ?

I, standing on this region of thy hate,
Pour forth, in swelling words of wrath and ruth,
Such storm of passionate woe, rebukeful rage,
As might bring down those heedless Heavens in floods
Of most astonished and remorseful tears !
   But thou ! oh, thou destroyer ! could the tears
Of woman or of Heaven move thy soul ;
Might their despairing or compassionate flow
Stir but one line the adamant of thy heart,—
It were too late ! One Victim more lies here
Than willed thy wild desire ? Was ever yet
A crime conceived that wore its course alone ?
An evil purpose wrought to ending, that
Bore on no further ill ?
                Oh, mighty Earl,
There's blood upon thy hands—upon thy heart !
There's blood been shed this day, that I foretell
Shall roll and gather like a rill, fount-shed,
Through days not distant ; till the drumlie ooze
From out thy death-wound swells it into speed,
Bearing thine infamy adown all Time,
To Oceans of the Future !
                See ! pale Death,

My dear desirèd Lord, holds to my sight
His wizard globe of crystal; and therein
I read a far Beyond!

      'No room (saidst thou)
For Randolph here—and Comyn.'

        Nay! but while
Thy name shall scarce in memory blight her bloom,
They shall abide to hold and worship still
This land thy life polluted!"

. . . .

       He had time
To gather him unto himself again;
And now, the only vestige of the fray
That tore him inly, hung in beaded drops
Cold on his brow, while he returned her gaze.
 "Foul sorceress! what art thou? Whence, animal?
I've known thee Lupola, apart those Eyes!
 What crime hath blasted thee with 'horrent view?
What Fate hath bid thee Randolph thus upbraid?
 Know, Wolf-eyed Woman, that whate'er betide
Of doom or death, I utterly defy
Without one thought repentant of regret
For any deed o' my life, save just yon blow
That, circling, caught Her life upon its edge
While snatching His.

      For the poor maiden there
Woke, with her gentle spell, some sense in me
Akin to softness, taught me Fatherhood,
And—earlier known—had trained my life's wild stream,
Belike, to gentler flowing.

       Thou! get thee gone!
Lest haply I may call thee to account
For thy and thy poor mistress' presence here:

And thank thy guardian powers that thou didst beard
John Randolph, and beholdest yet the day !
    Hark ! hide those eyes, else may their evil glare
Have opportunity to test the warmth
Of certain irons !"
                Thence Earl Moray moved.

    The woman hardly sensed him out of ken,
Than with a wild and wailing cry of woe
She leaned her o'er the dead, and tore her hands,
And moaned, "Ydonea ! Ydonea !"
    "Ah, God ! ah, God !" (on failing knees she fell),
"Art Thou, and this allowest ? 'Tis a scene
Of such great ruth as might accord these stones
A power to weep ; and raiseth up in me
Some new, strange sense.
                Hath my enshrouded heart
Risen through vicarious anguish to its Day ?
Needed it Death, hers—whom alone I loved—
To stir me,—as Thy Sacrifice, the world,
Thou of the Thornèd Brows ?
                Seems I would weep !
Tears have their source in Souls,—I have no Soul !
Whence then this burning drop, whence ?—from my sight,
Or from the o'erhanging Heavens ?   Nay ! meseems
My floods have burst their dams ; my prisoned heart,
Fetterless, leaps to greet the new-born Soul !

Divine Compassion ! child of Sympathy !
Born of th' Eternal Love, hast wrought in me
This marvel of melting anguish ?   Oh ! I bow,
I kneel, I bless, I lay my stony heart,
Mercy, before Thy Throne ! . . .

Have I o'ercome ?—Blest Vision of my youth,
Enough endured ?—or have these agonised hours
Filled years of woe ?   Or, do these waters clear
Mine earth-dulled sight ?—is't Thou hast finished all ?
Once more I see that Form, with lustre crowned,
But 'neath *my* fardel bending; now I hear
Again those tender accents, comfortful :
' Oh, heavy laden, I will give thee rest !
Behold ! they shall rejoice, who strong èndure.'

" Life's chords are sundering—this is surely Death !
O Friend most welcome, I do exhort thee !   Light !
Light all within me glows; without all's dark :
I see no more : I faint ! I fall ! I die !
Ydonea, loved one ! see ! I join thee now.
The Light, ah ! bright, within . . . ! "
                                        And by the form
Of her adorèd Ladye, Lupola
Laid her tired dust, and sent her new-born Soul
To seek its Heaven !

NOTES TO RETRIBUTION.

" From out thy death-wound swells it into speed."—P. 252, l. 29.

RANDOLPH, Earl of Moray, was killed at the battle of Neville's Cross, near Durham, in the year 1346.

" To seek its Heaven ! "—P. 255, l. 19.

The idea of the Wehr-wolf as a beautiful woman, wearing the brute's eyes in her female semblance, I borrowed from a weird story of Mr George Macdonald's, which appeared in the first edition of 'Robert Falconer,' and which he told me he had been advised to leave out for curtailment in after editions (more's the pity).

The fact of her becoming the Wolf only at the full moon is my own fancy, as also the idea of demonstrating, in her being, the war between the spiritual and animal natures. She, of course, like Ydonea and Denys (and Allan Shaw, save in the betrayal of his master), are all inventions, and apart the traditions which form the main story.

PEACE.

Let us to mirth, the tale is sad (they said);
Laugh with your living, leave me to my dead.

SHRINE thee, O sorrowing Shire, beneath the pall,
That, whitening, falls in snow upon thy Past—
That kindly lights above thy shattered Pride:
    The day is done, the season all is dead,
The doom's accomplished when the hope is fled.

    The Summers, and the Autumns, and the snow,
Of past five centuries have come and gone;
The gathering streams have babbled all they know
Of life and living long since dust and done!

Me fails the murmurous music of the tide;
For thirsty Summer, with his parchèd mouth,
Absorbs the flood, that gabbles, querulous,
Like meagre Eld, a-dwindling 'mid the prime.
    The trumpet blazon of the boisterous North
Afar, clangs through ice-wrackage of his home;
And westlin' winds lull me to apathy
In soft monotonous measures.
                Yet a word
Rests to be spoken: hear, and then—farewell!

R

Thou that canst heal the ills of Earth, O Death,
Art not aye merciful !   Ydonea lived :
'Twas a long swoon, whence rousing, through the Vale
Of Shadows must she pass, with 'horrent visions,
With frightful racking of distorted brain,
With youth, and youth's bright loveliness, forgone !
And long unconscious hours ; but still, she lived ;
Through weakling days, the Real to realise ;
Through force regained, to know her utter loss.

His cold ambitious life did Randolph yield
Ere evening drooped o'er Durham's sanguined field :
And not a son or daughter by his tomb
Mourned ; and his lands passed to another name.

Back to their Mother France by Denys borne
Ere this, Ydonea left the Northern scene
Of such tremendous sorrow.
                              Some there are
Who vow these widowed hearts, by youth's rebound,
Can spring and love anew ; for Time and Youth,
Uniting, conquer.   These see pictured dreams
Of Denys, loving ever ; made content,
And comforter, through peaceful wedded days,
When retrospection knew a chastened woe,   .
Not stabbing, as erst, with anguish.
                              These can hear
Still, in the fair dream-semblance of desire,
The laugh of children 'round mid-age's knee,
Unchecked, unchidden, by the memory
Of that deflowered Glen beyond the Sea,
And its enacted tragedy.   .   .   .

Dream this, if dream you will, but let me rest:
My pipe is riven wholly; and my Lute,
Strung to the golden chords of Alastair,
Shall sound responsive to no meaner strain!

I fain would slumber: wake me not again,
Ye winds, ye waters: see! your will is done,
And Sorrow sleeps beneath the genial Sun.

NOTE TO PEACE.

" Mourned ; and his lands passed to another name."—P. 258, l. 13.

The Dunbars, through the marriage of Randolph's sister, " Black Agnes," became Earls of Moray. *Vide* note, " John Randolph, Earl of Moray," p. 74.

APPENDIX

APPENDIX.

ACCORDING to promise—in the Preface—I copy portions of letters describing the origin of traditions that gave subject for the story of Comyn and Randolph feuds.

These letters appear to be sequels of a conversation between Sir Thomas Dick Lauder, Bart. of Grange, &c., then residing at Relugas (a place on Findhorn belonging to his wife, *née* Miss Cumming), and engaged upon his work on the Floods that had desolated the province of Moray the preceding year—and the Rev. Mr Rose, minister of Drainie, near Elgin, in the year 1830. The first letter bears date January 12th; and after speaking of the change from a Celtic to a Saxon population in the parishes of Edinkillie and Ardclach (in Moray), and the consequent disappearance of old tales and traditions, Mr Rose continues: "I presume you know that Randolph, Earl of Moray, is in Gaelic called Ranlach or Rannach. His Saxon origin, his antipathy to the Cumins, his inhuman treatment of Alister Bāne Cumin, the popular hero of the Clan Cumin on the banks of the Ern and vicinity of Dorb; rendered his name for a long time odious to the Highlanders; and if songs and traditions could establish the fact, my father, who in his

youth had imbibed the sentiments of the Highlanders, and felt
strongly inclined to credit their traditions, could have given
many proofs; and if the songs and traditions of his countrymen could in the least be relied upon, Randolph, notwithstanding all his military renown handed down by the Saxon
historians, was but an inhuman monster.   My father had most
of his songs, traditions, and heroic ballads from one of the
name of Miller, who lived in the neighbourhood of Aitnach—
an old man when my father was but a youth of fifteen.
Miller was in his early days a kind of minstrel by profession.
His father followed the same idle trade; an excellent musician,
forester, and fisher; attended weddings, merry-meetings, wakes,
and funerals; sang songs or psalms, and songs of any description.   He could neither read nor write, yet valued himself
highly on account of his Celtic lore.   He often complained of
the change of days, and gave it as a sad proof of degeneracy
that, though his father lived like a gentleman and among
gentlemen, he was obliged to turn fox-hunter, and lay the
country under a sort of voluntary contribution, if not for
music, at least for the preservation of their sheep and poultry.
His music and traditions were hailed with joy by the children;
and his polite and entertaining manners made him an accept-
able guest at the tables of rich and poor.   Miller had many
failings; yet with all his failings he was just the man to my
father's mind, who followed him when in the parish as constantly as one of his dogs—so constantly, that his father,
fearing that he would turn out nothing but a rhymer and
sportsman [*sic !*], sent him to the school of Fortrose to be out
of the way.   Of Miller's historical ballads and poems there
were two which my father particularly admired—one called
'The Lost Standard of the Cumins,' the other an 'Elegy on the
Death of Alister Bāne.'   The 'Standard' was of considerable
length, prefaced by a historical narration in measured prose;

the 'Elegy' short, but the composition more pathetic and elegant."

Mr Rose goes on to say that in his father's last illness recitations of Gaelic poems, &c., " were agreeable to him, and amusing to me"! His imagination was fired with the account of the "melancholy and undeserved fate of Alister Bāne"; and he went to seek out the scenes of the tragedy, finding the cave with some difficulty, and not till after his father's death. It was not then, as now, made easy of access, both from river and road, by the paths constructed by the late proprietor of Dunphail.

Mr Rose begged his father to write out and translate some of the historical ballads—who, " after some time, tried a verse or two of what is called the 'Gathering of the Clan,' but gave it up and said, 'If I attempt it, it must be in prose.' This was in July, and on the 12th of August he died of a stroke of paralysis, and with him the historical ballad, and the beautiful 'Elegy on the Death of Alister Bāne.'" Further on he continues: "The tradition, as far as my memory serves me, is that Cumming of Retz and his vassals had gone to assist the Chief of Lochy (perhaps Inverlochy), when notice was sent him that Randolph was preparing for hostilities, and he was entreated to return. 'With the help of God,' said Retz, 'I will fight this battle, and that too.' They were defeated, and the Chief of Lochy—whoever he was—slain. Retz snatched a spear and broke it, and besmeared that and his battle-axe in the blood of his kinsman; and on his return sent this bloody fiery cross, surmounted on his battle-axe, through all the Clans as an imperative summons to revenge. He was represented as returning to Retz with sorrow in his heart, and sadness depicted on his brow. While his daughters were burnishing up his armour, his son was grinding his sword, which was sadly hacked on the field at Lochy. The place of rendezvous was 'Cairnbar,' the

private pass-word, 'Live and die like a Cumin.' On a con-
certed signal, the lighting up of beacons, the whole was to
assemble at the place appointed. It was hoped they might be
able to attack Ranlach before he could collect his vassals.
Retz, Gorm, Dunearn, and Dunlugas were lighted up; all
hurried to Cairnbar; and when convened, set off for Ranlach's
place. All appeared still; no movement indicated danger till
they came to 'Boggan-gall' (now Whitemyre), when Randolph,
whose troops had been arranged in order of battle, issued
from the ravine. Retz endeavoured to fall back, but his error
was irreparable. It is said that he fell in this first engage-
ment, and was buried under the great cairn raised on the
moor, and that Randolph, when he had buried him, boasted
that he had buried the plague of Moray; and it is the opinion
of children yet—as it once was my own—that the plague was
actually buried there, and it would prove mortal to any one
who dared to violate its secret recesses. The defeat would
have become a complete rout but for Bāne, who collected and
reanimated the fugitives, which he did at Clune, where he
drew up on a rising ground where the farmhouse now stands
—inaccessible to cavalry, and difficult on two sides to in-
fantry. For a short time he put a stop to the slaughter, but
seeing himself like to be surrounded, he resolved to cut his
way through, and waving his sword, exclaimed: 'The man
that fears not to die, let him follow me.' They did, it was
said, cut their way through, and the retreat was conducted
with little loss till they came to the Rhait-cook [sic], 'narrow
pass of Ern,' which they found preoccupied by a strong detach-
ment of Randolph's troops, and posted on the opposite bank.
As the enemy was fast advancing, he commanded the rear as
the more honourable, and ordered Drummoin with his men to
take the ford, and take possession of the pass. A desperate
struggle ensued between Drummoin and Randolph's detach-

ment. Bāne, afraid of losing his Standard, flung it across the pass among the combatants, and cried aloud, 'Let the bravest keep it!' and Ern was said, in the hyperbolical language of the poet, to roll red with blood to the sea. The bravery of Drummoin, the courage and humanity of Alister Bāne in helping the wounded through the water, contrasted with the unrelenting cruelty of Ranlach and his men, who with their long spears thrust back the unarmed, and pushed down in the water the head that was drawing its last breath, concluded the ballad of the 'Lost Standard'; and the bridge over the Ern is called Rannoch's bridge till this day. In corroboration of the credibility of this tradition, I have to say that a cairn on the farm near the field of battle having been removed in my own time, a good many skeletons and the iron heads of pikes were found beneath it. They were not laid in any regular order: the nose or socket of the pike about 18, and the pike or head about 12 in. long: the iron so corroded that in most places it could be broken with ease. In another place a great many bones and pieces of skulls were found, but nothing like one whole or complete skeleton. My father would have it that the former was the grave of some distinguished Saxons, buried with the honours of war,—then in fashion,—as a cairn was raised over them. The latter the bones of the vulgar dead.

"The 'Elegy on the Death of Bāne' represented him flying from place to place,—sometimes in, sometimes out of the fortress—everywhere dreaded by his enemies—harassing and surprising them, and supplying the wants of an aged father and of his wounded kinsmen, crowded in that narrow space,— in spite of all the vigilance of Ranlach's men. Randolph put a price on his head, and one of Comyn's own clan betrayed his lurking-place in Slack-kaunin (Slack of heads). When asked to come out, he consented to come out if they would allow him to die like a Cumin. 'No!' said his murderers; 'die like a fox!' and rolling fragments of rock to the mouth of the cave to prevent his escape, pulled heather, set fire to it, and smoked him to death. When the cave was opened, Bāne and five or six of his men were found dead; Bāne with his head rolled in his plaid, and resting on the pommel of his sword. Their heads were severed from their bodies, and thrown one after another into the fortress. 'Your son has provided you in meal, and we send you flesh to eat with it.' The old man recognised the fair head of his son, and weeping over it, said: 'It is a bitter morsel indeed, but I will gnaw the last bone of it before I surrender.' The 'Elegy' concluded with the old weeping, the young weeping, the brave and the timid, the eagles and the victims, weeping."

Mr Rose says after this, that the ballad of the "Lost Standard" was perhaps as long as that of "Chevy Chase"; the "Elegy" not one-third as long. He then tells the story we have known so well: that outside the garden-wall of Dunphail was a knoll "called," when translated into English, "the grave of the Headless Cumins." This was opened in presence of his grandfather, John Rose of Aitnach ("who had heard the 'Elegy' a hundred times"), by the Dunbars, the then proprietors, intending to include the knoll in the garden-ground. It contained "five or six skeletons in rude-constructed stone chests; the skeletons fresher than might have been expected, but not a vestige of a skull or head on any one of them." We always heard that these skeletons were carefully buried in the churchyard of Edinkillie, close to the church-wall; but Mr Rose does not mention the fact. He—very provoking man— ends this first letter by saying: "Had I known that any one thought as much of them as I did myself, I might have obtained many heroic ballads in the Gaelic language. My father was a perfect enthusiast as to Gaelic poetry."

The second letter is dated January 22d. He begins by (evidently) answering some questions put to him by Sir Thomas, anent the cave in Slack-kaunin, as he persists in spelling it (I think it should be thus—Sleoch-nan-Ceann, vulgarised nowadays into Slaginnan); discusses the *locale* of the beacon-fires, and mentions having himself seen the pike-heads and skeletons found as aforenamed at Clune, where Alister Bāne was said to have rallied his flying troops. Then he says: "On looking over the few verses translated by my father of the heroic ballad called the 'Lost Standard of the Cumins,' the fields of battle appear to me distinctly marked out. They must have been fought near Whitemyre, Clune, and Rhait-cuik on the Earn. He valued the 'Standard' as a composition only for the little historical light which it threw on tradition, and for the muster of the clan, and number of men which the different districts were said to have brought to the field, which, though far beyond what was credible, gave some idea of the respective power of the Chiefs. The names of some of the districts were changed, or entirely forgotten; he could only guess at them. Some remained entire, or were translated to English. In his last illness he attempted at my request, as I told you, to translate some verses of the 'Standard.' These verses describe the scene of action; and it was my acquaintance with the scenery which impressed the tradition so strongly on my memory. He thought he could translate the 'Standard,' but despaired of doing justice to the 'Elegy on Cumin Bāne.' The kinds of verse he adopted, though far from being elegant, were perhaps necessary, either from the measure of the originals, or from the airs or tunes to which they were sung, to which perhaps he wished to adapt them. These verses were the production of a day, and that day a day of sickness. He gave up the task, disgusted with the difficulty of a faithful translation. . . . But the verses,

such as they were, I valued them; and if they can throw any
light on traditions in which you take an interest, you are
welcome to them, and here they are :—

" ' Hark ! the eagles loud are screaming, though the stars on high are
    gleaming ;
They flap upon their young to wing with speed away ;
The ravens leave the rock, and the crows together flock,
Afraid they are too late to feast on gory prey.
Hark ! Dorb's dark forest groans, and Earn sadly moans ;
They weep but for the good, they mourn but for the brave :
This is no tempest scowl—'tis the melancholy howl
Of the dogs who wail the hero's fate now marching to the grave. ,
Hark ! the horrid tramp of war, how it rolls from Cairn-bar ;
It strikes on Boggau-kall, and recoils on Clachan-Clune ;
It sounds on Knockan-righ, and it spreads on Blarna-fiegh ;
It thunders on the Ern, and it dies upon the Dune.
Who is that among the dead, with his helm on his head ?
'Tis the gallant Lord of Reits, and his sword is broke in twain ;
He has met the bowman's dart : there's a lance run through his heart,
And the best of Cumin blood flows fast from every vein.
Wield, Cumin Bāne, thy sword ! remember now the word :
Now like a Cumin stand, or like a Cumin fall !
Not Ranlach's length of spear, nor his horsemen on thy rear,
Can thy true courage daunt, nor yet thy heart appal.
Oh ! wield thy trusty brand, cut through the hostile band ;
Away to Rhait-cuik ; oh, day of piercing woe !
Drummoin thy clan will guide through Ern's bloody tide.
Oh, Bāne, protect the feeble from the fury of the foe !
    Too true is the vision ; 'tis no waking dream ;
    Reits' beacon is kindled, Bareven's in flame ;
    Old Gorm now mingles its fires with the clouds,
    And summons the heroes of Spey in their shrouds.
    Dunearn its warlike beacon doth raise ;
    Dunlugas replies, and is all in a blaze,
    And flashes its ire over Ranlach's place,
    Over Ranlach's men, and in Ranlach's face ;
    The fiery cross, smeared with the blood of the chief,
    Fills the brave soul with vengeance, the tender with grief ;
    The brave mourn the brave with hearts full of woe,
    But mingle their tears with the blood of the foe !

THE BAN.

{
Now curse on the Cumin that loiters behind ;
Let him hang in the air ; let him bleach in the wind ;
Pull his house to the ground ; give its roof to the flame ;
Disdaining his sire, let the son change his name.
Despised by the wise, and scorned by the good,
Let the daughter deny she inherits his blood ;
Let his memory to endless disgrace be consigned,
And his grave as the grave of the coward designed.
}

> The beacons are gleaming,
> The timid are screaming ;
> The pipers are playing,
> Old women are praying ;
> The banners are flying,
> Soft maidens are crying ;
> But the bold and the brave,
> All fearless of death,
> They pour down from the heath ;
> And swift as the roe,
> They descend on the foe—
> From hill and from dale,
> From wood and from vale,' &c.

Something like a muster-roll of glens and straths, with hundreds on hundreds of men, followed in the same short and rapped measure—all good men, true men, valiant men, brave men, &c. Nothing is said of the numbers of Randolph's men —by which I would judge that they were fewer in number— nor of his coadjutors ; the whole imprecations of the bard being poured out on Ranlach—his cruelty, and the length of their spears, and the impenetrable armour of his horsemen ; and after running over the various fate of the battle, it concluded, as I mentioned, with a contrast of the generous intrepidity of Cumin Bāne in protecting the feeble and wounded while they forded the Ern, with the cruelty of Ranlach, who slaughtered without mercy the weak and the wounded.

" Some of the places in the previous vision of the bard (for it seems they laid claim not only to a poetic, but to a prophetic spirit, or something like the second-sight) still go by the same names. . . . So much, dear Sir Thomas, about an old song, and idle tradition, &c.

"*P.S.*—I have sent you the verses of the 'Lost Standard of the Cumins' just as I found them. They have been by me for *thirty-six* years. . . .

"It would put my father's spirit mad if he could see what was done to please a boy, held out as a specimen of his rhyming talent. Unfinished as it is, I regret that he suited the first part to an old drawling mournful air called a Lament, to which the first and last parts were sung.

"I cannot conceive where Drummoin is. I have heard of the forest of Drummoin, which extends from Birnie to Spey; but know of no place of residence which goes by that name. It would, I suppose, at the time, be a place of some consequence, as next to A. Bāne he appears of most influence or tried courage." . . .

I have given these portions of Mr Rose's letters in his own words, and with his own spelling of proper names, &c.; omitting many of his private remarks, deductions, and fancies on the subject, and copying only what explains my story, or may interest those who value Gaelic poetry—which latter thought prompted the insertion of the fragment of translation by the elder Mr Rose. I myself sought out the battle-fields, and endeavoured to realise the various scenes and positions, with great success. Establishing Retz, Raites, or Reits, is a matter of difficulty; and the whence and who, with regard to Drummoin, is not assured.[1] I had always heard Alastair was tracked to the cave by bloodhounds, not betrayed by one of his clan. So I have in my version steered a middle course, making the traitor a Shaw, a sept always inimical to Clan Comyn.

[1] *Vide* notes, pp. 170 and 218.

This, my dear Elma, is all I can discover among Sir Thomas's papers. Would that one could live back 100 years, and make the acquaintance of Miller the minstrel, or even of Mr Rose's father—what fine old records and tales one might have saved from utter oblivion, and preserved airs and laments now lost for aye!

I perceive that in these letters there is no mention of the additional incident adduced by Sir T. Dick Lauder in the ' Moray Floods ' — *i.e.*, where Alastair and his people, disguised as peasants, supply, through a stratagem, the beleaguered garrison of Dunphail.

I feel sure that the author of that interesting work (so stamped afterwards by Sir Edwin Landseer's brush [1]) had been able to prosecute further researches among the old folk in the country, or that Mr Rose's brain was further ransacked when he paid Sir Thomas a visit promised in his letters, and that more facts were discovered, which, though not needful to his book, would have been valuable to my story.

Since copying the foregoing, another letter from the Rev. Mr Rose has turned up — of earlier date — namely, March 1820.

It is addressed to the minister of Edinkillie (in which parish, I think, is Dunphail). He says :—

" May not the tradition of the Wolf, killed in Edenkillie, have taken its rise or been connected with the death of Alastair Bān, who, when called upon to come out just before the fire was kindled, answered he would, 'if they would allow him to die like a Cumming, with his sword in his hand;' and the reply of his enemy: 'Die like a wolf [*sic*] as you are.' It is a pity you forgot, in narrating the tradition, Cumming's

---

[1] The picture called the " The Moray Floods," now in possession of Lord Cheylesmore, 16 Princes Gate, W.

answer, because there is something heroic in it, and probable, from there being no possibility of escape, or hope of mercy.

"That the last wolf [1] was killed in Edenkillie, derives much credibility from the fact that Edenkillie makes a part of the great forest of Drummoin, extending at one period its immense tract of pine from the parish of Birnie to the woods of Abernethy. It is the universal tradition of the people, that Castle Dorb, though now without a shrub within many miles of it, was, when in the hands of the Cummings, the heart of an immense forest. The remains of . . . are yet visible in the large tracts of moss, and nowhere more frequent than in the parish of Edenkillie. Mr Rose of Mountcoffer, who was better versed than any other of his day in the charters of Moray, informed me that many of them held as parts of the forest of Drummoin; and you may remember, that on the Monday after a Sacrament at Edenkillie, upon my mentioning that circumstance, Logie (the lairds of Logie are Cummings), then present, said, with much exultation: 'Drummoin is my property! Drummoin is my property!'

"As you have taken up the traditionary history of your parish, though I fear too late, I beg leave to call your attention to a noted refuge of Alastair Bān and his clan in your parish, as little known to *some* of the Antiquarians in your parish as the murderous cave of Slack-kaunin, and perhaps never heard of by the stupid mechanic race, who have within the course of these last sixty years supplanted the Gael—a race of heroes. I never was at [it?]. I must only say that from circumstances mentioned by my father, I *believe* that such a place exists, and perhaps some traditions in the west

---

[1] For the account of the killing of last wolves in Moray, *vide* 'Ballads' by the Lady Middleton—published by Kegan Paul & Co.

of your parish may yet be alive; but you need not look for them but among those who speak the Gaelic language—nor among them unless the family has been of considerable standing. The resort frequented so by Bān and his clan lies, I was informed, in the heart of a morass south or south-east of the Knock of Brae Moray. It once was, I have been told, almost inaccessible, and might be defended by a few; its Gaelic name I have forgotten, but little trouble will find out both the name and the place. Do, my good sir, take that trouble on some dry day, for I was told it could only be approached in dry weather. If my information was correct, there is yet the remains of a temporary fortification made up of loose stones. Mr Milne (?), when I repeated to him the tradition of Bān, never heard of such a place as Slack-kaunin, and assured me there was not on the Divie, from its source to its influx, a cave that could contain one man. He was then, however, but a year and a half minister of the parish. But for that, I might have been induced to ask a copy of the elegant Lamentation of Shennen Paul Glass [or *P. v.* (?)] [rather difficult to read.—E. M. M] to his people on the rock, over the head of his brave but unfortunate son; but my father's illness, which terminated in paralysis, and death a few months after, drove poems and traditions out of my mind. I have put you to the expense of postage for this, rather thoughtlessly. Your friend, Mr Lach. M'Pherson, can inform you of the tradition of the Wolf of Badenoch; and as Lach[n.] is famous as a genealogist, he may be able to trace your Wolf of Edenkillie to its parent stock.—I am, dear sir, yours truly, RICHARD ROSE.

" To the Rev. THOS. M'FARLANE,
    Edenkillie, Forres."

Alas for the death of Gaelic in Edinkillie! was that resort or refuge of Alastair Bhan ever found? I never heard of it; and if sixty and seventy years ago Mr Rose dreaded it was already too late to search for old traditions, what hope have we of ever finding the Lament of the bereaved father of the heroic Comyn?

———————

PRINTED BY WILLIAM BLACKWOOD AND SONS.

www.ingramcontent.com/pod-product-compliance
Lightning Source LLC
Chambersburg PA
CBHW060602030726
47498CB00005B/1508